THE INDIANS HAD THE HIGH GROUND, AND THEIR RIFLES WERE SMOKING . . .

Cassidy dove behind a pile of rocks, and they instantly pinned him down. With no place to run and very little room to hide, all he could do was sit.

Until he began to itch and saw he was on top of an ant hill.

Then came the metallic whir of copperheads from under the nearby rocks. Cassidy lurched reflexively, exposing himself to the Indians for just one second and a bullet smashed his collarbone.

He pitched backward, and a copperhead sensed its moment. Twisting out from under the rocks, it hissed and spat, its tongue flicking in and out.

As it writhed and undulated toward him, its rattles began to buzz . . .

**Clarence E. Mulford books by
Tom Doherty Associates, Inc.**

A HOPALONG CASSIDY NOVEL

BAR-20

Clarence E. Mulford

FORGE®

A TOM DOHERTY ASSOCIATES BOOK
NEW YORK

This is a work of fiction. All the characters and events portrayed in this book are either products of the author's imagination or are used fictitiously.

BAR-20

All materials in this edition copyright © 1992 by Tom Doherty Associates, LLC.

Cover art by Carl Cassler

A Forge Book
Published by Tom Doherty Associates, LLC
175 Fifth Avenue
New York, NY 10010

www.tor.com

Forge® is a registered trademark of Tom Doherty Associates, LLC.

ISBN-13: 978-0-765-35737-3
ISBN-10: 0-765-35737-2

First Tor Edition: October 1992
Second Tor Edition: December 2006

Printed in the United States of America

0 9 8 7 6 5 4 3 2 1

Introduction

IN JUNE, 1991 Bantam published the first of Louis L'Amour's acclaimed Hopalong Cassidy novels, *The Rustlers of West Fork*. Since then, there has been a tremendous ground swell of enthusiasm for Hopalong and his friends. Readers around the country want to know more about these Bar-20 boys—and above all, want more of their books.

Consequently, Tor Books is bringing back the original novels, written by Clarence E. Mulford, the man who created Cassidy and company. It's a good thing too. These are really first-rate books, full of true grit and pulse-pounding action, the kind of books you can't put down.

If you liked Louis L'Amour's Hopalong Cassidy novel—*The Rustlers of West Fork*—you'll *love* this one. This is no imitation but the real thing.

A lot of western writers—people like Richard S. Wheeler, Earl Murray, Al Dempsey and yours truly—when we get together for a few beers, we sometimes talk about books. We talk about the books that inspired us; the authors who made us love the West and even want to write ourselves. For whatever it's worth, it's a short list. And for a lot of us, the guy at the top is Clarence Mulford.

Clarence, old hoss, wherever you are, here's a Lone Star beer to you.

—Jackson Cain,
author of *Hellbreak Country*
and *Hangman's Whip*

CHAPTER I

Buckskin

THE TOWN lay sprawled over half a square mile of alkali plain, its main street depressing in its width, for those who were responsible for its inception had worked with a generosity born of the knowledge that they had at their immediate and unchallenged disposal the broad lands of Texas and New Mexico on which to assemble a grand total of twenty buildings, four of which were of wood. As this material was scarce, and had to be brought from where the waters of the Gulf lapped against the flat coast, the last-mentioned buildings were a matter of local pride, as indicating the progressiveness of their owners. These creations of hammer and saw were of one story, crude and unpainted; their cheap weather sheathing warped and shrunken by the pitiless sun, curled back on itself and allowed unrestricted entrance to alkali dust and air. The other shacks were of adobe and owned by Indians and Mexicans.

It was an incident of the Cattle Trail, that most

unique and stupendous of all modern migrations, and
its founders must have been inspired with a mali-
cious desire to perpetrate a crime against geogra-
phy, or else they reveled in a perverse cussedness,
for within a mile on every side lay broad prairies,
and two miles to the east flowed the indolent waters
of the Rio Pecos itself. The distance separating the
town from the river was excusable, for at certain
seasons of the year the placid stream swelled might-
ily and swept down in a broad expanse of turbulent,
yellow flood.

Buckskin was a town of one hundred inhabitants,
located in the valley of the Rio Pecos fifty miles south
of the Texas–New Mexico line. The census claimed
two hundred, but it was a well-known fact that it was
exaggerated. One instance of this is shown at the
name of Tom Flynn. Those who once knew Tom
Flynn, alias Johnny Redmond, alias Bill Sweeney,
alias Chuck Mullen, by all four names, could find
them in the census list. Furthermore, he had been
shot and killed in the March of the year preceding
the census, and now occupied a grave in the young
but flourishing cemetery. Perry's Bend, twenty miles
up the river, was cognizant of this and other facts,
and, laughing in open derision at the padded list,
claimed to be the better town in all ways, including
marksmanship.

One year before this tale opens, Buck Peters, an
example for the more recent Billy the Kid, had paid
Perry's Bend a short but busy visit. He had ridden
in at the north end of Main Street and out at the
south. As he came in he was fired at by a group of
ugly cowboys from a ranch known as the C-80. He
was hit twice, but he unlimbered his artillery, and
before his horse had carried him, half dead, out on

the prairie, he had killed one of the group. Several citizens had joined the cowboys and added their bullets against Buck. The deceased had been the best bartender in the country, and the rage of the suffering citizens can well be imagined. They swore vengeance on Buck, his ranch, and his stamping ground.

The difference between Buck and Billy the Kid is that the former never shot a man who was not trying to shoot him, or who had not been warned by some action against Buck that would call for it. He minded his own business, never picked a quarrel, and was quiet and pacific up to a certain point. After that had been passed he became like a raging cyclone in a tenement house, and storm cellars were much in demand.

"Fanning" is the name of a certain style of gunplay and was universal among the bad men of the West. While Buck was not a bad man, he had to rub elbows with them frequently, and he believed that the sauce for the goose was the sauce for the gander. So he had removed the trigger of his revolver and worked the hammer with the thumb of the "gun hand" or the thumb of the unencumbered hand. The speed thus acquired was greater than that of the more modern double-action weapon. Six shots in three seconds was his average speed when that number was required, and when it is thoroughly understood that at least five of them found their intended billets it is not difficult to realize that fanning was an operation of danger when Buck was doing it.

He was a good rider, as all cowboys are, and was not afraid of anything that lived. At one time he and his chums, Red Connors and Hopalong Cassidy, had successfully routed a band of fifteen Apaches who wanted their scalps. Of these, twelve never hunted scalps again, nor anything else on this earth, and the other three returned to their tribe with the report that three evil spirits had chased them with "wheel guns" (cannons).

So now, since his visit to Perry's Bend, the rivalry of the two towns had turned to hatred and an alert and eager readiness to increase the inhabitants of each other's graveyard. A state of war existed, which for a time resulted in nothing worse than acrimonious suggestions. But the time came when the score was settled to the satisfaction of one side, at least.

Four ranches were also concerned in the trouble. Buckskin was surrounded by two, the Bar-20 and the Three Triangle. Perry's Bend was the common point for the C-80 and the Double Arrow. Each of the two ranch contingents accepted the feud as a matter of course, and as a matter of course took sides with their respective towns. As no better class of fighters ever lived, the trouble assumed Homeric proportions and insured a danger zone well worth watching.

Bar-20's northern line was C-80's southern one, and Skinny Thompson took his turn at outriding one morning after the season's roundup. He was to follow the boundary and turn back stray cattle. When he had covered the greater part of his journey he saw Shorty Jones riding toward him on a course parallel to his own and about long revolver range away. Shorty and he had "crossed trails" the year before and the best of feelings did not exist between them.

Shorty stopped and stared at Skinny, who did likewise at Shorty. Shorty turned his mount around and applied the spurs, thereby causing his indignant horse to raise both heels at Skinny. The latter took it all in gravely and, as Shorty faced him again, placed his left thumb to his nose, wiggling his fingers suggestively. Shorty took no apparent notice of this but began to shout:

"Yu wants to keep yore busted-down cows on yore own side. They was all over us day afore yisterday. I'm goin' to salt any more what comes over, and don't yu fergit it, neither."

Thompson wigwagged with his fingers again and shouted in reply: "Yu c'n salt all yu wants to, but if I ketch yu adoin' it yu won't have to work no more. An' I kin say right here thet they's more C-80 cows over here than they's Bar-20's over there."

Shorty reached for his revolver and yelled, "Yore a liar!"

Among the cowboys in particular and the Westerners in general at that time, the three suicidal terms, unless one was an expert in drawing quick and shooting straight with one movement, were the words "liar," "coward," and "thief." Any man who was called one of these in earnest, and he was the judge, was expected to shoot if he could and save his life, for the words were seldom used without a gun coming with them. The movement of Shorty's hand toward his belt before the appellation reached him was enough for Skinny, who let go at long range—and missed.

The two reports were as one. Both urged their horses nearer and fired again. This time Skinny's sombrero gave a sharp jerk and a hole appeared in the crown. The third shot of Skinny's sent the horse of the other to its knees and then over on its side. Shorty very promptly crawled behind it and, as he did so, Skinny began a wide circle, firing at intervals as Shorty's smoke cleared away.

Shorty had the best position for defense, as he was in a shallow coulée, but he knew that he could not leave it until his opponent had either grown tired of the affair or had used up his ammunition. Skinny knew it, too. Skinny also knew that he could get back to the ranch house and lay in a supply of food and ammunition and return before Shorty could cover the twelve miles he had to go on foot.

Finally Thompson began to head for home. He had carried the matter as far as he could without it being murder. Too much time had elapsed now, and, besides, it was before breakfast and he was hungry. He would go away and settle the score at some time when they would be on equal terms.

He rode along the line for a mile and chanced to look back. Two C-80 punchers were riding after him, and as they saw him turn and discover them they fired at him and yelled. He rode on for some distance and cautiously drew his rifle out of its long holster at his right leg. Suddenly he turned around in the saddle and fired twice. One of his pursuers fell forward on the neck of his horse, and his comrade turned to help him. Thompson wigwagged again and rode on, reaching the ranch as the others were finishing their breakfast.

At the table Red Connors remarked that the tardy one had a hole in his sombrero, and asked its owner how and where he had received it.

"Had a argument with C-80 out'n th' line."

"Go 'way! Ventilate enny?"

"One."

"Good boy, sonny! Hey, Hopalong, Skinny perforated C-80 this mawnin'!"

Hopalong Cassidy was struggling with a mouthful of beef. He turned his eyes toward Red without ceasing, and grinning as well as he could under the cir-

cumstances managed to grunt out "Gu—," which was
as near to "Good" as the beef would allow.

Lanky Smith now chimed in as he repeatedly stuck
his knife into a reluctant boiled potato, "How'd yu
do it, Skinny?"

"Bet he sneaked up on him," joshed Buck Peters;
"did yu ask his pardin, Skinny?"

"Ask nothin'," remarked Red, "he jest nachurly
walks up to C-80 an' sez, 'Kin I have the pleasure of
ventilatin' yu?' an' C-80 he sez, 'If yu do it easy
like,' sez he. Didn't he, Thompson?"

'They'll be some ventilatin' under th' table if yu
fellows don't lemme alone; I'm hungry," complained
Skinny.

"Say, Hopalong, I bets yu I kin clean up C-80 all
by my lonesome," announced Buck, winking at Red.

"Yah! Yu onct tried to clean up the Bend, Buckie,
an' if Pete an' Billy hadn't afound yu when they come
by Eagle Pass that night yu wouldn't be here eatin'
beef by th' pound," glancing at the hard-working
Hopalong. "It was plum' lucky fer yu that they was
acourtin' that time, wasn't it, Hopalong?" suddenly
asked Red. Hopalong nearly strangled in his efforts
to speak. He gave it up and nodded his head.

"Why can't yu git it straight, Connors? I wasn't
doin' no courtin', it was Pete. I runned into him on
th' other side o' th' pass. I'd look fine acourtin',
wouldn't I?" asked the downtrodden Williams.

Pete Wilson skillfully flipped a potato into that
worthy's coffee, spilling the beverage of the ques-
tionable name over a large expanse of blue flannel
shirt. "Yu's all right, yu are. Why, when I meets yu,
yu was lost in th' arms of yore ladylove. All I could
see was yore feet. Go an' git tangled up with a two
hundred and forty pound half-breed squaw an' then

try to lay it onter me! When I proposed drownin'
yore troubles over at Cowan's, yu went an' got mad
over what yu called th' insinooation. An' yu shore
didn't look any too blamed fine, neither."

"All th' same," volunteered Thompson, who had
taken the edge from his appetite, "we better go over
an' pay C-80 a call. I don't like what Shorty said
about saltin' our cattle. He'll shore do it, unless I
camps on th' line, which same I hain't hankerin' after."

"Oh, he wouldn't stop th' cows that way, Skinny;
he was only afoolin'," exclaimed Connors meekly.

"Foolin' yore gran'mother! That there bunch'll do
anything if we wasn't lookin'," hotly replied Skinny.

"That's shore nuff gospel, Thomp. They's sore fer
mor'n one thing. They got aplenty when Buck went
on th' warpath, an' they's hankerin' to git square,"
remarked Johnny Nelson, stealing the pie, a rare
treat, of his neighbor when that unfortunate individual was not looking. He had it halfway to his mouth
when its former owner, Jimmy Price, a boy of eighteen, turned his head and saw it going.

"Hi-yi! Yu clay-bank coyote, drap thet pie! Did yu
ever see such a son-of-a-gun fer pie?" he plaintively
asked Red Connors, as he grabbed a mighty handful
of apples and crust. "Pie'll kill yu some day, yu bobtailed jack! I had an uncle that died onct. He et too
much pie an' he went an' turned green, an' so'll yu
if yu don't let it alone."

"Yu ought'r seed th' pie Johnny had down in Eagle
Flat," murmured Lanky Smith reminiscently. "She
had feet that'd stop a stam*pede*. Johnny was shore
loco about her. Swore she was the finest blossom
that ever growed." Here he choked and tears of
laughter coursed down his weather-beaten face as

he pictured her. "She was about fifteen han's high an' about sixteen han's around. Johnny used to chalk off when he hugged her, usen't yu, Johnny? One night when he had got purty well around on th' second lap he run inter a man jest startin' out on his fust. They hain't caught that Mexican yet."

Nelson was pelted with everything in sight. He slowly wiped off the pie crust and bread and potatoes. "Anybody'd think I was a busted grub wagon," he grumbled. When he had fished the last piece of beef out of his ear he went out and offered to stand treat. As the roundup was over, they slid into their saddles and raced for Cowan's saloon at Buckskin.

CHAPTER II

The Rashness of Shorty

BUCKSKIN WAS very hot; in fact it was never anything else. Few people were on the streets and the town was quiet. Over in the Houston hotel a crowd of cowboys was lounging in the barroom. They were very quiet—a condition as rare as it was ominous. Their mounts, twelve in all, were switching flies from their quivering skins in the corral at the rear. Eight of these had a large C-80 branded on their flanks; the other four, a Double Arrow.

In the barroom a slim, wiry man was looking out of the dirty window up the street at Cowan's saloon. Shorty was complaining, "They shore oughter be here now. They rounded up last week." The man nearest assured him that they would come. The man at the window turned and said, "They's yer now."

In front of Cowan's a crowd of nine happy-go-lucky, daredevil riders were sliding from their saddles. They threw the reins over the heads of their mounts and filed in to the bar. Laughter issued from the open door and the clink of glasses could be heard. They stood in picturesque groups, strong, self-reliant, humorous, virile. Their expensive sombreros were pushed far back on their heads and their hairy chaps were covered with the alkali dust from their ride.

Cowan, bottle in hand, pushed out several more glasses. He kicked a dog from under his feet and looked at Buck. "Rounded up yet?" he inquired.

"Shore, day afore yesterday," came the reply. The rest were busy removing the dust from their throats, and gradually drifted into groups of two or three. One of these groups strolled over to the solitary card table, and found Jimmy Price resting in a cheap chair, his legs on the table.

"I wisht yu'd extricate yore delicate feet from off'n this hyar table, James," humbly requested Lanky Smith, morally backed up by those with him.

"Ya-as, they shore is delicate, Mr. Smith," responded Jimmy, without moving.

"We wants to play draw, Jimmy," explained Pete.

"Yore shore welcome to play if yu wants to. Didn't I tell yu when yu growed that mustache that yu didn't have to ask me anymore?" queried the placid James, paternally.

"Call 'em off, sonny. Pete sez he kin clean me out. Anyhow, yu kin have the fust deal," compromised Lanky.

"I'm shore sorry fer Pete if he cayn't. Yu don't reckon I has to have fust deal to beat yu fellers, do yu? Go way an' lemme alone; I never seed such a bunch fer buttin' in as yu fellers."

Billy Williams returned to the bar. Then he walked along it until he was behind the recalcitrant possessor of the table. While his aggrieved friends shuffled

their feet uneasily to cover his approach, he tiptoed
up behind Jimmy and, with a nod, grasped that indignant individual firmly by the neck while the others grabbed his feet. They carried him, twisting and
bucking, to the middle of the street and deposited
him in the dust, returning to the now-vacant table.

Jimmy rested quietly for a few seconds and then
slowly arose, dusting the alkali from him. "Th' wall-
eyed piruts," he muttered, and then scratched his
head for a way to "play hunk." As he gazed sorrow-
fully at the saloon he heard a snicker from behind
him. He, thinking it was one of his late tormentors,
paid no attention to it. Then a cynical, biting laugh
stung him. He wheeled, to see Shorty leaning against
a tree, a sneering leer on his flushed face. Shorty's
right hand was suspended above his holster, hooked
to his belt by the thumb—a favorite position of his
when expecting trouble.

"One of yore reg'lar habits?" he drawled.

Jimmy began to dust himself in silence, but his lips
were compressed to a thin white line.

"Does they hurt yu?" pursued the onlooker.

Jimmy looked up. "I heard tell that they make glue
outen cayuses, sometimes," he remarked.

Shorty's eyes flashed. The loss of the horse had
been rankling in his heart all day.

"Does they git yu frequent?" he asked. His voice
sounded hard.

"Oh, 'bout as frequent as yu lose a cayuse, I
reckon," replied Jimmy hotly.

Shorty's hand streaked to his holster and Jimmy
followed his lead. Jimmy's Colt was caught. He had
bucked too much. As he fell Shorty ran for the Houston House.

Pistol shots were common, for they were the uni-

versal method of expressing emotions. The poker
players grinned, thinking their victim was letting off
his indignation. Lanky sized up his hand and remarked half audibly, "He's a shore good kid."

The bartender, fearing for his new beveled, gilt-
framed mirror, gave a hasty glance out the window.
He turned around, made change and remarked to
Buck, "Yore kid, Jimmy, is plugged." Several of the
more credulous craned their necks to see, Buck being the first. "Hell!" he shouted, and ran out to where
Jimmy lay coughing, his toes twitching. The saloon
was deserted and a crowd of angry cowboys surrounded their chum—a boy. Buck had seen Shorty
enter the door of the Houston House and he swore.
"Chase them damn cayuses behind th' saloon, Pete,
an' git under cover."

Jimmy was choking and he coughed up blood.
"He's shore—got me. My—gun stuck," he added
apologetically. He tried to sit up, but was not able
and he looked surprised. "It's purty—damn hot—out
here," he suggested. Johnny and Billy carried him in
the saloon and placed him by the table, in the chair
he had previously vacated. As they stood up he fell
across the table and died.

Billy placed the dead boy's sombrero on his head
and laid the refractory revolver on the table. "I wonder who th' shooter was." He looked at the slim figure and started to go out, followed by Johnny. As
he reached the threshold a bullet zipped past him
and thudded into the frame of the door. He backed
away and looked surprised. "That's Shorty's shootin'—he allus misses 'bout that much." He looked out
and saw Buck standing behind the live oak that
Shorty had leaned against, firing at the hotel. Turn-

ing around he made for the rear, remarking to Johnny that "they's in th' Houston." Johnny looked at the quiet figure in the chair and swore softly. He followed Billy. Cowan, closing the door and taking a .60-caliber buffalo gun from under the bar, went out also and slammed the rear door forcibly.

CHAPTER III

The Argument

UP THE street two hundred yards from the Houston House Skinny and Pete lay hidden behind a boulder. Three hundred yards on the other side of the hotel Johnny and Billy were stretched out in an arroyo. Buck was lying down now, and Hopalong, from his position in the barn belonging to the hotel, was methodically dropping the horses of the besieged, a job he hated as much as he hated poison. The corral was their death trap. Red and Lanky were emitting clouds of smoke from behind the store, immediately across the street from the barroom. A .60-caliber buffalo gun roared down by the plaza and several Sharps cracked a protest from different points. The town had awakened and the shots were dropping steadily.

Strange noises filled the air. They grew in tone and volume and then dwindled away to nothing. The hum of the buffalo gun and the sobbing *pi-in-in-ing* of the Winchesters were liberally mixed with the sharp whines of the revolvers.

There were no windows in the hotel now. Raw furrows in the bleached wood showed yellow, and splinters mysteriously sprang from the casings. The panels of the door were producing cracks and the cheap door handle flew many ways at once. An empty whisky keg on the stoop boomed out mournfully at intervals and finally rolled down the steps with a rumbling protest. Wisps of smoke slowly climbed up the walls and seemed to be waving defiance to the curling wisps in the open.

Pete raised his shoulder to refill the magazine of his smoking rifle and dropped the cartridges all over his lap. He looked sheepishly at Skinny and began to load with his other hand.

"Yore plum' loco, yu are. Don't yu reckon they kin hit a blue shirt at two hundred?" Skinny cynically inquired. "Got one that time," he announced a second later.

"I wonder who's got th' buffalo," grunted Pete. "Mus' be Cowan," he replied to his own question and settled himself to use his left hand.

"Don't yu git Shorty; he's my meat," suggested Skinny.

"Yu better tell Buck—he ain't got no love fer Shorty," replied Pete, aiming carefully.

The panic in the corral ceased and Hopalong was now sending his regrets against the panels of the rear door. He had cut his last initial in the near panel and was starting a wobbly "H" in its neighbor. He was in a good position. There were no windows in the rear wall, and as the door was a very dangerous place he was not fired at.

He began to get tired of this one-sided business and crawled up on the window ledge, dangling his feet on the outside. He occasionally sent a bullet at a different part of the door, but amused himself by annoying Buck.

"Plenty hot down there?" he pleasantly inquired, and as he received no answer he tried again. "Better save some of them cartridges fer some other time, Buck."

Buck was sending .45 Winchesters into the shattered window with a precision that presaged evil to any of the defenders who were rash enough to try to gain the other end of the room.

Hopalong bit off a chew of tobacco and drowned a green fly that was crawling up the side of the barn. The yellow liquid streaked downward a short distance and was eagerly sucked up by the warped boards.

A spurt of smoke leaped from the battered door and the bored Hopalong promptly tumbled back inside. He felt of his arm, and then, delighted at the notice taken of his artistic efforts, shot several times from a crack on his right. "This yer's shore gittin' like home," he gravely remarked to the splinter that whizzed past his head. He shot again at the door and it sagged outward, accompanied by the thud of a falling body. "Pies like mother used to make," he announced to the empty loft as he slipped the magazine full of .45's. "An' pills like popper used to take," he continued when he had lowered the level of the liquor in his flask.

He rolled a cigarette and tossed the match into the air, extinguishing it by a shot from his Colt.

"Got any cigarettes, Hoppy?" said a voice from below.

"Shore," replied the joyous puncher, recognizing Pete; "how'd yu git here?"

"Like a cow. Busy?"

"None whatever. Comin' up?"

"Nope. Skinny wants a smoke too."

Hopalong handed tobacco and papers down the hole. "So long."

"So long," replied the daring Pete, who risked death twice for a smoke.

The hot afternoon dragged along and about three o'clock Buck held up an empty cartridge belt to the gaze of the curious Hopalong. That observant worthy nodded and threw a double handful of cartridges, one by one, to the patient and unrelenting Buck, who filled his gun and piled the few remaining ones up at his side. "Th' lives of mice and men gang aft all wrong," he remarked at random.

"Th' son-of-a-gun's talkin' Shakespeare," marveled Hopalong.

"Satiate any, Buck?" he asked as that worthy settled down to await his chance.

"Two," he replied, "Shorty an' another. Plenty damn hot down here," he complained. A spurt of alkali dust stung his face but the hand that made it never made another. "Three," he called. "How many, Hoppy?"

"One. That's four. Wonder if th' others got any?"

"Pete said Skinny got one," replied the intent Buck.

"Th' son-of-a-gun, he never said nothin' about it, an' me a fillin' his ornery paws with smokin'." Hopalong was indignant.

"Bet yu ten we don't git 'em afore dark," he announced.

"Got yu. Go yu ten more I gits another," promptly responded Buck.

"That's a shore cinch. Make her twenty."

"She is."

"Yu'll have to square it with Skinny, he shore

wanted Shorty plum' bad," Hopalong informed the unerring marksman.

"Why didn't he say suthin' about it? Anyhow, Jimmy was my bunkie."

Hopalong's cigarette disintegrated and the board at his left received a hole. He promptly disappeared and Buck laughed. He sat up in the loft and angrily spat the soaked paper out from between his lips.

"All that trouble fer nothin', th' white-eyed coyote," he muttered. Then he crawled around to one side and fired at the center of his "C." Another shot hurtled at him and his left arm fell to his side. "That's funny—wonder where th' damn pirut is?" He looked out cautiously and saw a cloud of smoke over a knothole which was situated close up under the eaves of the barroom; and it was being agitated. Someone was blowing at it to make it disappear. He aimed very carefully at the knot and fired. He heard a sound between a curse and a squawk and was not molested any further from that point.

"I knowed he'd git hurt," he explained to the bandage, torn from the edge of his kerchief, which he carefully bound around his last wound.

Down in the arroyo Johnny was complaining.

"This yer's a no-good bunk," he plaintively remarked.

"It shore ain't—but it's th' best we kin find," apologized Billy.

"That's th' sixth that feller sent up there. He's a damn poor shot," observed Johnny; "must be Shorty."

"Shorty kin shoot plum' good—tain't him," contradicted Billy.

"Yas—with a six-shooter. He's off'n his feed with a rifle," explained Johnny.

"Yu wants to stay down from up there, yu ijit," warned Billy as the disgusted Johnny crawled up the bank. He slid down again with a welt on his neck.

"That's somebody else now. He oughter a done better'n that," he said.

Billy had fired as Johnny started to slide and he smoothed his aggrieved chum. "He could onct, yu means."

"Did yu git him?" asked the anxious Johnny, rubbing his welt.

"Plum' center," responded the businesslike Billy. "Go up agin, mebby I kin git another," he suggested tentatively.

"Mebby you kin go to hell. I ain't no gallery," grinned the now-exuberant owner of the welt.

"Who's got th' buffalo?" he inquired as the .60 caliber roared.

"Mus' be Cowan. He's shore all right. Sounds like a bloomin' cannon," replied Billy. "Lemme alone with yore fool questions, I'm busy," he complained as his talkative partner started to ask another. "Go an' git me some water—I'm alkalied. An' git some .45's, mine's purty near gone."

Johnny crawled down the arroyo and reappeared at Hopalong's barn.

As he entered the door a handful of empty shells fell on his hat and dropped to the floor. He shook his head and remarked, "That mus' be that fool Hopalong."

"Yore shore right. How's business?" inquired the festive Cassidy.

"Purty fair. Billy's got one. How many's gone?"

"Buck's got three, I got two and Skinny's got one. That's six, an' Billy's is seven. They's five more," he replied.

"How'd yu know?" queried Johnny as he filled his flask at the horse trough.

"Because they's twelve cayuses behind th' ho*tel*. That's why."

"They might git away on 'em," suggested the practical Johnny.

"Can't. They's all cashed in."

"Yu said that they's five left," ejaculated the puzzled water-carrier.

"Yah; yore a smart cuss, ain't yu?"

Johnny grinned and then said, "Got any smokin'?"

Hopalong looked grieved. "I ain't no store. Why don't yu git generous and buy some?"

He partially filled Johnny's hand, and as he put the sadly depleted bag away he inquired, "Got any papers?"

"Nope."

"Got any matches?" he asked cynically.

"Nope."

"Kin yu smoke 'em?" he yelled, indignantly.

"Sure nuff," placidly replied the unruffled Johnny. "Billy wants some .45's."

Hopalong gasped. "Don't he want my gun, too?"

"Nope. Got a better one. Hurry up, he'll git mad."

Hopalong was a very methodical person. He was the only one of his crowd to carry a second cartridge strap. It hung over his right shoulder and rested on his left hip, holding one hundred cartridges and his second Colt. His waist belt held fifty cartridges and all would fit both the rifle and revolvers. He extracted twenty from that part of the shoulder strap hardest to get at, the back, by simply pulling it over his shoulder and plucking out the bullets as they came into reach.

"That's all yu kin have. I'm *Buck's* ammernition

jackass," he explained. "Bet yu ten we gits 'em afore dark"—he was hedging.

"Any fool knows that. I'll take yu if yu bets th' other way," responded Johnny, grinning. He knew Hopalong's weak spot.

"Yore on," promptly responded Hopalong, who would bet on anything.

"Well, so long," said Johnny as he crawled away.

"Hey, yu, Johnny!" called out Hopalong, "don't yu go an' tell anybody I got any pills left. I ain't no ars'nal."

Johnny replied by elevating one foot and waving it. Then he disappeared.

Behind the store, the most precarious position among the besiegers, Red Connors and Lanky Smith were ensconced and commanded a view of the entire length of the barroom. They could see the dark mass they knew to be the rear door and derived a great amount of amusement from the spots of light which were appearing in it.

They watched the "C" (reversed to them) appear and be completed. When the wobbly "H" grew to completion they laughed heartily. Then the hardwood bar had been dragged across their field of vision and up to the front windows, and they could only see the indiscriminate holes which appeared in the upper panels at frequent intervals.

Every time they fired they had to expose a part of themselves to a return shot, with the result that Lanky's forearm was seared its entire length. Red had been more fortunate and only had a bruised ear.

They laboriously rolled several large rocks out in the open, pushing them beyond the shelter of the store with their rifles. When they had crawled behind them they each had another wound. From their new position they could see Hopalong sitting in his window. He promptly waved his sombrero and grinned.

They were the most experienced fighters of all except Buck, and were saving their shots. When they did shoot they always had some portion of a man's body to aim at, and the damage they inflicted was considerable. They said nothing, being older than the rest and more taciturn, and they were not reckless. Although Hopalong's antics made them laugh, they grumbled at his recklessness and were not tempted to emulate him. It was noticeable, too, that they shoved their rifles out simultaneously and, although both were aiming, only one fired. Lanky's gun cracked so close to the enemy's that the whirr of the bullet over Red's head was merged in the crack of his partner's reply.

When Hopalong saw the rocks roll out from behind the store he grew very curious. Then he saw a flash, followed instantly by another from the second rifle. He saw several of these follow shots and could sit in silence no longer. He waved his hat to attract attention and then shouted, "How many?" A shot was sent straight up in the air and he notified Buck that there were only four left.

The fire of these four grew less rapid—they were saving their ammunition. A potshot at Hopalong sent that gentleman's rifle hurtling to the ground. Another tore through his hat, removing a neat amount of skin and hair and giving him a lifelong part. He fell back inside and proceeded to shoot fast and straight with his revolvers, his head burning as though on fire. When he had vented the dangerous pressure of his anger he went below and tried to fish the rifle in with a long stick. It was obdurate, so he

sent three more shots into the door, and, receiving
no reply, ran out around the corner of his shelter
and grasped the weapon. When halfway back he
sank to the ground. Before another shot could be
fired at him with any judgment a ripping, spitting
rifle was being frantically worked from the barn. The
bullets tore the door into seams and gaps; the lowest
panel, the one having the "H" in it, fell inward in
chunks. Johnny had returned for another smoke.

Hopalong, still grasping the rifle, rolled rapidly
around the corner of the barn. He endeavored to
stand, but could not. Johnny, hearing rapid and flu-
ent swearing, came out.

"Where'd they git yu?" he asked.

"In th' off leg. Hurts like hell. Did yu git him?"

"Nope. I jest come fer another cig; got any left?"

"Up above. Yore gall is shore appallin'. Help me
in, yu two-laigged jackass."

"Shore. We'll shore pay our 'tentions to that door.
She'll go purty soon—she's as full of holes as th' Bad
Lan's," replied Johnny. "Git aholt an' hop along,
Hopalong."

He helped the swearing Hopalong inside, and then
the lead they pumped into the wrecked door was
scandalous. Another panel fell in and Hopalong's "C"
was destroyed. A wide crack appeared in the one
above it and grew rapidly. Its mate began to gape
and finally both were driven in. The increase in the
light caused by these openings allowed Red and
Lanky to secure better aim and soon the fire of the
defenders died out.

Johnny dropped his rifle and, drawing his six-
shooter, ran out and dashed for the dilapidated door,
while Hopalong covered that opening with a fusillade.

As Johnny's shoulder sent the framework flying inward he narrowly missed sudden death. As it was he staggered to the side, out of range, and dropped full-length to the ground, flat on his face. Hopalong's rifle cracked incessantly, but to no avail. The man who had fired the shot was dead. Buck got him immediately after he had shot Johnny.

Calling to Skinny and Red to cover him, Buck sprinted to where Johnny lay gasping. The bullet had entered his breast, just missed his lungs and had passed out his back. Buck, Colt in hand, leaped through the door, but met with no resistance. He signaled to Hopalong, who yelled, "They's none left."

The trees and rocks and gullies and buildings yielded men who soon crowded around the hotel. A young doctor, lately graduated, appeared. It was his first case, but he eased Johnny and saved his life. Then he went over to Hopalong, who was now raving, and attended to him. The others were patched up as well as possible and the struggling young physician had his pockets crammed full of gold and silver coins.

The scene of the wrecked barroom was indescribable. Holes, furrows, shattered glass and bottles, the liquor oozing down the walls of the shelves and running over the floor; the ruined furniture, a wrecked bar, seared and shattered and covered with blood; bodies as they had been piled in the corners; ropes, shells, hats; and liquor everywhere, over everything, met the gaze of those who had caused the chaos.

Perry's Bend had failed to wipe out the score.

CHAPTER IV

The Vagrant Sioux

BUCKSKIN GRADUALLY readjusted itself to the conditions which had existed before its sudden leap into the limelight as a town which did things. The soirée at the Houston House had drifted into the past, and was now substantially established as an epoch in the history of the town. Exuberant joy gave way to dignity and deprecation, and to solid satisfaction; and the conversations across the bar brought forth parallels of the affair to be judged impartially—and the impartial judgment was, unanimously, that while there had undoubtedly been good fights before Perry's Bend had disturbed the local quiet, they were not quite up to the new standard of strenuous hospitality. Finally the heat blistered everything back into the old state, and the shadows continued to be in demand.

One afternoon, a month after the reception of the honorable delegation from Perry's Bend, the town of Buckskin seemed desolated, and the earth and the buildings thereon were as huge furnaces radiating a visible heat, but when the blazing sun had begun to settle in the west it awoke with a clamor which might have been laid to the efforts of a zealous Satan. At this time it became the Mecca of two score or more joyous cowboys from the neighboring ranches, who livened things as those knights of the saddle could.

In the scant but heavy shadow of Cowan's saloon sat a picturesque figure from whom came guttural, resonant rumblings which mingled in a spirit of loneliness with the fretful sighs of a flea-tormented dog. Both dog and master were vagrants, and they were tolerated because it was a matter of supreme indifference as to who came or how long they stayed as long as the ethics and the unwritten law of the cow country were inviolate. And the breaking of these caused no unnecessary anxiety, for justice was both speedy and sure.

When the outcast Sioux and his yellow dog had drifted into town some few months before they had caused neither expostulation nor inquiry, as the cardinal virtue of that whole broad land was to ask a man no questions which might prove embarrassing to all concerned; judgment was of observation, not of history, and a man's past would reveal itself through actions. It mattered little whether he was an embezzler or the wild chip from some prosperous eastern block, as men came to the range to forget and to lose touch with the pampered East; and the range absorbed them as its own. A man was only a man when he had the qualities necessary; and the illiterate who could ride and shoot and live to himself was far more esteemed than the educated who could not do those things. The more a man depends upon himself and the closer is his contact to a quick judgment the more laconic and even-poised he becomes. And the knowledge that he is himself a judge tends to create caution and judgment. He has no court to uphold his honor and to offer him protection, so he must be quick to protect himself and to maintain his own standing. His nature saved him, or it executed; and the range absolved him of all unpaid penalties of a careless past. He became a man born again and he took up his burden, the exactions of a new environment, and he lived as long as those exactions gave him the right to live. He must tolerate no restrictions of his natural rights, and he must not restrict; for the one would proclaim him a coward, the other a bully; and both received short shrifts in that land of the self-protected. The basic law of nature is the survival of the fittest.

So, when the wanderers found their level in Buckskin they were not even asked by what name men knew them. Not caring to hear a name which might not harmonize with their idea of the fitness of things, the cowboys of the Bar-20 had, with a freedom born of excellent livers and fearless temperaments, bestowed names befitting their sense of humor and adaptability. The official title of the Sioux was By-and-by; the dog was known as Fleas. Never had names more clearly described the objects to be represented, for they were excellent examples of cowboy discernment and aptitude.

In their eyes By-and-by was a man. He could feel and he could resent insults. With them he had a right to enjoy his life as he saw fit so long as he did not trespass on or restrict the rights of others. They were not analytic in temperament, neither were they moralists. He was not a menace to society, because society had superb defenses. So they vaguely rec-

ognized his many poor qualities and clearly saw his
few good ones. He could shoot, when permitted,
with the best; no horse, however refractory, had ever
been known to throw him; he was an adept at following the trails left by rustlers, and that was an
asset; he became of value to the community; he was
an economic factor. His ability to consume liquor
with indifferent effects raised him another notch in
their estimation. He was not always talking when
someone else wished to—another count. There remained about him that stoical indifference to the
petty; that observant nonchalance; and a dignity common to chieftains. He was a log of grave deference
which tossed on their sea of mischievous hilarity.

He wore a pair of corduroy trousers, known to the
carefree as "pants," which were held together by
numerous patches of what had once been brilliantly
colored calico. A pair of suspenders, torn into two
separate straps, made a belt for himself and a collar
for his dog. The trousers had probably been secured
during a fit of absentmindedness on his part when
their former owner had not been looking. Tucked at
intervals in the top of the corduroys (the exceptions
making convenient shelves for alkali dust) was what
at one time had been a stiff-bosomed shirt. This was
open down the front and back, the weight of the
trousers on the belt holding it firmly on the square
shoulders of the wearer, thus precluding the necessity of collar buttons. A pair of moccasins, beautifully
worked with wampum, protected his feet from the
onslaughts of cacti and the inquisitive and pugnacious sand flies; and lying across his lap was a repeating Winchester rifle.

The two were contented and happy. They had no
cares nor duties, and their pleasures were simple and

easily secured, as they consisted of sleep and a proneness to avoid moving. Like the untrammeled coyote, their bed was where sleep overtook them; their food, what the night wrapped in a sense of security, or the generosity of the cowboys of the Bar-20. No cowboy ever knew so little of responsibility or as much unadulterated content. There is a penalty even to civilization and ambition.

When the sun had cast its shadows beyond By-and-by's feet the air became charged with noise; shouts, shots and the rolling thunder of madly pounding hoofs echoed flatly throughout the town. By-and-by yawned, stretched and leaned back, reveling in the semiconscious ecstasy of the knowledge that he did not have to immediately get up. Fleas opened one eye and cocked an ear in inquiry, and then rolled over on his back, squirmed and sighed contentedly and long. The outfit of the Bar-20 had come to town.

The noise came rapidly nearer and increased in volume as the riders turned the corner and drew rein suddenly, causing their mounts to slide on their haunches in ankle-deep dust.

"Hullo, old Buck-with-th'-pants, how's yore liver?"

"Come up an' irrigate, old tank!"

"Chase th' flea ranch an' trail along!"

These were a few of the salutations discernible among the medley of playful yells, the safety valves of supercharged good-nature.

"Skr-e-e!" yelled Hopalong Cassidy, letting off a fusillade of shots in the vicinity of Fleas, who rapidly retreated around the corner, where he wagged his tail in eager expectation. He was not disappointed, for a cow pony tore around in pursuit and Hopalong leaned over and scratched the yellow back, thumping it heartily, and, tossing a chunk of beef into the open jaws of the delighted dog, departed as he had come. The advent of the outfit meant a square meal, and the dog knew it.

In Cowan's, lined up against the bar, the others were earnestly and assiduously endeavoring, with a promise of success, to get By-and-by drunk, which endeavors coincided perfectly with By-and-by's idea of the fitness of things. The fellowship and the liquor combined to thaw out his reserve and to loosen his tongue. After gazing with an air of injured surprise at the genial loosening of his knees he gravely handed his rifle with an exaggerated sweep of his arm, to the cowboy nearest him, and wrapped his arms around the recipient to insure his balance. The rifle was passed from hand to hand until it came to Buck Peters, who gravely presented it to its owner as a new gun.

By-and-by threw out his stomach in an endeavor to keep his head in line with his heels, and grasping the weapon with both hands turned to Cowan, to whom he gave it.

"Yu hab this un. Me got two. Me keep new un, mebbyso." Then he loosened his belt and drank long and deep.

A shadow darkened the doorway and Hopalong limped in. Spying By-and-by pushing the bottle into his mouth, while Red Connors propped him, he grinned and took out five silver dollars, which he jingled under By-and-by's eyes, causing that worthy to lay aside the liquor and erratically grab for the tantalizing fortune.

"Not yet," said Hopalong, changing the position of the money. "If yu wants to corral this here herd of simoleons yu has to ride a cayuse what Red bet

me yu can't ride. Yu has got to grow on that there
saddle and stayed growed for five whole minutes by
Buck's ticker. I ain't a-goin' to tell yu he's any saw-
horse, and yu'd know better, as yu reckons Red
wouldn't bet on no losin' proposition if he knowed better, which same he don't. Yu straddles that four-laigged
cloudburst an' yu gets these. I ain't seen th' cayuse yet
that yu couldn't freeze to, an' I'm backin' my opinions
with my moral support an' one month's pay."

By-and-by's eyes began to glitter as the meaning
of the words sifted through his befuddled mind. Ride
a horse—five dollars—then he straightened up and
began to speak in an incoherent jumble of Sioux and
bad English. He, the mighty rider of the Sioux; he,
the bravest warrior and the greatest hunter; could
he ride a horse for five dollars? Well, he rather
thought he could. Grasping Red by the shoulder, he
tacked for the door and narrowly missed hitting the
bottom step first, landing, as it happened, in the soft
dust. Somewhat sobered by the jar, he stood up and
apologized to the crowd.

The outfit of the Bar-20 was, perhaps, the most
famous of all from Canada to the Rio Grande. The
foreman, Buck Peters, controlled a crowd of men
(who had all the instincts of boys) that had shown no
quarter to many rustlers, and who, while always
carefree and easygoing (even fighting with great
good humor and carelessness), had established the
reputation of being the most reckless gang of daredevil gunfighters that ever pounded leather. Crooked
gaming houses, from El Paso to Cheyenne and from
Phœnix to Leavenworth, unanimously and enthusiastically damned them from their boots to their
sombreros, and the sheriffs and marshals of many
localities had received from their hands most timely

assistance—and some trouble. Wiry, indomitable, boyish and generous, they were splendid examples of virile manhood; and, surrounded as they were with great dangers and a unique civilization, they should not, in justice, be judged by opinions born of the commonplace.

They were real cowboys, which means, public opinion to the contrary notwithstanding, that they were not lawless, nor drunken, shooting bullies who held life cheaply, as their kin has been unjustly pictured; but while these men were naturally peaceable they had to continually rub elbows with men who were not. Gamblers, criminals, bullies and the riffraff that fled from the protected East had drifted among them in great numbers, and it was this class that caused the trouble. The hardworking "cowpunchers" lived according to the law of the land, and they obeyed that greatest of all laws, that of self-preservation. Their fun was boisterous, but they paid for all the damage they inflicted; their work was one continual hardship, and the reaction of one extreme swings far toward the limit of its antithesis. Go back to the Apple if you would trace the beginning of self-preservation and the need.

Buck Peters was a man of mild appearance, somewhat slow of speech and correspondingly quick of action, who never became flurried. His was the master hand that controlled, and his Colts enjoyed the reputation of never missing when a hit could have been expected with reason. Many floods, stampedes and blizzards had assailed his nerves, but he yet could pour a glass of liquor, held at arm's length, through a knothole in the floor without wetting the wood.

Next in age came Lanky Smith, a small, undersized man of retiring disposition. Then came Skinny

Thompson, six feet four on his bared soles, and true to his name; Hopalong described him as "th' shadow of a chalk mark." Pete Wilson, the slow-witted and very taciturn, and Billy Williams, the wavering pessimist, were of ordinary height and appearance. Red Connors, with hair that shamed the name, was the possessor of a temper which was as dry as tinder; his greatness weakness was his regard for the rifle as a means of preserving peace. Johnny Nelson was the protégé, and he could do no wrong. The last, Hopalong Cassidy, was a combination of irresponsibility, humor, good nature, love of fighting, and nonchalance when face-to-face with danger. His most prominent attribute was that of always getting into trouble without any intention of so doing; in fact, he was much aggrieved and surprised when it came. It seemed as though when any "bad man" desired to add to his reputation he invariably selected Hopalong as the means (a fact due, perhaps, to the perversity of things in general). Bad men became scarce soon after Hopalong became a fixture in any locality. He had been crippled some years before in a successful attempt to prevent the assassination of a friend, Sheriff Harris, of Albuquerque, and he still possessed a limp.

When Red had relieved his feelings and had dug the alkali out of his ears and eyes, he led the Sioux to the rear of the saloon, where a "pinto" was busily engaged in endeavoring to pitch a saddle from his back, employing the intervals in trying to see how much of the picket rope he could wrap around his legs.

When By-and-bye saw what he was expected to ride he felt somewhat relieved, for the pony did not appear to have more than the ordinary amount of cussedness. He waved his hand, and Johnny and Red bandaged

the animal's eyes, which quieted him at once, and then
they untangled the rope from around his legs and saw
that the cinches were secure. Motioning to By-and-by
that all was ready, they jerked the bandage off as the
Indian settled himself in the saddle.

Had By-and-by been really sober he would have
taken the conceit out of that pony in chunks, and as it
was he experienced no great difficulty in holding his
seat; but in his addled state of mind he grasped the end
of the cinch strap in such a way that when the pony
jumped forward in its last desperate effort the buckle
slipped and the cinch became unfastened; and By-and-
by, still seated in the saddle, flew headforemost into
the horse trough, where he spilled much water.

As this happened Cowan turned the corner, and
when he saw the wasted water (which he had to
carry, bucketful at a time, from the wells a good
quarter of a mile away) his anger blazed forth, and
yelling, he ran for the drenched Sioux, who was just
crawling out of his bath. When the unfortunate saw
the irate man bearing down on him he sputtered in
rage and fear, and, turning, he ran down the street,
with Cowan thundering flat-footedly behind on a fat
man's gallop, to the hysterical cheers of the delighted outfit, who saw in it nothing but a good joke.

When Cowan returned from his hopeless task, blowing and wheezing, he heard sundry remarks, which
were not calculated to increase his opinion of his
physical condition.

"Seems to me," remarked the irrepressible Hopalong, "that one of those cayuses has got th' heaves."

"It shore sounds like it," acquiesced Johnny, red
in the face from holding in his laughter, "an' say,
somebody interferes."

"All knock-kneed animals do, yu heathen," supplied Red.

"Hey, yu, let up on that an' have a drink on th' house," invited Cowan. "If I gits that damn Sioux I'll make yu think there's been a cyclone. I'll see how long that bum hangs around this here place, I will."

Red's eyes narrowed and his temper got the upper hand. "He ain't no bum when yu gives him rotgut at a quarter of a dollar a glass, is he? Anytime that 'bum' gits razzled out for nothin' more'n this, why, I goes too; an' I ain't sayin' nothin' about goin' peaceable-like, neither."

"I knowed somethin' like this 'ud happen," dolefully sang out Billy Williams, strong on the side of his pessimism.

"For th' Lord's sake, have yu broke out?" asked Red, disgustedly. "I'm goin' to hit the trail—but just keep this afore yore mind: if By-and-by gits in any accidents or ain't in sight when I comes to town again, this here climate'll be a damn sight hotter'n it is now. No hard feelings? It's just a casual bit of advice. Come on, fellows, let's amble—I'm hungry."

As they raced across the plain toward the ranch a pair of beady eyes, snapping with a drunken rage, watched them from an arroyo; and when Cowan entered the saloon the next morning he could not find By-and-by's rifle, which he had placed behind the bar. He also missed a handful of cartridges from the box near the cash drawer; and had he looked closely at his bottled whiskey he would have noticed a loss there. A horse was missing from a Mexican's corral and there were rumors that several Indians had been seen far out on the plain.

CHAPTER V

The Law of the Range

"Phew! I'm shore hungry," said Hopalong, as he and Red dismounted at the ranch the next morning for breakfast. "Wonder what's good for it?"

"They's three things that's good for famine," said Red, leading the way to the bunkhouse. "Yu can pull in yore belt, yu can drink, an' yu can eat. Yore getting as bad as Johnny—but he's young yet."

The others met their entrance with a volley of good-humored banter, some of which was so personal and evoked such responses that it sounded like the preliminary skirmish to a fight. But under all was that soft accent, that drawl of humorous appreciation and eyes twinkling in suppressed merriment. Here they were thoroughly at home and the spirit of comradeship manifested itself in many subtle ways; the wit became more daring and sharp. Billy lost some of his pessimism, and the alertness disappeared from their manner.

Skinny left off romping with Red and yawned. "I

wish that cook'ud wake up an' git breakfast. He's the cussedest thing I ever saw—he kin go to sleep standin' up an' not know it. *Johnny's* th' boy that worries him—th' kid comes in an' whoops things up till he's gorged himself."

"Johnny's got th' most appallin' feel for grub of anybody I knows," added Red. "I wonder what's keepin' him—he's usually bangin' around here bawlin' for his grub like a spoiled calf, long afore cookie's got th' fire goin'."

"Mebby he rustled some grub out with him—I saw him tiptoein' out of th' gallery this mornin' when I come back for my cigs," remarked Hopalong, glancing at Billy.

Billy groaned and made for the gallery. Emerging half a minute later he blurted out his tale of woe: "Every time I blows myself an' don't drink it all in town some slab-sided maverick freezes to it. It's gone," he added, dismally.

"Too bad, Billy—but what is it?" asked Skinny.

"What is it? Wha'd yu think it was, yu emaciated match? *Jewelry? Cayuses?* It's whisky—two dollars' worth. Somethin's allus wrong. This here whole yearth's wrong."

"Will yu let up?" yelled Red, throwing a sombrero at the grumbling unfortunate. "Yu ask Buck where yore tanglefoot is."

"I'd shore look nice askin' th' *boss* if he'd rustled my whisky, *wouldn't I*? An' would yu mind throwin' somebody else's hat? I paid twenty wheels for that eight years ago, and I don't want it mussed none."

"Gee, yore easy! Why, Ah Sing, over at Albuquerque, gives them away every time yu gits yore shirt washed," gravely interposed Hopalong as he went out to cuss the cook.

"Well, what'd yu think of that?" exclaimed Billy in an injured tone.

"Oh, yu needn't be hikin' for Albuquerque—Washee-Washee'ud charge yu double for washin' yore shirt. Yu ought to fall in th' river someday—then he might talk business," called Hopalong over his shoulder as he heaved an old boot into the gallery. "Hey, yu hibernatin' son of morphine, if yu don't git them flapjacks in here pretty sudden-like I'll scatter yu all over th' landscape. Yu just wait till Johnny comes!"

"Wonder where th' kid is?" asked Lanky, rolling a cigarette.

"Off somewhere lookin' at th' sun through th' bottom of my bottle," grumbled Billy.

Hopalong started to go out, but halted on the sill and looked steadily off toward the northwest. "That's funny. Hey, fellows, here comes Buck an' Johnny ridin' double—on a walk, too!" he exclaimed. "Wonder what th'—thunder! Red, Buck's carryin' him! Somethin's busted!" he yelled, as he dashed for his pony and made for the newcomers.

"I told yu he was hittin' my bottle," pertly remarked Billy, as he followed the rest outside.

"Did yu ever see Johnny drunk? Did yu ever see him drink more'n two glasses? Shut yore wailin' face—they's somethin' worse'n that in this here," said Red, his temper rising. "Hopalong an' me took yore cheap liquor—it's under Pete's bunk," he added.

The trio approached on a walk and Johnny, delirious and covered with blood, was carried into the bunkhouse. Buck waited until all had assembled again and then, his face dark with anger, spoke sharply and without the usual drawl: "Skragged from behind, damn them! Get some grub an' water an' be quick. We'll see who the gent with th' grudge is."

At this point the expostulations of the indignant cook, who, not understanding the cause, regarded the invasion of china-shop bulls as sacrilegious, came to his ears. Striding quickly to the door, he grabbed the pan the Mexican was about to throw and, turning the now frightened man around, thundered, "Keep quiet an' get 'em some grub."

When rifles and ammunition had been secured they mounted and followed him at a hard gallop along the back trail. No words were spoken, for none were necessary. All knew that they would not return until they had found the man for whom they were looking, even if the chase let to Canada. They did not ask Buck for any of the particulars, for the foreman was not in the humor to talk, and all, save Hopalong, whose curiosity was always on edge, recognized only two facts and cared for nothing else: Johnny had been ambushed and they were going to get the one who was responsible. They did not even conjecture as to who it might be, because the trail would lead them to the man himself, and it mattered nothing who or what he was—there was only one course to take with an assassin. So they said nothing, but rode on with squared jaws and set lips, the seven ponies breast to breast in a close arc.

Soon they came to an arroyo which they took at a leap. As they approached it they saw signs in the dust which told them that a body had lain there huddled up; and there were brown spots on the baked alkali. The trail they followed was now single, Buck having ridden along the bank of the arroyo when hunting for Johnny, for whom he had orders. This trail was very irregular, as if the horse had wan-dered at will. Suddenly they came upon five tracks, all pointing one way, and four of these turned abruptly and disappeared in the northwest. Half a mile beyond the point of separation was a chaparral, which was an important factor to them.

Each man knew just what had taken place as if he had been an eyewitness, for the trail was plain. The assassins had waited in the chaparral for Johnny to pass, probably having seen him riding that way. When he had passed and his back had been turned to them they had fired and wounded him severely at the first volley, for Johnny was of the stuff that fights back and his revolvers had showed full chambers and clean barrels when Red had examined them in the bunkhouse. Then they had given chase for a short distance and, from some inexplicable motive, probably fear, they had turned and ridden off without knowing how bad he was hit. It was this trail that led to the northwest, and it was this trail that they followed without pausing.

When they had covered fifty miles they sighted the Cross Bar O ranch, where they hoped to secure fresh mounts. As they rode up to the ranch house the owner, Bud Wallace, came around the corner and saw them.

"Hullo, boys! What deviltry are yu up to now?" he asked.

Buck leaped from his mount, followed by the others, and shoved his sombrero back on his head as he started to remove the saddle.

"We're trailin' a bunch of murderers. They ambushed Johnny an' damn near killed him. I stopped here to get fresh cayuses."

"Yu did right!" replied Wallace heartily. Then raising his voice he shouted to some of his men who were near the corral to bring up the seven best horses they could rope. Then he told the cook to bring out plenty of food and drink.

"I got four punchers what ain't doin' nothin' but eat," he suggested.

"Much obliged, Wallace, but there's only four of 'em, an' we'd rather get 'em ourselves—Johnny'ud feel better," replied Buck, throwing his saddle on the horse that was led up to him.

"How's yore cartridges—got plenty?" persisted Wallace.

"Two hundred apiece," responded Buck, springing into his saddle and riding off. "So long," he called.

"So long, an' plug hell out of them," shouted Wallace as the dust swept over him.

At five in the afternoon they forded the Black River at a point where it crossed the state line from New Mexico, and at dusk camped at the base of the Guadalupe Mountains. At daybreak they took up the chase, grim and merciless, and shortly afterward they passed the smoldering remains of a camp fire, showing that the pursued had been in a great hurry, for it should have been put out and masked. At noon they left the mountains to the rear and sighted the Barred Horseshoe, which they approached.

The owner of the ranch saw them coming, and from their appearance surmised that something was wrong.

"What is it?" he shouted. "Rustlers?"

"Nope. Murderers. I wants to swap cayuses quick," answered Buck.

"There they are. Th' boys just brought 'em in. Anything else I can let yu have?"

"Nope," shouted Buck as they galloped off.

"Somebody's goin' to get plugged full of holes,"

murmured the ranch owner as he watched them kicking up the dust in huge clouds.

After they had forded a tributary of the Rio Penasco near the Sacramento Mountains and had surmounted the opposite bank, Hopalong spurred his horse to the top of a hummock and swept the plain with Pete's field glasses, which he had borrowed for the occasion, and returned to the rest, who had kept on without slacking the pace. As he took up his former position he grunted, "Indians" and unslung his rifle, an example followed by the others. The ponies were now running at top speed, and as they shot over a rise their riders saw their quarry a mile and a half in advance. One of the Indians looked back and discharged his rifle in defiance, and it now became a race worthy of the name—Death fled from Death. The fresher mounts of the cowboys steadily cut down the distance and, as the rifles of the pursuers began to speak, the hard-pressed Indians made for the smaller of two knolls, the plain leading to the larger one being too heavily strewn with boulders to permit speed.

As the fugitives settled down behind the rocks which fringed the edge of their elevation a shot from one of them disabled Billy's arm, but had no other effect than to increase the score to be settled. The pursuers rode behind a rise and dismounted, from where, leaving their mounts protected, they scattered out to surround the knoll.

Hopalong, true to his curiosity, finally turned up on the highest point of the other knoll, a spur of the range in the west, for he always wanted to see all he could. Skinny, due to his fighting instinct, settled one hundred yards to the north and on the same spur. Buck lay hidden behind an enormous boulder

eight hundred yards to the northeast of Skinny, and
the same distance southeast of Buck was Red Connors, who was crawling up the bed of an arroyo.
Billy, nursing his arm, lay in front of the horses, and
Pete, from his position between Billy and Hopalong,
was crawling from rock to rock in an endeavor to
get near enough to use his Colts, his favorite and
most effective weapons. Intermittent puffs of smoke
arising from a point between Skinny and Buck
showed where Lanky Smith was improving each
shining hour.

There had been no directions given, each man
choosing his own position, yet each was of strategic
worth. Billy protected the horses, Hopalong and
Skinny swept the knoll with a plunging fire, and
Lanky and Buck lay in the course the besieged would
most likely take if they tried a dash. Off to the east
Red barred them from creeping down the arroyo,
and from where Pete was he could creep up to within
sixty yards if he chose the right rocks. The ranges
varied from four hundred yards for Buck to sixty for
Pete, and the others averaged close to three hundred, which allowed very good shooting on both
sides.

Hopalong and Skinny gradually moved nearer to
each other for companionship, and as the former
raised his head to see what the others were doing
he received a graze on the ear.

"Wow!" he yelled, rubbing the tingling member.

Two puffs of smoke floated up from the knoll, and
Skinny swore.

"Where'd he get yu, Fat?" asked Hopalong.

"G'wan, don't get funny, son," replied Skinny.

Jets of smoke arose from the north and east, where
Buck and Red were stationed, and Pete was halfway

to the knoll. So far he hadn't been hit as he dodged in and out, and, emboldened by his luck, he made a run of five yards and his sombrero was shot from his head. Another dash and his empty holster was ripped from its support. As he crouched behind a rock he heard a yell from Hopalong, and saw that interested individual waving his sombrero to cheer him on. An angry *pang!* from the knoll caused that enthusiastic rooter to drop for safety.

"Locoed son-of-a-gun," complained Pete. "He'll shore git potted." Then he glanced at Billy, who was the center of several successive spurts of dust.

"How's business, Billy?" he called pleasantly.

"Oh, they'll git me yet," responded the pessimist. "Yu needn't git anxious. If that off buck wasn't so green he'd 'a' had me long ago."

"Ya-*hoo!* Pete! Oh, Pete!" called Hopalong, sticking his head out at one side and grinning as the wondering object of his hail craned his neck to see what the matter was.

"Huh?" grunted Pete, and then remembering the distance he shouted, "What's th' matter?"

"Got any cigarettes?" asked Hopalong.

"Yu damn sheep!" said Pete, and turning back to work he drove a .44 into a yellow moccasin.

Hopalong began to itch and he saw that he was near an ant hill. Then the cactus at his right boomed out mournfully and a hole appeared in it. He fired at the smoke and a yell informed him that he had made a hit. "Go 'way!" he complained as a green fly buzzed past his nose. Then he scratched each leg with the foot of the other and squirmed incessantly, kicking out with both feet at once. A warning metallic *whir-r-r!* on his left caused him to yank them in again, and turning his head quickly he had the pleasure of lopping off the head of a rattlesnake with his Colt's.

"Glad yu wasn't a copperhead," he exclaimed. "Somebody had ought 'a' shot that fool Noah. Damn the ants!" He drowned with a jet of tobacco juice a Gila monster that was staring at him and took a savage delight in its frantic efforts to bury itself.

Soon he heard Skinny swear and he sung out: 'What's the matter, Skinny? Git plugged again?"

"Naw, bugs—ain't they hell?" plaintively asked his friend.

"They ain't none over here. What kind of bugs?"

"Sufferin' Moses, I ain't no bugologist! All kinds!"

But Hopalong got it at last. He had found tobacco and rolled a cigarette, and in reaching for a match exposed his shoulder to a shot that broke his collarbone. Skinny's rifle cracked in reply and the offending brave rolled out from behind a rock. From the fuss emanating from Hopalong's direction Skinny knew that his neighbor had been hit.

"Don't yu care, Hoppy. I got th' cuss," he said consolingly. "Where'd he git yu?" he asked.

"In th' heart, yu pie-faced nuisance. Come over here an' corral this cussed bandage an' gimme some water," snapped the injured man.

Skinny wormed his way through the thorny chaparral and bound up the shoulder. "Anything else?" he asked.

"Yes. Shoot that bunch of warts an' blow that tobacco-eyed Gila to Cheyenne. This here's worse than the time we cleaned out th' C-80 outfit!" Then he kicked the dead toad and swore at the sun.

"Close yore yap; yore worse than a kid! Anybody'd think yu never got plugged afore," said Skinny indignantly.

"I can cuss all I wants," replied Hopalong, proving his assertion as he grabbed his gun and fired at the dead Indian. A bullet whined above his head and Skinny fired at the smoke. He peeped out and saw that his friends were getting nearer to the knoll.

"They's closin' in now. We'll soon be gittin' home," he reported.

Hopalong looked out in time to see Buck make a dash for a boulder that lay ten yards in front of him, which he reached in safety. Lanky also ran in and Pete added five more yards to his advance. Buck made another dash but leaped into the air, and, coming down as if from an intentional high jump, staggered and stumbled for a few paces and then fell flat, rolling over and over toward the shelter of a split rock, where he lay quiet. A leering red face peered over the rocks on the knoll, but the whoop of exultation was cut short, for Red's rifle cracked and the warrior rolled down the steep bank, where another shot from the same gun settled him beyond question.

Hopalong choked and, turning his face away, angrily dashed his knuckles into his eyes. "Damn 'em! Damn 'em! They've got Buck! They've got Buck, damn 'em! They've got Buck, Skinny! Good old Buck! They've got him! Jimmy's gone, Johnny's plugged, and now Buck's gone! Come on!" he sobbed in a frenzy of vengeance. "Come on, Skinny! We'll tear their cussed hides into a deeper red than they are now! Oh, damn it, I can't see—where's my gun?" He groped for the rifle and fought Skinny when the latter, red-eyed but cool, endeavored to restrain him. "Lemme go, curse yu! Don't yu know they got Buck? Lemme go!"

"Down! Red's got th' skunk. *Yu* can't do nothin'— they'd drop yu afore yu took five steps. *Red's* got

him, I tell yu! We'll pay 'em with th' coals of hell if
yu'll keep yore head!" exclaimed Skinny, throwing
the crazed man heavily.

Musical tones, rising and falling in weird octaves,
whining pityingly, diabolically, sobbing in a fascinat-
ing monotone and slobbering in ragged chords, calling as they swept over the plain, always calling and
exhorting, they mingled in barbaric discord with the
defiant barks of the six-shooters and the inquiring
cracks of the Winchesters. High up in the air several
specks sailed and drifted, more coming up rapidly
from all directions. Buzzards know well where food
can be found.

As Hopalong leaned back against a rock he was
hit in the thigh by a ricochet that tore its way out,
whirling like a circular saw, a span above where it
entered. The wound was very nasty, being ripped
twice the size made by an ordinary shot, and it bled
profusely. Skinny crawled over and attended to it,
making a tourniquet of his neckerchief and clumsily
bandaging it with a strip torn from his shirt.

"Yore shore lucky, yu are," he grumbled as he
made his way back to his post, where he vented his
rancor by emptying the semi-depleted magazine of
his Winchester at the knoll.

Hopalong began to sing and shout and he talked
of Jimmy and his childhood, interspersing the broken narrative with choice selections as sung in the
music halls of Leavenworth and Abilene. He wound
up by yelling and struggling, and Skinny had his
hands full in holding him.

"Hopalong! Cassidy! Come out of that! Keep
quiet—yu'll shore git plugged if yu don't stop that
plungin'. For God's sake, did yu hear that?" A bullet
viciously hissed between them and flattened out on

a nearby rock; others cut their way through the chaparral to the sound of falling twigs, and Skinny threw himself on the struggling man and strapped Hopalong with his belt to the base of a honey mesquite that grew at his side.

"Hold still, now, and let that bandage alone. Yu allus goes off th' range when yu gets plugged," he complained. He cut down a cactus and poured the sap over the wounded man's face, causing him to gurgle and look around. His eyes had a sane look now and Skinny slid off his chest.

"Git that—belt loose; I ain't—no cow," brokenly blazed out the picketed Hopalong. Skinny did so, handed the irate man his Colts and returned to his own post, from where he fired twice, reporting the shots.

"I'm tryin' to get him on th' glance—th' first one went high an' th' other fell flat," he explained.

Hopalong listened eagerly, for this was shooting that he could appreciate. "Lemme see," he commanded. Skinny dragged him over to a crack and settled down for another try.

"Where is he, Skinny?" asked Hopalong.

"Behind that second big one. No, over on this here side. See that smooth granite? If I can get her there on th' right spot he'll shore know it." He aimed carefully and fired.

Through Pete's glasses Hopalong saw a leaden splotch appear on the rock and he notified the marksman that he was shooting high. "Put her on that bump closer down," he suggested. Skinny did so and another yell reached their ears.

"That's a dandy. Yore shore all right, yu old cuss," complimented Hopalong, elated at the success of the experiment.

Skinny fired again and a brown arm flopped out into sight. Another shot struck it and it jerked as though it were lifeless.

"He's cashed. See how she jumped? Like a rope," remarked Skinny with a grin. The arm lay quiet.

Pete had gained his last cover and was all eyes and Colts. Lanky was also very close in and was intently watching one particular rock. Several shots echoed from the far side of the knoll and they knew that Red was all right. Billy was covering a cluster of rocks that protruded above the others and, as they looked, his rifle rang out and the last defender leaped down and disappeared in the chaparral. He wore yellow trousers and an old boiled shirt.

"By-an'-by, by all that's bad!" yelled Hopalong. "Th' measly coyote! An' me a-fillin' his ornery hide with liquor. Well, they'll have to find him all over again now," he complained, astounded by the revelation. He fired into the chaparral to express his pugnacious disgust and scared out a huge tarantula, which alighted on Skinny's chaps, crawling rapidly toward the unconscious man's neck. Hopalong's face hardened and he slowly covered the insect and fired, driving it into the sand, torn and lifeless. The bullet touched the leathern garment and Skinny remonstrated, knowing that Hopalong was in no condition for fancy shooting.

"Huh!" exclaimed Hopalong. "That was a tarantula what I plugged. He was headin' for yore neck," he explained, watching the chaparral with apprehension.

"Go 'way, was it? Bully for yu!" exclaimed Skinny, tarantulas being placed at par with rattlesnakes, and he considered that he had been saved from a horrible death. "Thought yu said they wasn't no bugs over here," he added in an aggrieved tone.

"They wasn't none. Yu brought 'em. I only had th' main show—Gilas, rattlers an' toads," he replied, and then added, "Ain't it cussed hot up here?"

"She is. Yu won't have no cinch ridin' home with that leg. Yu better take my cayuse—he's busted more'n yourn," responded Skinny.

"Yore cayuse is at th' Cross Bar O, yu wall-eyed pirute."

"Shore 'nuff. Funny how a feller forgets sometimes. Lemme alone now, they's goin' to git By-an'-by. Pete an' Lanky has just went in after him."

That was what had occurred. The two impatient punchers had grown tired of waiting, and risked what might easily have been death in order to hasten matters. The others kept up a rapid fire, directed at the far end of the chaparral on the knoll, in order to mask the movements of their venturesome friends, intending also to drive By-and-by toward them so that he would be the one to get picked off as he advanced.

Several shots rang out in quick succession on the knoll and the chaparral became agitated. Several more shots sounded from the depth of the thicket and a mounted Indian dashed out of the northern edge and headed in Buck's direction. His course would take him close to Buck, whom he had seen fall, and would let him escape at a point midway between Red and Skinny, as Lanky was on the knoll and the range was very far to allow effective shooting by these two.

Red saw him leave the chaparral and in his haste to reload jammed the cartridge, and By-and-by swept on toward temporary safety, with Red dancing in a paroxysm of rage, swelling his vocabulary with words he had forgotten existed.

By-and-by, rising to his full height in the saddle, turned and wiggled his fingers at the frenzied Red and made several other signs that the cowboy was in the humor to appreciate to the fullest extent. Then he turned and shook his rifle at the marksmen on the larger knoll, whose best shots kicked up the dust fully fifty yards too short. The pony was sweeping toward the reservation and friends only fifteen miles away, and By-and-by knew that once among the mountains he would be on equal footing at least with his enemies. As he passed the rock behind which Buck lay sprawled on his face he uttered a piercing whoop of triumph and leaned forward on his pony's neck. Twenty leaps farther and the spiteful crack of an unerring rifle echoed from where the foreman was painfully supporting himself on his elbows. The pony swept on in a spurt of nerve-racking speed, but alone. By-and-by shrieked again and crashed heavily to the ground, where he rolled inertly and then lay still. Men like Buck are dangerous until their hearts have ceased to beat.

CHAPTER VI

Trials of the Convalescent

THE DAYS at the ranch passed in irritating idleness for those who had obstructed the flight of hostile lead, and worse than any of the patients was Hopalong, who fretted and fumed at his helplessness, which retarded his recovery. But at last the day came when he was fit for the saddle again, and he gave notice of his joy in whoops and forthwith announced that he was entitled to a holiday; and Buck had not the heart to refuse him. So he started forth in his quest of peace and pleasure, but instead had found only trouble and had been forced to leave his card at almost every place he had visited.

There was that affair in Red Hot Gulch, Colorado, where, under pressure, he had invested sundry pieces of lead in the persons of several obstreperous citizens and then had paced the zealous and excitable sheriff to the state line.

He next was noticed in Cheyenne, where his deformity was vividly dwelt upon, to the extent of six words, by one Tarantula Charley, the aforesaid Charley not being able to proceed to greater length on account of heart failure. As Charley had been a ubiquitous nuisance, those present availed themselves of the opportunity offered by Hopalong to indulge in a free drink.

Laramie was his next stopping place, and shortly after his arrival he was requested to sing and dance by a local terror, who informed all present that he was the only seventeen-buttoned rattlesnake in the cow country. Hopalong, hurt and indignant at being treated like a common tenderfoot, promptly knocked the terror down. After he had irrigated several square feet of parched throats belonging to the audience he again took up his journey and spent a day at Denver, where he managed to avoid any further trouble.

Santa Fé loomed up before him several days later and he entered it shortly before noon. At this time the old Spanish city was a bundle of high-strung nerves, and certain parts of it were calculated to furnish any and all kinds of excitement except revival meetings and church fairs. Hopalong straddled a lively nerve before he had been in the city an hour. Two local bad men, Slim Travennes and Tex Ewalt, desiring to establish the fact that they were roaring prairie fires, attempted to consume the placid and innocent stranger as he limped across the plaza in search of a game of draw poker at the Black Hills Emporium, with the result that they needed repairs, to the chagrin and disgust of their immediate acquaintances, who endeavored to drown their mortification and sorrow in rapid but somewhat wild gunplay, and soon remembered that they had pressing engagements elsewhere.

Hopalong reloaded his guns and proceeded to the Emporium, where he found a game all prepared for him in every sense of the word. On the third deal he objected to the way in which the dealer manipulated the cards, and when the smoke cleared away he was the only occupant of the room, except a dog belonging to the bartender that had intercepted a stray bullet.

Hunting up the owner of the hound, he apologized for being the indirect cause of the animal's death, deposited a sum of Mexican dollars in that gentleman's palm and went on his way to Alameda, which he entered shortly after dark, and where an insult, simmering in its uncalled-for venom, met him as he limped across the floor of the local dispensary on his way to the bar. There was no time for verbal argument and precedent had established the manner of his reply, and his repartee was as quick as light and most effective. Having resented the epithets he gave his attention to the occupants of the room.

Smoke drifted over the table in an agitated cloud and dribbled lazily upward from the muzzle of his six-shooter, while he looked searchingly at those around him. Strained and eager faces peered at his opponent, who was sliding slowly forward in his chair, and for the length of a minute no sound but the guarded breathing of the onlookers could be heard. This was broken by a nervous cough from the rear of the room, and the faces assumed their ordinary nonchalant expressions, their rugged lines heavily shadowed in the light of the flickering oil lamps, while the shuffling of cards and the clink of silver became audible. Hopalong Cassidy had objected to insulting remarks about his affliction.

Hopalong was very sensitive about his crippled leg

and was always prompt to resent any scorn or curiosity directed at it, especially when emanating from strangers. A young man of twenty-three years, when surrounded by nearly perfect specimens of physical manhood, is apt to be painfully self-conscious of any such defect, and it reacted on his nature at times, even though he was well known for his happy-go-lucky disposition and playfulness. He consoled himself with the knowledge that what he lost in symmetry was more than balanced by the celerity and certainty of his gun hand, which was right or left, or both, as the occasion demanded.

Several hours later, as his luck was vacillating, he felt a heavy hand on his shoulder, and was overjoyed at seeing Buck and Red, the latter grinning as only Red could grin, and he withdrew from the game to enjoy his good fortune.

While Hopalong had been wandering over the country the two friends had been hunting for him and had traced him successfully, that being due to the trail he had blazed with his six-shooters. This they had accomplished without harm to themselves, as those of whom they inquired thought that they must want Hopalong "bad," and cheerfully gave the information required.

They had started out more for the purpose of accompanying him for pleasure, but that had changed to an urgent necessity in the following manner:

While on the way from Denver to Santa Fé they had met Pete Willis of the Three Triangle, a ranch that adjoined their own, and they paused to pass the compliments of the season.

"Purty far from th' grub wagon, Pie," remarked Buck.

"Oh, I'm only goin' to Denver," responded Pie.

"Purty hot," suggested Red.

"She shore is. Seen anybody yu knows?" Pie asked.

"One or two—Billy of th' Star Crescent an' Panhandle Lukins," answered Buck.

"That so? Panhandle's goin' to punch for us next year. I'll hunt him up. I heard down south of Albuquerque that 'Thirsty Jones an' his brothers are lookin' for trouble," offered Pie.

"Yah! They ain't lookin' for no trouble—they just goes around blowin' off. Trouble? Why, they don't know what she is," remarked Red contemptuously.

"Well, they's been dodgin' th' sheriff purty lively lately, an' if that ain't trouble I don't know what is," said Pie.

"It shore is, an' hard to dodge," acquiesced Buck.

"Well, I has to amble. Is Panhandle in Denver? Yes? I calculates as how me an' him'll buck th' tiger for a whirl—he's shore lucky. Well, so long," said Pie as he moved on.

"So long," responded the two.

"Hey, wait a minute," yelled Pie after he had ridden a hundred yards. "If yu sees Hopalong yu might tell him that th' Joneses are goin' to hunt him up when they gits to Albuquerque. They's shore sore on him. 'Tain't none of my funeral, only they ain't always a-carin' how they goes after a feller. So long," and soon he was a cloud of dust on the horizon.

"Trouble!" snorted Red; "well, between dodgin' Harris an' huntin' Hopalong I reckons they'll shore find her." Then to himself he murmured, "Funny how everthin' comes his way."

"That's gospel shore enough, but, as Pie said, they ain't a whole lot particular as how they deal th' cards. We better get a move on an' find that ornery little cuss," replied Buck.

"O.K., only I ain't losin' no sleep about Hoppy. His gun's too lively for me to do any worryin'," asserted Red.

"They'll get lynched sometime, shore," declared Buck.

"Not if they find Hoppy," grimly replied Red.

They tore through Santa Fé, only stopping long enough to wet their throats, and after several hours of hard riding entered Alameda, where they found Hopalong in the manner narrated.

After some time the three left the room and headed for Albuquerque, twelve miles to the south. At ten o'clock they dismounted before the Nugget and Rope, an unpainted wooden building supposed to be a clever combination of barroom, dance and gambling hall and hotel. The cleverness lay in the man who could find the hotel part.

CHAPTER VII

The Open Door

THE PROPRIETOR of the Nugget and Rope, a German named Baum, not being troubled with police rules, kept the door wide open for the purpose of inviting trade, a proceeding not to the liking of his patrons for obvious reasons. Probably not one man in ten was fortunate enough to have no one "looking for him," and the lighted interior assured good hunting to anyone in the dark street. He was continually opening the door, which every newcomer promptly and forcibly slammed shut. When he saw men walk across the room for the express purpose of slamming it he began to cherish the idea that there was a conspiracy on foot to anger him and thus force him to bring about his own death. After the door had been slammed three times in one evening by one man, the last slam being so forcible as to shake two bottles from the shelf and to crack the door itself, he became positive that his suspicions were correct, and so was very careful to smile and take it as a joke.

Finally, wearied by his vain efforts to keep it open and fearing for the door, he hit upon a scheme, the brilliancy of which inflated his chest and gave him the appearance of a prize-winning bantam. When his patrons strolled in that night there was no door to slam, as it lay behind the bar.

When Buck and Red entered, closely followed by Hopalong, they elbowed their way to the rear of the room, where they could see before being seen. As yet they had said nothing to Hopalong about Pie's warning and were debating in their minds whether they should do so or not, when Hopalong interrupted their thoughts by laughing. They looked up and he nodded toward the front, where they saw that anxious eyes from all parts of the room were focused on the open door. Then they noticed that it had been removed. The air of semihostile, semi-anxious inquiry of the patrons and the smile of satisfaction covering the face of Baum appealed to them as the most ludicrous sight their eyes had seen for months, and they leaned back and roared with laughter, thus calling forth sundry looks of disapproval from the innocent causers of their merriment. But they were too well known in Albuquerque to allow the disapproval to approach a serious end, and finally, as the humorous side of the situation dawned on the crowd, they joined in the laugh and all went merrily.

At the psychologic moment someone shouted for a dance and the suggestion met with uproarious approval. At that moment Harris, the sheriff, came in and volunteered to supply the necessary music if the crowd would pay the fine against a straying fiddler he had corraled the day before. A hat was quickly passed and a sum was realized which would pay several fines to come and Harris departed for the music.

A chair was placed on the bar for the musician and, to the tune of "Old Dan Tucker" and an assortment of similar airs, the board floor shook and trembled. It was a comical sight and Hopalong, the only wallflower besides Baum and the sheriff, laughed until he became weak. Cowpunchers play as they work, hard and earnestly, and there was plenty of action. Sombreros flapped like huge wings and the baggy chaps looked like small, distorted balloons.

The Virginia reel was a marvel of supple, exaggerated grace and the quadrille looked like a free-for-all for unbroken colts. The honor of prompter was conferred upon the sheriff, and he gravely called the changes as they were usually called in that section of the country:

> "Oh, th' ladies trail in
> An' th' gents trail out,
> An' all stampede down th' middle.
> If yu ain't got th' tin
> Yu can dance an' shout,
> But yu must keep up with th' fiddle."

As the dance waxed faster and the dancers grew hotter Hopalong, feeling lonesome because he wouldn't face ridicule, even if it was not expressed, went over and stood by the sheriff. He and Harris were good friends, for he had received the wound that crippled him in saving the sheriff from assassination. Harris killed the man who had fired that shot, and from this episode on the burning desert grew a friendship that was as strong as their own natures.

Harris was very well liked by the majority and

feared by the rest, for he was a "square" man and the best sheriff the county had ever known. Quiet and unassuming, small of stature and with a kind word for everyone, he was a universal favorite among the better class of citizens. Quick as a flash and unerring in his shooting, he was a nightmare to the "bad men." No profane word had ever been known to leave his lips, and he was the possessor of a widespread reputation for generosity. His face was naturally frank and open; but when his eyes narrowed with determination it became blank and cold. When he saw his young friend sidle over to him he smiled and nodded a hearty welcome.

"They's shore cuttin' her loose," remarked Hopalong.

"First two pairs forward an' back!—they shore is," responded the prompter.

"Who's th' gent playin' lady to Buck?" queried Hopalong.

"Forward again an' ladies change!—Billy Jordan."

Hopalong watched the couple until they swung around and then he laughed silently. "Buck's got too many feet," he seriously remarked to his friend.

"Swing th' girl yu loves th' best!—he ain't lonesome, look at that—"

Two shots rang out in quick succession and Harris stumbled, wheeled and pitched forward on his face as Hopalong's sombrero spun across his body. For a second there was an intense silence, heavy, strained and sickening. Then a roar broke forth and the crowd of frenzied merrymakers, headed by Hopalong, poured out into the street and spread out to search the town. As daylight dawned the searchers began to straggle back with the same report of failure. Buck and Red met on the street near the door and each looked questioningly at the other. Each shook his head and looked around, their fingers toying absentmindedly at their belts. Finally Buck cleared his throat and remarked casually, "Mebby he's following 'em."

Red nodded and they went over toward their horses. As they were hesitating which route to take, Billy Jordan came up.

"Mebby yu'd like to see yore pardner—he's out by Buzzard's Spring. We'll take care of *him*," jerking his thumb over his shoulder toward the saloon where Harris's body lay. "And we'll *all* git th' *others* later. They can't git away for long."

Buck and Red nodded and headed for Buzzard's Spring. As they neared the water hole they saw Hopalong sitting on a rock, his head resting in one hand while the other hung loosely from his knee. He did not notice them when they arrived, and with a ready tact they sat quietly on their horses and looked in every direction except toward him. The sun became a ball of molten fire and the sand flies annoyed them incessantly, but still they sat and waited, silent and apologetic.

Hopalong finally arose, reached for his sombrero, and, finding it gone, swore long and earnestly at the scene its loss brought before him. He walked over to his horse and, leaping into the saddle, turned and faced his friends. "Yu old sons-of-guns," he said. They looked sheepish and nodded negatively in answer to the look of inquiry in his eyes. "They ain't got 'em yet," remarked Red slowly. Hopalong straightened up, his eyes narrowed and his face became hard and resolute as he led the way back toward the town.

Buck rode up beside him and, wiping his face with his shirtsleeve, began to speak to Red. "We *might*

look up th' Joneses, Red. They had been dodgin' th'
sheriff purty lively lately, an' they was huntin' Hopalong. Ever since we had to kill their brother in
Buckskin they has been yappin' as how they was
goin' to wipe us out. Hopalong an' Harris was standin' clost together an' they tried for both. They shot
twice, one for Harris an' one for Hopalong, an' what
more do yu want?"

"It shore looks thataway, Buck," replied Red, biting into a huge plug of tobacco which he produced
from his chaps. "Anyhow, they wouldn't be no loss
if they didn't. 'Member what Pie said?"

Hopalong looked straight ahead, and when he
spoke the words sounded as though he had bitten
them off: "Yore right, Buck, but I gits first try at
Thirsty. He's my meat an' I'll plug th' fellow what
says he ain't. Damn him!"

The others replied by applying their spurs, and in
a short time they dismounted before the Nugget and
Rope. Thirsty wouldn't have a chance to not care
how he dealt the cards.

Buck and Red moved quickly through the crowd,
speaking fast and earnestly. When they returned to
where they had left their friend they saw him half a
block away and they followed slowly, one on either
side of the street. There would be no bullets in his
back if they knew what they were about, and they
usually did.

As Hopalong neared the corner, Thirsty and his
two brothers turned it and saw him. Thirsty said
something in a low voice, and the other two walked
across the street and disappeared behind the store.
When assured that they were secure, Thirsty walked
up to a huge boulder on the side of the street farthest
from the store and turned and faced his enemy, who

approached rapidly until about five paces away, when he slowed up and finally stopped.

For a number of seconds they sized each other up, Hopalong quiet and deliberate with a deadly hatred; Thirsty pale and furtive with a sensation hitherto unknown to him. It was Right meeting Wrong, and Wrong lost confidence. Often had Thirsty Jones looked death in the face and laughed, but there was something in Hopalong's eyes that made his flesh creep.

He glanced quickly past his foe and took in the scene with one flash of his eyes. There was the crowd, eager, expectant, scowling. There were Buck and Red, each lounging against a boulder, Buck on his right, Red on his left. Before him stood the only man he had ever feared. Hopalong shifted his feet and Thirsty, coming to himself with a start, smiled. His nerve had been shaken, but he was master of himself once more.

"Well!" he snarled, scowling.

Hopalong made no response, but stared him in the eyes.

Thirsty expected action, and the deadly quiet of his enemy oppressed him. He stared in turn, but the insistent searching of his opponent's eyes scorched him and he shifted his gaze to Hopalong's neck.

"Well!" he repeated uneasily.

"Did yu have a nice time at th' dance last night?" asked Hopalong, still searching the face before him.

"Was there a dance? I was over in Alameda," replied Thirsty shortly.

"Ya-as, there was a dance, an' yu can shoot purty damn far if yu was in Alameda," responded Hopalong, his voice low and monotonous.

Thirsty shifted his feet and glanced around. Buck

and Red were still lounging against their boulders and apparently were not paying any attention to the proceedings. His fickle nerve came back again, for he knew he would receive fair play. So he faced Hopalong once more and regarded him with a cynical smile.

"Yu seems to worry a whole lot about me. Is it because yu has a tender feelin', or because it's none of yore damn business?" he asked aggressively.

Hopalong paled with sudden anger, but controlled himself.

"It's because yu murdered Harris," he replied.

"An how does yu figger it out?" asked Thirsty, jauntily.

"He was huntin' yu hard an' yu thought yu'd stop it, so yu came in to lay for him. When you saw me an' him together yu saw th' chance to wipe out another score. That's how I figger it out," replied Hopalong quietly.

"Yore a reg'lar 'tective, ain't yu?" Thirsty asked ironically.

"I've got common sense," responded Hopalong.

"Yu has? Yu better tell th' rest that, too," replied Thirsty.

"I know yu shot Harris, an' yu can't get out of it by makin' funny remarks. Anyhow, yu won't be much loss, an' th' stage company'll feel better, too."

"An' suppose I did shoot him, I done a good job, didn't I?"

"Yu did the worst job you could do, yu highway robber," softly said Hopalong, at the same time moving nearer. "Harris knew yu stopped th' stage last month, an' that's why yu've been dodgin' him."

"Yore a liar!" shouted Thirsty, reaching for his gun. The movement was fatal, for before he could draw, the Colt in Hopalong's holster leaped out and flashed from its owner's hip and Thirsty fell sideways, face-down in the dust of the street.

Hopalong started toward the fallen man, but as he did so a shot rang out from behind the store and he pitched forward, stumbled and rolled behind the boulder. As he stumbled his left hand streaked to his hip, and when he fell he had a gun in each hand.

As he disappeared from sight Goodeye and Bill Jones stepped from behind the store and started to run away. Not able to resist the temptation to look again, they stopped and turned and Bill laughed.

"Easy as hell," he said.

"Run, yu fool—Red an' Buck'll be here. Want to git plugged?" shouted Goodeye angrily.

They turned and started for a group of ponies twenty yards away, and as they leaped into the saddles two shots were fired from the street. As the reports died away Buck and Red turned the corner of the store, Colts in hand, and, checking their rush as they saw the saddles emptied, they turned toward the street and saw Hopalong, with blood oozing from an abrasion on his cheek, sitting up cross-legged, with each hand holding a gun, from which came thin wisps of smoke.

"Th' son-of-a-gun!" cried Buck, proud and delighted.

"Th' son-of-a-gun!" echoed Red, grinning.

CHAPTER VIII

Hopalong Keeps His Word

THE WATERS of the Rio Grande slid placidly toward the Gulf, the hot sun branding the sleepy waters with streaks of molten fire. To the north arose from the gray sandy plain the Quitman Mountains, and beyond them lay Bass Cañon. From the latter emerged a solitary figure astride a broncho, and as he ascended the topmost rise he glanced below him at the placid stream and beyond it into Mexico. As he sat quietly in his saddle he smiled and laughed gently to himself. The trail he had just followed had been replete with trouble which had suited the state of his mind and he now felt humorous, having cleaned up a pressing debt with his six-shooter. Surely there ought to be a mild sort of excitement in the land he faced, something picturesque and out of the ordinary. This was to be the finishing touch to his trip, and he had left his two companions at Albuquerque in order that he might have to himself all that he could find.

Not many miles to the south of him lay the town which had been the rendezvous of Tamale José, whose weakness had been a liking for other people's cattle. Well he remembered his first manhunt: the discovery of the theft, the trail and pursuit and—the ending. He was scarcely eighteen years of age when that event took place, and the wisdom he had absorbed then had stood him in good stead many times since. He had even now a touch of pride at the recollection how, when his older companions had failed to get Tamale José, he with his undeveloped strategy had gained that end. The fight would never be forgotten, as it was his first, and no sight of wounds would ever affect him as did those of Red Connors as he lay huddled up in the dark corner of that old adobe hut.

He came to himself and laughed again as he thought of Carmencita, the first girl he had ever known—and the last. With a boy's impetuosity he had wooed her in a manner far different from that of the peons who sang beneath her window and talked to her mother. He had boldly scaled the wall and did his courting in her house, trusting to luck and to his own ability to avoid being seen. No hidden meaning lay in his words; he spoke from his heart and with no concealment. And he remembered the treachery that had forced him, fighting, to the camp of his outfit; and when he had returned with his friends she had disappeared. To this day he hated that mud-walled convent and those sisters who so easily forgot how to talk. The fragrance of the old days wrapped themselves around him, and although he had ceased to pine for his black-eyed Carmencita—well, it would be nice if he chanced to see her again. Spurring his mount into an easy canter he swept down to and across the river, fording it where he had crossed it when pursuing Tamale José.

The town lay indolent under the Mexican night, and the strumming of guitars and the tinkle of spurs and tiny bells softly echoed from several houses. The convent of St. Maria lay indistinct in its heavy shadows and the little church farther up the dusty street showed dim lights in its stained windows. Off to the north became audible the rhythmic beat of a horse and soon a cowboy swept past the convent with a mocking bow. He clattered across the stone-paved plaza and threw his mount back on its haunches as he stopped before a house. Glancing around and determining to find out a few facts as soon as possible, he rode up to the low door and pounded upon it with the butt of his Colt. After waiting for possibly half a minute and receiving no response he hammered a tune upon it with two Colts and had the satisfaction of seeing half a score of heads protrude from the windows in the nearby houses.

"If I could scare up another gun I might get th' whole blamed town up," he grumbled whimsically, and fell on the door with another tune.

"Who is it?" came from within. The voice was distinctly feminine and Hopalong winked to himself in congratulation.

"Me," he replied, twirling his fingers from his nose at the curious, forgetting that the darkness hid his actions from sight.

"Yes, I know; but who is 'me'?" came from the house.

"Ain't I a fool!" he complained to himself, and raising his voice he replied coaxingly, "Open th' door a bit an' see. Are yu Carmencita?"

"O-o-o! But you must tell me who it is first."

"Mr. Cassidy," he replied, flushing at the 'mister,' "an' I wants to see Carmencita."

"Carmencita who?" teasingly came from behind the door.

Hopalong scratched his head. "Gee, yu've roped me—I suppose she has got another handle. Oh, yu know—she used to live here about seven years back. She had great big black eyes, pretty cheeks an' a mouth that 'ud stampede anybody. Don't yu know now? She was about so high," holding out his hands in the darkness.

The door opened a trifle on a chain and Hopalong peered eagerly forward.

"Ah, it is you, the brave Americano! You must go away quick or you will meet with harm. Manuel is awfully jealous and he will kill you! Go at once, please!"

Hopalong pulled at the half-hearted down upon his lip and laughed softly. Then he slid the guns back in their holsters and felt of his sombrero.

"Manuel wants to see me first, Star Eyes."

"No! no!" she replied, stamping upon the floor vehemently. "You must go now—at once!"

"I'd shore look nice hittin' th' trail because Manuel Somebody wants to get hurt, wouldn't I? Don't yu remember how I used to shinny up this here wall an' skin th' cat gettin' through that hole up there what yu said was a window? Ah, come on an' open th' door—I'd shore like to see yu again!" pleaded the irrepressible.

"No! no! Go away. Oh, won't you please go away!"

Hopalong sighed audibly and turned his horse. As he did so he heard the door open and a sigh reached his ears. He wheeled like a flash and found the door closed again on its chain. A laugh of delight came from behind it.

"Come out, please!—just for a minute," he begged, wishing that he was brave enough to smash the door to splinters and grab her.

"If I do, will you go away?" asked the girl. "Oh, what will Manuel say if he comes? And all those people, they'll tell him!"

"Hey, yu!" shouted Hopalong, brandishing his Colts at the protruding heads. "Git scarce! I'll shore plug th' last one in!" Then he laughed at the sudden vanishing.

The door slowly opened and Carmencita, fat and drowsy, wobbled out to him. Hopalong's feelings were interfering with his breathing as he surveyed her. "Oh, yu shore are mistaken, Mrs. Carmencita. I wants to see yore *daughter!*"

"Ah, you have forgotten the little Carmencita who used to look for you. Like all the men, you have forgotten," she cooed reproachfully. Then her fear predominated again and she cried, "Oh, if my husband should see me now!"

Hopalong mastered his astonishment and bowed. He had a desire to ride madly into the Rio Grande and collect his senses.

"Yu are right—this *is* too dangerous—I'll amble on some," he replied hastily. Under his breath he prayed that the outfit would never learn of this. He turned his horse and rode slowly up the street as the door closed.

Rounding the corner he heard a soft footfall, and swerving in his saddle he turned and struck with all his might in the face of a man who leaped at him, at the same time grasping the uplifted wrist with his other hand. A curse and the tinkle of thin steel on

the pavement accompanied the fall of his opponent.
Bending down from his saddle he picked up the
weapon and the next minute the enraged assassin
was staring into the unwavering and, to him, grow-
ing muzzle of a Colt's .45.

"Yu shore had a bum teacher. Don't you know
better'n to *push* it in? An' me a cowpuncher, too! I'm
most grieved at yore conduct—it shows you don't
appreciate cow-wrastlers. This is safer," he remarked, throwing the stilleto through the air and
into a door, where it rang out angrily and quivered.
"I don't know as I wants to ventilate yu; we mostly
poisons coyotes up my way," he added. Then a
thought struck him. "Yu must be that dear Manuel
I've been hearin' so much about?"

A snarl was the only reply and Hopalong grinned.

"Yu shore ain't got no call to go loco that way,
none whatever. I don't want yore Carmencita. I only
called to say hulloo," responded Hopalong, his sym-
pathies being aroused for the wounded man before
him from his vivid recollection of the woman who
had opened the door.

"Yah!" snarled Manuel. "You wants to poison my
little bird. You with your fair hair and your cursed
swagger!"

The six-shooter tentatively expanded and then
stopped six inches from the Mexican's nose. "Yu
wants to ride easy, hombre. I ain't no angel, but I
don't poison no woman; an' don't yu amble off with
th' idea in yore head that she wants to be poisoned.
Why, she near stuck a knife in me!" he lied.

The Mexican's face brightened somewhat, but it
would take more than that to wipe out the insult of
the blow. The horse became restless, and when Hopalong had effectively quieted it he spoke again.

"Did yu ever hear of Tamale José?"

"Yes."

"Well, I'm th' fellow that stopped him in th' 'dobe hut by th' arroyo. I'm tellin' yu this so yu won't do nothin' rash an' leave Carmencita a widow."

The hate on the Mexican's face redoubled and he took a short step forward, but stopped when the muzzle of the Colt kissed his nose. He was the brother of Tamale José. As he backed away from the cool touch of the weapon he thought out swiftly his revenge. Some of his brother's old companions were at that moment drinking mescal in a saloon down the street, and they would be glad to see this Americano die. He glanced past his house at the saloon and Hopalong misconstrued his thoughts.

"Shore, go home. I'll just circulate around some for exercise. No hard feelings, only yu better throw it next time," he said as he backed away and rode off. Manuel went down the street and then ran into the saloon, where he caused an uproar.

Hopalong rode to the end of the plaza and tried to sing, but it was a dismal failure. Then he felt thirsty and wondered why he hadn't thought of it before. Turning his horse and seeing the saloon he rode up to it and in, lying flat on the animal's neck to avoid being swept off by the door frame. His entrance scared white some half a dozen loungers, who immediately sprang up in a decidedly hostile manner. Hopalong's Colts peeped over the ears of his horse and he backed into a corner near the bar.

"One, two, three—now, altogether, *breathe*! Yu acts like yu never saw a real puncher afore. All th' same," he remarked, nodding at several of the crowd, "I've seen yu afore. Yu are th' gents with th' hotfoot getaway that vamoosed when we got Tamale."

Curses were flung at him and only the humorous mood he was in saved trouble. One, bolder than the rest, spoke up: "The señor will not see any 'hotfoot getaway,' as he calls it, now! The señor was not wise to go so far away from his friends!"

Hopalong looked at the speaker and a quizzical grin slowly spread over his face. "They'll shore feel glad when I tells them yu was askin' for 'em. But didn't yu see too much of 'em once, or was yu poundin' leather in the other direction? Yu don't want to worry none about me—*an' if yu don't get yore hands closter to yore neck they'll be hell to pay!* There, that's more like home," he remarked, nodding assurance.

Reaching over he grasped a bottle and poured out a drink, his Colt slipping from his hand and dangling from his wrist by a thong. As the weapon started to fall several of the audience involuntarily moved as if to pick it up. Hopalong noticed this and paused with the glass halfway to his lips. "Don't bother yoreselves none; I can git it again," he said, tossing off the liquor.

"Wow! Holy smoke!" he yelled. "This ain't drink! Sufferin' coyotes, nobody can accuse yu of sellin' liquor! Did yu make this all by yoreself?" he asked incredulously of the proprietor, who didn't know whether to run or to pray. Then he noticed that the crowd was spreading out and his Colts again became the center of interest.

"Yu with th' lovely face, *sit down!*" he ordered as the person addressed was gliding toward the door. "I ain't a-goin' to let you pot me from th' street. Th' first man who tries to get scarce will stop somethin' hot. An' yu *all* better sit down," he suggested, sweeping them with his guns. One man, more obdurate than the rest, was slow in complying and Hopalong sent a bullet through the top of his high sombrero, which had a most gratifying effect.

"You'll regret this!" hissed a man in the rear, and a murmur or assent arose. Someone stirred slightly in searching for a weapon and immediately a blazing Colt froze him into a statue.

"Yu shore looks funny; eeny, meeny, miny, mo," counted off the daring horseman; "move a bit an' off yu go," he finished. Then his face broke out in another grin as he thought of more enjoyment.

"That there gent on th' left," he said, pointing out with a gun the man he meant. "Yu sing us a song. Sing a nice little song."

As the object of his remarks remained mute he let his thumb ostentatiously slide back with the hammer of the gun under it. "Sing! Quick!" The man sang.

As Hopalong leaned forward to say something a stiletto flashed past his neck and crashed into the bottle beside him. The echo of the crash was merged into a report as Hopalong fired from his waist. Then he backed out into the street and, wheeling, galloped across the plaza and again faced the saloon. A flash split the darkness and a bullet hummed over his head and thudded into an adobe wall at his back. Another shot and he replied, aiming at the flash. From down the street came the sound of a window opening and he promptly caused it to close again. Several more windows opened and hastily closed, and he rode slowly toward the far end of the plaza. As he faced the saloon once more he heard a command to throw up his hands and saw the glint of a gun, held by a man who wore the insignia of sheriff. Hopalong complied, but as his hands went up two spurts of fire shot forth and the sheriff dropped his weapon, reeled and sat down. Hopalong rode over to him and, swinging down, picked up the gun and looked the officer over.

"Shoo, yu'll be all right soon—yore only plugged in th' arms," he remarked as he glanced up the street. Shadowy forms were gliding from cover to cover and he immediately caused consternation among them by his accuracy.

"Ain't it hell?" he complained to the wounded man. "I never starts out but what somebody makes me shoot 'em. Came down here to see a girl an' find she's married. Then when I moves on peaceable-like her husband makes me hit him. Then I wants a drink an' he goes an' fans a knife at me, an' me just teachin' him how! Then yu has to come along an' make more trouble. Now look at them fools over there," he said, pointing at a dark shadow some fifty paces off. "They're pattin' their backs because I don't see 'em, an' if I hurts them they'll git mad. Guess I'll make 'em dust along," he added, shooting into the spot. A howl went up and two men ran away at top speed.

The sheriff nodded his sympathy and spoke. "I reckons you had better give up. You can't get away. Every house, every corner and shadow holds a man. You are a brave man—but, as you say, unfortunate. Better help me up and come with me—they'll tear you to pieces."

"Shore I'll help yu up—I ain't got no grudge against nobody. But my friends know where I am an' they'll come down here an' raise a ruction if I don't show up. So, if it's all th' same to you, I'll be ambling right along," he said as he helped the sheriff to his feet.

"Have you any objections to telling me your name?" asked the sheriff as he looked himself over.

"None whatever," answered Hopalong heartily. "I'm Hopalong Cassidy of th' Bar-20, Texas."

"You don't surprise me—I've heard of you," replied the sheriff wearily. "You are the man who killed Tamale José, whom I hunted for unceasingly. I found him when you had left and I got the reward. Come again sometime and I'll divide with you; two hundred and fifty dollars," he added craftily.

"I shore will, but I don't want no money," replied Hopalong as he turned away. "Adios, señor," he called back.

"Adios," replied the sheriff as he kicked a nearby door for assistance.

The cow pony tied itself up in knots as it pounded down the street toward the trail, and although he was fired on he swung into the dusty trail with a song on his lips. Several hours later he stood dripping wet on the American side of the Rio Grande and shouted advice to a score of Mexican cavalrymen on the opposite bank. Then he slowly picked his way toward El Paso for a game at Faro Dan's.

The sheriff sat in his easy chair one night some three weeks later, gravely engaged in rolling a cigarette. His arms were practically well, the wounds being in the fleshy parts. He was a philosopher and was disposed to take things easy, which accounted for his being in his official position for fifteen years. A gentleman at the core, he was well educated and had visited a goodly portion of the world. A book of Horace lay open on his knees and on the table at his side lay a shining new revolver, Hopalong having carried off his former weapon. He read aloud several lines and in reaching for a light for his cigarette noticed the new six-shooter. His mind leaped from Horace to Hopalong, and he smiled grimly at the latter's promise to call.

Glancing up, his eyes fell on a poster which conveyed the information in Spanish and in English that there was offered

> ## FIVE HUNDRED DOLLARS ($500)
> # R E W A R D
> For Hopalong Cassidy, of the Ranch Known as the Bar-20, Texas, U.S.A.

and which gave a good description of that gentleman.

Sighing for the five hundred, he again took up his book and was lost in its pages when he heard a knock, rather low and timid. Wearily laying aside his reading, he strode to the door, expecting to hear a lengthy complaint from one of his townsmen. As he threw the door wide open the light streamed out and lighted up a revolver and behind it the beaming face of a cowboy, who grinned.

"Well, I'll be damned!" ejaculated the sheriff, starting back in amazement.

"Don't say that, sheriff; you've got lots of time to reform," replied a humorous voice. "How's th' wings?"

"Almost well: you were considerate," responded the sheriff.

"Let's go in—somebody might see me out here an' get into trouble," suggested the visitor, placing his foot on the sill.

"Certainly—pardon my discourtesy," said the sheriff. "You see, I wasn't expecting you tonight," he explained, thinking of the elaborate preparations that he would have gone to if he had thought the irrepressible would call.

"Well, I was down this way, an' seeing as how I had promised to drop in I just natchurally dropped," replied Hopalong as he took the chair proferred by his host.

After talking awhile on everything and nothing the sheriff coughed and looked uneasily at his guest.

"Mr. Cassidy, I am sorry you called, for I like men of your energy and courage and I very much dislike to arrest you," remarked the sheriff. "Of course you understand that you are under arrest," he added with anxiety.

"Who, me?" asked Hopalong with a rising inflection.

"Most assuredly," breathed the sheriff.

"Why, this is the first time I ever heard anything about it," replied the astonished cowpuncher. "I'm an American—don't that make any difference?"

"Not in this case, I'm afraid. You see, it's for manslaughter."

"Well, don't that beat th' devil, now?" said Hopalong. He felt sorry that a citizen of the glorious United States should be prey for troublesome sheriffs, but he was sure that his duty to Texas called upon him never to submit to arrest at the hands of a Mexican. Remembering the Alamo, and still behind his Colt, he reached over and took up the shining weapon from the table and snapped it open on his knee. After placing the cartridges in his pocket he tossed the gun over on the bed and, reaching inside his shirt, drew out another and threw it after the first.

"That's yore gun; I forgot to leave it," he said, apologetically. "Anyhow yu needs two," he added.

Then he glanced around the room, noticed the poster and walked over and read it. A full swift sweep of his gloved hand tore it from its fastenings and crammed it under his belt. The glimmer of anger in his eyes gave way as he realized that his head was worth a definite price, and he smiled at what the boys would say when he showed it to them. Planting his feet far apart and placing his arms akimbo he faced his host in grim defiance.

"Got any more of these?" he inquired, placing his hand on the poster under his belt.

"Several," replied the sheriff.

"Trot 'em out," ordered Hopalong shortly.

The sheriff sighed, stretched and went over to a shelf, from which he took a bundle of the articles in question. Turning slowly he looked at the puncher and handed them to him.

"I reckons they's all over this here town," remarked Hopalong.

"They are, and you may never see Texas again."

"So? Well, yu tell yore most particular friends that the job is worth five thousand, and that it will take so many to do it that when th' money is divided up it won't buy a meal. There's only one man in this country tonight that can earn that money, an' that's me," said the puncher. "An' I don't need it," he added, smiling.

"But you are my prisoner—you are under arrest," enlightened the sheriff, rolling another cigarette. The sheriff spoke as if asking a question. Never before had five hundred dollars been so close at hand and yet so unobtainable. It was like having a checkbook but no bank account.

"I'm shore sorry to treat yu mean," remarked Hopalong, "but I was paid a month in advance an' I'll have to go back an' earn it."

"You can—if you say that you will return," replied the sheriff tentatively. The sheriff meant what he said and for the moment had forgotten that he was powerless and was not the one to make terms.

Hopalong was amazed and then he smiled sympathetically.

"Never like to promise nothin'," he replied. "I might get plugged, or something might happen that wouldn't let me." Then his face lighted up as a thought came to him. "Say, I'll cut th' cards with yu to see if I comes back or not."

The sheriff leaned back and gazed at the cool youngster before him. A smile of satisfaction, partly at the self-reliance of his guest and partly at the novelty of his situation, spread over his face. He reached for a pack of Mexican cards and laughed. "God! You're a cool one—I'll do it. What do you call?"

"Red," answered Hopalong.

The sheriff slowly raised his hand and revealed the ace of hearts.

Hopalong leaned back and laughed, at the same time taking from his pocket the six extracted cartridges. Arising and going over to the bed he slipped them in the chambers of the new gun and then placed the loaded weapon at the sheriff's elbow.

"Well, I reckon I'll amble, sheriff," he said as he opened the door. "If yu ever sifts up my way drop in an' see me—th' boys'll give yu a good time."

"Thanks; I will be glad to," replied the sheriff. "You'll take your pitcher to the well once too often someday, my friend. This courtesy," glancing at the restored revolver, "might have cost you dearly."

"Shoo! I did that once an' th' feller tried to use it," replied the cowboy as he backed through the door. "Some people are awfully careless," he added. "So long—"

"So long," replied the sheriff, wondering what sort of a man he had been entertaining.

The door closed softly and soon after a joyous whoop floated in from the street. The sheriff toyed with the new gun and listened to the low caress of a distant guitar.

"Well, don't that beat hell?" he ejaculated.

CHAPTER IX

The Advent of McAllister

THE BLAZING sun shone pitilessly on an arid plain which was spotted with dust-gray clumps of mesquite and thorny chaparral. Basking in the burning sand and alkali lay several Gila monsters, which raised their heads and hissed with wide-open jaws as several faint, whip-like reports echoed flatly over the desolate plain, showing that even they had learned that danger was associated with such sounds.

Off to the north there became visible a cloud of dust and at intervals something swayed in it, something that rose and fell and then became hidden again. Out of that cloud came sharp, splitting sounds, which were faintly responded to by another and larger cloud in its rear. As it came nearer and finally swept past, the Gilas, to their terror, saw a madly pounding horse, and it carried a man. The latter turned in his saddle and raised a gun to his shoulder and the thunder that issued from it caused the creeping audience to throw up their tails in sudden panic and bury themselves out of sight in the sand.

The horse was only a broncho, its sides covered with hideous yellow spots, and on its near flank was a peculiar scar, the brand. Foam flecked from its crimsoned jaws and found a resting place on its sides and on the hairy chaps of its rider. Sweat rolled and streamed from its heaving flanks and was greedily sucked up by the drought-cursed alkali. Close to the rider's knee a bloody furrow ran forward and one of the broncho's ears was torn and limp. The broncho was doing its best—it could run at that pace until it dropped dead. Every ounce of strength it possessed was put forth to bring those hind hoofs well in front of the forward ones and to send them pushing the sand behind in streaming clouds. The horse had done this same thing many times—when would its master learn sense?

The man was typical in appearance with many of that broad land. Lithe, sinewy and bronzed by hard riding and hot suns, he sat in his Cheyenne saddle like a centaur, all his weight on the heavy, leather-guarded stirrups, his body rising in one magnificent straight line. A bleached mustache hid the thin lips, and a gray sombrero threw a heavy shadow across his eyes. Around his neck and over his open, blue flannel shirt lay loosely a knotted silk kerchief, and on his thighs a pair of open-flapped holsters swung uneasily with their ivory-handled burdens. He turned abruptly, raised his gun to his shoulder and fired, then he laughed recklessly and patted his mount, which responded to the confident caress by lying flatter to the earth in a spurt of heartbreaking speed.

"I'll show 'em who they're trailin'. This is th' sec-

ond time I've started for Muddy Wells, an' I'm goin'
to git there, too, for all th' Apaches out of Hades!"

To the south another cloud of dust rapidly approached and the rider scanned it closely, for it was
directly in his path. As he watched it he saw something wave and it was a sombrero! Shortly afterward
a real cowboy yell reached his ears. He grinned and
slid another cartridge in the greasy, smoking barrel
of the Sharp's and fired again at the cloud in his rear.
Some few minutes later a whooping, bunched crowd
of madly riding cowboys thundered past him and he
was recognized.

"Hullo, Frenchy!" yelled the nearest one. "Comin'
back?"

"Come on, McAllister!" shouted another; "we'll
give 'em blazes!" In response the straining broncho
suddenly stiffened, bunched and slid on its haunches,
wheeled and retraced its course. The rear cloud suddenly scattered into many smaller ones and all swept
off to the east. The rescuing band overtook them
and, several hours later, when seated around a table
in Tom Lee's saloon, Muddy Wells, a count was taken
of them, which was pleasing in its facts.

"We was huntin' coyotes when we saw yu," said
a smiling puncher who was known as Salvation
Carroll chiefly because he wasn't.

"Yep! They've been stalkin' Tom's chickens," supplied Waffles, the champion poker player of the outfit. Tom Lee's chickens could whip anything of their
kind for miles around and were reverenced accordingly.

"Sho! Is that so?" asked Frenchy with mild incredulity, such a state of affairs being deplorable.

"She shore is!" answered Tex Le Blanc, and then,

as an afterthought, he added, "Where'd yu hit th' Indians?"

" 'Bout four hours back. This here's th' second time I've headed for this place—last time they chased me to Las Cruces."

"That so?" asked Bigfoot Baker, a giant. "Ain't they *allus* interferin', now? Anyhow, they're better 'n coyotes."

"They was purty well heeled," suggested Tex, glancing at a bunch of repeating Winchesters of late model which lay stacked in a corner. "Charley here said he thought they was from th' way yore cayuse looked, didn't yu, Charley?" Charley nodded and filled his pipe.

" 'Pears like a feller can't amble around much nowadays without havin' to fight," grumbled Lefty Allen, who usually went out of his way hunting up trouble.

"We're goin' to th' Hills as soon as our cookie turns up," volunteered Tenspot Davis, looking inquiringly at Frenchy. "Heard any more news?"

"Nope. Same old story—lots of gold. Shucks, I've bit on so many of them rumors that they don't feaze me no more. One man who don't know nothin' about prospectin' goes an' stumbles over a fortune an' those who know it from A to Izzard goes 'round pullin' in their belts."

"*We* don't pull in no belts—*we* knows just where to look, *don't* we, Tenspot?" remarked Tex, looking very wise.

"Ya-as we do," answered Tenspot, "if yu hasn't dreamed about it, we do."

"Yu wait; I wasn't dreamin', none whatever," assured Tex. "I *saw* it!"

"Ya-as, I saw it too onct," replied Frenchy with

sarcasm. "Went and lugged fifty pound of it all th' way to th' assay office—took me two days; an' that there four-eyed cuss looks at it and snickers. Then he takes me by th' arm an' leads me to th' window. 'See that pile, my friend? That's all like yourn,' sez he. 'It's worth about one dollar a ton at th' coast. They use it for ballast.' "

"Aw! But this what *I* saw was *gold*!" exploded Tex.

"So was mine, for a while!" laughed Frenchy, nodding to the bartender for another round.

"Well, we're tired of punchin' cows! Ride sixteen hours a day, year in an' year out, an' what do we get? Fifty a month an' no chance to spend it, an' grub that 'd make a coyote sniffle! I'm for a vacation, an' if I goes broke, why, I'll punch again!" asserted Waffles, the foreman, thus revealing the real purpose of the trip.

"What'd yore boss say?" asked Frenchy.

"Whoop! What didn't he say! Honest, I never thought he had it in him. It was fine. He cussed an hour frontways an' then trailed back on a dead gallop, with us a-laughin' fit to bust. *Then* he rustles for his gun an' we rustles for town," answered Waffles, laughing at his remembrance of it.

As Frenchy was about to reply his sombrero was snatched from his head and disappeared. If he "got mad" he was to be regarded as not sufficiently well acquainted for banter and he was at once in hot water; if he took it good-naturedly he was one of the crowd in spirit; but in either case he didn't get his hat without begging or fighting for it. This was a recognized custom among the O-Bar-O outfit and was not intended as an insult.

Frenchy grabbed at the empty air and arose. Punching Lefty playfully in the ribs he passed his hands behind that person's back. Not finding the lost headgear he laughed and, tripping Lefty up, fell with him and, reaching up on the table for his glass, poured the contents down Lefty's back and arose.

"Yu son-of-a-gun!" indignantly wailed that unfortunate. "Gee, it feels funny," he added, grinning as he pulled the wet shirt away from his spine.

"Well, I've got to be amblin'," said Frenchy, totally ignoring the loss of his hat. "Goin' down to Buckskin," he offered, and then asked, "When's yore cook comin'?"

"Day after tomorrow, if he don't get loaded," replied Tex.

"Who is he?"

"A one-eyed Mexican—Antonio."

"*I* used to know him. He's a hell of a cook. Dished up th' grub one season when I was punchin' for th' Tin-Cup up in Montana," replied Frenchy.

"Oh, he kin cook *now*, all right," replied Waffles.

"That's about all he can cook. Useter wash his knives in th' coffeepot an' blow on th' tins. I chased him a mile one night for leavin' sand in th' skillet. Yu can have him—I don't envy yu none whatever."

"He don't sand no skillet when little Tenspot's around," assured that person, slapping his holster. "Does he, Lefty?"

"If he does, yu oughter be lynched," consoled Lefty.

"Well, so long," remarked Frenchy, riding off to a small store, where he bought a cheap sombrero.

Frenchy was a jack-of-all-trades, having been cowpuncher, prospector, proprietor of a "hotel" in Albuquerque, foreman of a ranch, sheriff, and at one time had played angel to a venturesome but poor show troupe. Besides his versatility he was well

known as the man who took the stage through
the Sioux country when no one else volunteered. He
could shoot with the best, but his one pride was the
brand of poker he handed out. Furthermore, he had
never been known to take an unjust advantage over
any man and, on the contrary, had frequently vol-
untarily handicapped himself to make the event
more interesting. But he must not be classed as being hampered with self-restraint.

His reasons for making this trip were twofold: he
wished to see Buck Peters, the foreman of the Bar-
20 outfit, as he and Buck had punched cows together
twenty years before and were firm friends; the other
was that he wished to get square with Hopalong Cassidy, who had decisively cleaned him out the year
before at poker. Hopalong played either in great
good luck or the contrary, while Frenchy played an
even, consistent game and usually left off richer than
when he began, and this decisive defeat bothered
him more than he would admit, even to himself.

The roundup season was at hand and the Bar-20
was short of ropers, the rumors of fresh gold discov-
eries in the Black Hills having drawn all the more
restless men north. The outfit also had a slight touch
of the gold fever, and only their peculiar loyalty to
the ranch and the assurance of the foreman that
when the work was over he would accompany them,
kept them from joining the rush of those who desired
sudden and much wealth as the necessary preliminary of painting some cow town in all the "bang-
up" style such an event would call for. Therefore
they had been given orders to secure the required
assistance, and they intended to do so, and were prepared to kidnap, if necessary, for the glamour of

wealth and the hilarity of the vacation made the hours falter in their speed.

As Frenchy leaned back in his chair in Cowan's saloon, Buckskin, early the next morning, planning to get revenge on Hopalong and then to recover his sombrero, he heard a medley of yells and whoops and soon the door flew open before the strenuous and concentrated entry of a mass of twisting and kicking arms and legs, which magically found their respective owners and reverted to the established order of things. When the alkali dust had thinned he saw seven cowpunchers sitting on the prostrate form of another, who was earnestly engaged in trying to push Johnny Nelson's head out in the street with one foot as he voiced his lucid opinion of things in general and the seven in particular. After Red Connors had been stabbed in the back several times by the victim's energetic elbow he ran out of the room and presently returned with a pleased expression and a sombrero full of water, his finger plugging an old bullet hole in the crown.

"Is he any better, Buck?" anxiously inquired the man with the reservoir.

"About a dollar's worth," replied the foreman. "Jest put a little right here," he drawled as he pulled back the collar of the unfortunate's shirt.

"Ow! wow! WOW!" wailed the recipient, heaving and straining. The unengaged leg was suddenly wrested loose, and as it shot up and out Billy Williams, with his pessimism aroused to a blue-ribbon pitch, sat down forcibly in an adjacent part of the room, from where he lectured between gasps on the follies of mankind and the attributes of army mules.

Red tiptoed around the squirming bunch, looking

for an opening, his pleased expression now having added a grin.

"Seems to be gittin' violent-like," he soliloquized, as he aimed a stream at Hopalong's ear, which showed for a second as Pete Wilson strove for a half-nelson, and he managed to include Johnny and Pete in his effort.

Several minutes later, when the storm had subsided, the woeful crowd enthusiastically urged Hopalong to the bar, where he "bought."

"Of all th' ornery outfits I ever saw—" began the man at the table, grinning from ear to ear at the spectacle he had just witnessed.

"Why, hullo, Frenchy! Glad to see yu, yu old son-of-a-gun! What's th' news from th' Hills?" shouted Hopalong.

"Rather locoed, an' there's a locoed gang that's headin' that way. Goin' up?" he asked.

"Shore, after roundup. Seen any punchers trailin' around loose?"

"Ya-as," drawled Frenchy, delving into the possibilities suddenly opened to him and determining to utilize to the fullest extent the opportunity that had come to him unsought. "There's nine over to Muddy Wells that yu might git if yu wants them bad enough. They've got a sombrero of mine," he added deprecatingly.

"Nine! Twisted Jerusalem, Buck! Nine whole cowpunchers a-pinin' for work," he shouted, but then added thoughtfully, "Mebby they's engaged," it being one of the courtesies of the land not to take another man's help.

"Nope. They've stampeded for th' Hills an' left their boss *all* alone," replied Frenchy, well knowing that such desertion would not, in the minds of the

Bar-20 men, add any merits to the case of the distant outfit.

"Th' sons-of-guns," said Hopalong, "let's go an' get 'em," he suggested, turning to Buck, who nodded a smiling assent.

"Oh, what's the hurry?" asked Frenchy, seeing his projected game slipping away into the uncertain future and happy in the thought that he would be avenged on the O-Bar-O outfit. "They'll be there till tomorrow noon—they's waitin' for their cookie, who's goin' with them."

"A cook! A cook! Oh, joy, a cook!" exulted Johnny, not for one instant doubting Buck's ability to capture the whole outfit and seeing a whirl of excitement in the effort.

"Anybody we knows?" inquired Skinny Thompson.

"Shore. Tenspot Davis, Waffles, Salvation Carroll, Bigfoot Baker, Charley Lane, Lefty Allen, Kid Morris, Curley Tate an' Tex Le Blanc," responded Frenchy.

"Umm-m. Might as well rope a blizzard," grumbled Billy. "Might as well try to git th' Seventh Cavalry. We'll have a pious time corralling that bunch. Them's th' fellows that hit that bunch of inquirin' Crow braves that time up in th' Bad Lands an' then said by-bye to th' Ninth."

"Aw, shut up! They's only two that's very much, an' Buck an' Hopalong can sing 'em to sleep," interposed Johnny, afraid that the expedition would fall through.

"How about Curley and Tex?" pugnaciously asked Billy.

"Huh, jest because they buffaloed yu over to Las Vegas yu needn't think they's dangerous. Salvation an' Tenspot are th' only ones who can shoot," stoutly maintained Johnny.

"Here yu, get mum," ordered Buck to the pair. "When this outfit goes after anything it generally gets it. All in favor of kidnappin' that outfit signify th' same by kickin Billy," whereupon Bill swore.

"Do yu want yore hat?" asked Buck, turning to Frenchy.

"I shore do," answered that individual.

"If yu helps us at th' roundup we'll get it for yu. Fifty a month an' grub," offered the foreman.

"O.K.," replied Frenchy, anxious to even matters.

Buck looked at his watch. "Seven o'clock—we ought to get there by five if we relays at th' Barred-Horseshoe. Come on."

"How are we goin' to git them?" asked Billy.

"Yu leave that to me, son. Hopalong an' Frenchy 'll tend to that part of it," replied Buck, making for his horse and swinging into the saddle, an example which was followed by the others, including Frenchy.

As they swung off Buck noticed the condition of Frenchy's mount and halted. "Yu take that cayuse back an' get Cowan's," he ordered.

"That cayuse is good for Cheyenne—she eats work, an' besides I wants my own," laughed Frenchy.

"Yu must had a reg'lar picnic from th' looks of that crease," volunteered Hopalong, whose curiosity was mastering him.

"Shoo! I had a little argument with some feather dusters—th' O-Bar-O crowd cleaned them up."

"That so?" asked Buck.

"Yep! They sorter got into th' habit of chasin' me to Las Cruces an' forgot to stop."

"How many 'd yu get?" asked Lanky Smith.

"Twelve. Two got away. I got two before th' crowd showed up—that makes fo'teen."

"Now th' cavalry 'll be huntin' yu," croaked Billy.

"Hunt nothin'! They was in war paint—think I was a target?—think I was goin' to call off their shots for 'em?"

They relayed at the Barred-Horseshoe and went on their way at the same pace. Shortly after leaving the last-named ranch Buck turned to Frenchy and asked, "Any of that outfit think they can play poker?"

"Shore. Waffles."

"Does th' reverend Mr. Waffles think so very hard?"

"He shore does."

"Do th' rest of them mavericks think so too?"

"They'd bet their shirts on him."

At this juncture all were startled by a sudden eruption from Billy. "Haw! Haw! Haw!" he roared as the drift of Buck's intentions struck him. "Haw! Haw! Haw!"

"Here, yu long-winded coyote," yelled Red, banging him over the head with his quirt, "If yu don't 'Haw! Haw!' away from my ear I'll make it a Wow! Wow! What d'yu mean? Think I am a echo cliff? Yu slab-sided doodlebug, yu!"

"G'way, yu crimson topknot, think my head's a hunk of quartz? Fer a plugged peso I'd strew yu all over th' scenery!" shouted Billy, feigning anger and rubbing his head.

"There ain't no scenery around here," interposed Lanky. "This here be-utiful prospect is a sublime conception of th' devil."

"Easy, boy! Them highfalutin' words 'll give yu a cramp someday. Yu talk like a newly made sergeant," remarked Skinny.

"He learned them words from that sky pilot over at El Paso," volunteered Hopalong, winking at Red. "He used to amble down th' aisle afore the lights was lit so's he could get a front seat. That was all hunky for a while, but every time he'd go out to irrigate, that female organ-wrastler would seem to call th' music off for his special benefit. So in a month he'd sneak in an' freeze to a chair by th' door, an' after a while he'd shy like blazes every time he got within eye range of th' church."

"Shore. But do yu know what made him get religion all of a sudden? He used to hang around on th' outside after th' joint let out an' trail along behind th' music-slinger, lookin' like he didn't know what to do with his hands. Then when he got woozy one time she up an' told him that she had got a nice long letter from her hubby. Then Mr. Lanky hit th' trail for Santa Fé so hard that there wasn't hardly none of it left. I didn't see him for a whole month," supplied Red innocently.

"Yore shore funny, ain't yu?" sarcastically grunted Lanky. "Why, I can tell things on yu that'd make yu stand treat for a year."

"I wouldn't sneak off to Santa Fé an' cheat yu out of them. Yu ought to be ashamed of yoreself."

"Yah!" snorted the aggrieved little man. "I had business over to Santa Fé!"

"Shore," endorsed Hopalong. "We've all had business over to Santa Fé. Why, about eight years ago I had business—"

"Choke up," interposed Red. "About eight years ago yu was washin' pans for cookie an' askin' me for cartridges. Buck used to larrup yu about four times a day eight years ago."

To their roars of laughter Hopalong dropped to

the rear, where, red-faced and quiet, he bent his thoughts on how to get square.

"We'll have a *pleasant* time corralling that gang," began Billy for the third time.

"For heaven's sake get off that trail!" replied Lanky. "We ain't goin' to hold 'em up. De-plomacy's th' game."

Billy looked dubious and said nothing. If he hadn't proven that he was as nervy as any man in the outfit they might have taken more stock in his grumbling.

"What's the latest from Abilene way?" asked Buck of Frenchy.

"Nothin' much 'cept th' barb-wire ruction," replied the recruit.

"What's that?" asked Red, glancing apprehensively back at Hopalong.

"Why, th' settlers put up barb-wire fence so's th' cattle wouldn't get on their farms. That would a been all right, for there wasn't much of it. But some Britishers who own a couple of big ranches out there got smart all of a sudden an' strung wire all along their lines. Punchers crossin' th' country would run plumb into a fence an' would have to ride a day an' a half, mebby, afore they found th' corner. Well, naturally, when a man has been used to ridin' where he blame pleases an' as straight as he pleases he ain't goin' to chase along a five-foot fence to 'Frisco when he wants to get to Waco. So th' punchers got to totin' wire-snips, an' when they runs up agin a fence they cuts down half a mile or so. Sometimes they'd tie their ropes to a strand an' pull off a couple of miles an' then go back after th' rest. Th' ranch bosses sent out men to watch th' fences an' told 'em to shoot any festive puncher that monkeyed with th' hardware. Well, yu know what happens when a puncher gets shot at."

"When fences grow in Texas there'll be th' devil to pay," said Buck. He hated to think that someday the freedom of the range would be annulled, for he knew that it would be the first blow against the cowboys' occupation. When a man's cattle couldn't spread out all over the land he wouldn't have to keep so many men. Farms would spring up and the sun of the free-and-easy cowboy would slowly set.

"I reckons th' cutters are classed th' same as rustlers," remarked Red with a gleam of temper.

"By th' owners, but not by th' punchers; an' it's th' punchers that count," replied Frenchy.

"Well, we'll give them a fight," interposed Hopalong, riding up. "When it gets so I can't go where I please I'll start on th' warpath. I won't buck the cavalry, but I'll keep it busy huntin' for me an' I'll have time to 'tend to th' wire-fence men, too. Why, we'll be told we can't tote our guns!"

"They're sayin' that now," replied Frenchy. "Up in Topeka, Smith, who's now marshal, makes yu leave 'em with th' bartenders."

"I'd like to see any two-laigged cuss get my guns if I didn't want him to!" began Hopalong, indignant at the idea.

"Easy, son," cautioned Buck. "Yu would do what th' rest did because yu are a square man. I'm about as hardheaded a puncher as ever straddled leather an' I've had to use my guns purty considerable, but I reckons if any decent marshal asked me to cache them in a decent way, why, I'd do it. An' let me brand somethin' on yore mind—I've heard of Smith of Topeka, an' he's mighty nifty with his hands. He don't stand off an' tell yu to unload yore lead-ranch, but he ambles up close an' taps yu on yore shirt; if yu makes a gunplay he naturally knocks yu clean across th' room an' unloads yu afore yu gets yore senses back. He weighs about a hundred an' eighty an' he's shore got sand to burn."

"Yah! When I makes a gunplay she plays! I'd look nice in Abilene or Paso or Albuquerque without my guns, wouldn't I? Just because I totes them in plain sight I've got to hand 'em over to some liquor-wrastler? I reckons not! Some hip-pocket skunk would plug me afore I could wink. I'd shore look nice loping around a keno layout without my guns, in th' same town with some cuss huntin' me, wouldn't I? A whole lot of good a marshal would a done Jimmy, an' didn't Harris get his from a cur in th' dark?" shouted Hopalong, angered by the prospect.

"We're talkin' about Topeka, where everybody has to hang up their guns," replied Buck. "An' there's th' law—"

"To blazes with th' law!" whooped Hopalong in Red's ear as he unfastened the cinch of Red's saddle and at the same time stabbing that unfortunate's mount with his spurs, thereby causing a hasty separation of the two. When Red had picked himself up and things had quieted down again the subject was changed, and several hours later they rode into Muddy Wells, a town with a little more excuse for its existence than Buckskin. The wells were in an arid valley west of Guadaloupe Pass, and were not only muddy but more or less alkaline.

CHAPTER X

Peace Hath Its Victories

As THEY neared the central group of buildings they heard a hilarious and assertive song which sprang from the door and windows of the main saloon. It was in jig time, rollicking and boisterous, but the words had evidently been improvised for the occasion, as they clashed immediately with those which sprang to the minds of the outfit, although they could not be clearly distinguished. As they approached nearer and finally dismounted, however, the words became recognizable and the visitors were at once placed in harmony with the air of jovial recklessness by the roaring of the verses and the stamping of the time.

Oh we're red-hot cowpunchers playin' on our luck,
An' there ain't a proposition that we won't buck;

*From sunrise to sunset we've ridden on the
 range,
But now we're off for a howlin' change.*

Chorus.
*Laugh a little, sing a little, all th' day;
Play a little, drink a little—we can pay;
Ride a little, dig a little an' rich we'll grow.
Oh, we're that bunch from th' O-Bar-O!*

*Oh, there was a little tenderfoot an' he had a
 little gun,
An' th' gun an' him went a-trailin' up some fun.
They ambles up to Santa Fé to find a quiet
 game,
An' now they're planted with some more of th'
 same!*

As Hopalong, followed by the others, pushed open
the door and entered he took up the chorus with
all the power of Texan lungs and even Billy joined
in. The sight that met their eyes was typical of the
men and the mood and the place. Leaning along the
walls, lounging on the table and straddling chairs
with their forearms crossed on the backs were nine
cowboys, ranging from old twenty to young fifty in
years, and all were shouting the song and keeping
time with their hands and feet. In the center of the
room was a large man dancing a fair buck-and-wing
to the time so uproariously set by his companions.
Hatless, neckerchief loose, holsters flapping, chaps
rippling out and close, spurs clinking and perspira-
tion streaming from his tanned face, danced Bigfoot
Baker as though his life depended on speed and
noise. Bottles shook and the air was fogged with

smoke and dust. Suddenly, his belt slipping and letting his chaps fall around his ankles, he tripped and sat down heavily. Gasping for breath, he held out his hand and received a huge plug of tobacco, for Bigfoot had won a contest.

Shouts of greeting were hurled at the newcomers and many questions were fired at them regarding "th' latest from th' Hills." Waffles made a rush for Hopalong, but fell over Bigfoot's feet and all three were piled up in a heap. All were beaming with good nature, for they were as so many schoolboys playing truant. Prosaic cowpunching was relegated to the rear and they looked eagerly forward to their several missions. Frenchy told of the barb-wire fence war and of the new regulations of "Smith of Topeka" regarding cowpunchers' guns, and from the caustic remarks explosively given it was plain to be seen what a wire fence could expect, should one be met with, and there were many imaginary Smiths put *hors de combat*.

Kid Morris, after vainly trying to slip a bluebottle fly inside of Hopalong's shirt, gave it up and slammed his hand on Hopalong's back instead, crying: "Well, I'll be doggoned if here ain't Hopalong! How's th' missus an' th' deacon an' all th' folks to hum? I hears yu an' Frenchy's reg'lar poker fiends!"

"Oh, we plays onct in a while, but we don't want none of yore dust. Yu'll shore need it all afore th' Hills get through with yu," laughingly replied Hopalong.

"Oh, yore shore kind! But I was a sort of reckonin' that we needs some more. Perfesser P. D. Q. Waffles is our poker man an' he shore can clean out anything I ever saw. Mebby yu fellers feel reckless-like an' would like to make a pool," he cried, addressing the outfit of the Bar-20, "an' back yore boss of th' full house agin ourn?"

Red turned slowly around and took a full minute in which to size the Kid up. Then he snorted and turned his back again.

The Kid stared at him in outraged dignity. "Well, what t'ell!" he softly murmured. Then he leaped forward and walloped Red on the back. "Hey, yore royal highness!" he shouted. "Yu-yu-yu—oh, hang it—*yu*! Yu slab-sided, ring-boned, saddle-galled shade of a coyote, do yu think I'm only meanderin' in th' misty vales of—of——"

Suggestions intruded from various sources. "Hades?" offered Hopalong. "Cheyenne?" murmured Johnny. "Misty mistiness of misty?" tentatively supplied Waffles.

Red turned around again. "Better come up an' have somethin'," he sympathetically invited, wiping away an imaginary tear.

"An' he's so young!" sobbed Frenchy.

"An' so fair!" wailed Tex.

"An' so ornery!" howled Lefty, throwing his arms around the discomfited youngster. Other arms went around him, and out of the sobbing mob could be heard earnest and heartfelt cussing, interspersed with imperative commands, which were gradually obeyed.

The Kid straightened up his wearing apparel. "Come on, yu locoed——"

"Angels?" queried Charley Lane, interrupting him. "Sweet things?" breathed Hopalong in hopeful expectancy.

"Oh, damn it!" yelled the Kid as he ran out into the street to escape the persecution.

"Good Kid, all right," remarked Waffles. "He'll go

around an' lick someone an' come back sweet as honey."

"Did somebody say poker?" asked Bigfoot, digressing from the Kid.

"Oh, yu fellows don't want no poker. Of course yu don't. Poker's mighty uncertain," replied Red.

"Yah!" exclaimed Tex Le Blanc, pushing forward. "I'll just bet you to a standstill that Waffles an' Salvation 'll round up all th' festive dollars yu can get together! An' I'll throw in Frenchy's hat as an inducement."

"Well, if yore shore set on it make her a pool," replied Red, "an' th' winners divide with their outfit. Here's a starter," he added, tossing a buckskin bag on the table. "Come on, pile 'em up."

The crowd divided as the players seated themselves at the table, the O-Bar-O crowd grouping themselves behind their representatives; the Bar-20 behind theirs. A deck of cards was brought and the game was on.

Red, true to his nature, leaned back in a corner, where, hands on hips, he awaited any hostile demonstration on the part of the O-Bar-O; then, suddenly remembering, he looked half ashamed of his warlike position and became a peaceful citizen again. Buck leaned with his broad back against the bar, talking over his shoulder to the bartender, but watching Tenspot Davis, who was assiduously engaged in juggling a handful of Mexican dollars. Up by the door Bigfoot Baker, elated at winning the buck-and-wing contest, was endeavoring to learn a new step, while his late rival was drowning his defeat at Buck's elbow. Lefty Allen was softly singing a Mexican love song, humming when the words would not come. At the table could be heard low-spoken card terms and good-natured banter, interspersed with the clink of gold and silver and the soft pat-pat of the onlookers' feet unconsciously keeping time to Lefty's song. Notwithstanding the grim assertiveness of belts full of .45's and the peeping handles of long-barreled Colts, set off with picturesque chaps, sombreros and tinkling spurs, the scene was one of peaceful content and good-fellowship.

"Ugh!" grunted Johnny, walking over to Red and informing that person that he, Red, was a worm-eaten prune and that for half a wink he, Johnny, would prove it. Red grabbed him by the seat of his corduroys and the collar of his shirt and helped him outside, where they strolled about, taking potshots at whatever their fancy suggested.

Down the street in a cloud of dust rumbled the Las Cruces–El Paso stage and the two punchers went up to meet it. Raw furrows showed in the woodwork, one mule was missing and the driver and guard wore fresh bandages. A tired tenderfoot leaped out with a sigh of relief and hunted for his baggage, which he found to be generously perforated. Swearing at the godforsaken land where a man had to fight highwaymen and Indians inside of half a day he grumblingly lugged his valise toward a forbidding-looking shack which was called a hotel.

The driver released his teams and then turned to Red. "Hullo, old hoss, how's th' gang?" he asked genially. "We've had a hell of a time this yere trip," he went on without waiting for Red to reply. "Five miles out of Las Cruces we stood off a son-of-a-gun that wanted th' dude's wealth. Then just this side of the San Andre foothills we runs into a bunch of young bucks who turned us off this yere way an' gave us a runnin' fight purty near all th' way. I'm a whole lot farther from Paso now than I was when I started, an' seein' as I lost a jack I'll be some time gittin' there. Yu don't happen to know of a jack I can borrow, do yu?"

"I don't know about no jack, but I'll rope yu a bronch," offered Red, winking at Johnny.

"I'll pull her myself before I'll put dynamite in th' traces," replied the driver. "Yu fellers might amble back a ways with me—them buddin' warriors 'll be layin' for me."

"We shore will," responded Johnny eagerly. "There's nine of us now an' there'll be nine more an' a cook tomorrow, mebby."

"Gosh, yu grows some," replied the guard. "Eighteen'll be a plenty for them glory hunters."

"We won't be able to," contradicted Red, "for things are peculiar."

At this moment the conversation was interrupted by the tenderfoot, who sported a new cheap sombrero and also a belt and holster complete.

"Will you gentlemen join me?" he asked, turning to Red and nodding at the saloon. "I am very dry and much averse to drinking alone."

"Why, shore," responded Red heartily, wishing to put the stranger at ease.

The game was running about even as they entered and Lefty Allen was singing "The Insult," the rich tenor softening the harshness of the surroundings.

THE INSULT

*I've swum th' Colorado where she runs down
   clost to hell,
   I've braced th' faro layouts in Cheyenne;*

I've fought for muddy water with a howlin'
  bunch of Sioux,
  An' swallowed hot tamales, an' cayenne.

I've rid a pitchin' broncho 'till th' sky was
  underneath,
  I've tackled every desert in th' land;
I've sampled XXXX whiskey 'till I couldn't
  hardly see,
  An' dallied with th' quicksands of the
  Grande.

I've argued with th' marshals of a half-a-dozen
  burgs,
  I've been dragged free an' fancy by a cow;
I've had three years' campaignin' with th'
  fightin', bitin' Ninth,
  An' never lost my temper 'till right now.

I've had the yaller fever an' I've been shot full
  of holes,
  I've grabbed an army mule plumb by its tail;
I've never been so snortin', really highfalutin'
  mad
  As when y'u up an' hands me ginger ale!

Hopalong laughed joyously at a remark made by
Waffles and the stranger glanced quickly at him. His
merry, boyish face, underlined by a jaw showing
great firmness and set off with an expression of ag-
gressive self-reliance, impressed the stranger and he
remarked to Red, who lounged lazily near him, that
he was surprised to see such a face on so young a
man and he asked who the player was.

"Oh, his name's Hopalong Cassidy," answered Red.

"He's th' cuss that raised that ruction down in Mexico last spring. Rode his cayuse in a saloon and played with the loungers and had to shoot one before he got out. When he did get out he had to fight a whole bunch of Mexicans an' even potted their marshal, who had th' drop on him. Then he returned and visited the marshal about a month later, took his gun away from him an' then cut th' cards to see if he was a prisoner or not. He's a shore funny cuss."

The tenderfoot gasped his amazement. "Are you not fooling with me?" he asked.

"Tell him yu came after that five hundred dollars reward and see," answered Red good-naturedly.

"Holy smoke!" shouted Waffles as Hopalong won his sixth consecutive pot. "Did yu ever see such luck?" Frenchy grinned and some time later raked in his third. Salvation then staked his last cent against Hopalong's flush and dropped out.

Tenspot flipped to Waffles the money he had been juggling and Lefty searched his clothes for wealth. Buck, still leaning against the bar, grinned and winked at Johnny, who was pouring hair-raising tales into the receptive ears of the stranger. Thereupon Johnny confided to his newly found acquaintance the facts about the game, nearly causing that person to explode with delight.

Waffles pushed back his chair, stood up and stretched. At the finish of a yawn, he grinned at his late adversary. "I'm all in, yu old son-of-a-gun. Yu shore can play draw. I'm goin' to try yu again sometime. I was beat fair an' square an' I ain't got no kick comin', none whatever," he remarked, as he shook hands with Hopalong.

" 'Oh, we're that gang from th' O-Bar-O,' " hummed the Kid as he sauntered in. One cheek was slightly swollen and his clothes shed dust at every step. "Who wins?" he inquired, not having heard Waffles.

"They did, damn it!" exploded Bigfoot.

One of the Kid's peculiarities was revealed in the unreasoning and hasty conclusions he arrived at. From no desire to imply unfairness, but rather because of his bitterness against failure of any kind and his loyalty to Waffles, came his next words: "Mebby they skinned yu."

Like a flash Waffles sprang before him, his hand held up, palm out. "He don't mean nothin'—he's only a damn-fool kid!" he cried.

Buck smiled and wrested the Colt from Johnny's ever-ready hand. "Here's another," he said. Red laughed softly and rolled Johnny on the floor. "Yu jackass," he whispered, "don't yu know better'n to make a gunplay when we needs them all?"

"What are we goin' to do?" asked Tex, glancing at the bulging pockets of Hopalong's chaps.

"We're goin' to punch cows again, that's what we're goin' to do," answered Bigfoot dismally.

"An' whose are we goin' to punch? We can't go back to the old man," grumbled Tex.

Salvation looked askance at Buck and then at the others. "Mebby," he began, "mebby we kin git a job on th' Bar-20." Then turning to Buck again he bluntly asked, "Are yu short of punchers?"

"Well, I might use some," answered the foreman, hesitating. "But I ain't got only one cook, an'——"

"We'll git yu th' cook all O.K.," interrupted Charley Lane vehemently. "Hi, yu cook!" he shouted, "amble in here an' git a rustle on!"

There was no reply, and after waiting for a minute he and Waffles went into the rear room, from which there immediately issued great chunks of profanity and noise. They returned looking pugnacious and disgusted, with a wildly fighting man who was more full of liquor than was the bottle which he belligerently waved.

"This here animated distillery what yu sees is our cook," said Waffles. "*We* eats his grub, nobody else. If he gits drunk that's *our* funeral; *but he won't get drunk*! If yu wants us to punch for yu say so an' we does; if yu don't, we don't."

"Well," replied Buck thoughtfully, "mebby I *can* use yu." Then with a burst of recklessness he added, "Yes, if I lose my job! But yu might sober that cook up if yu let him fall in th' horse trough."

As the procession wended its way on its mission of wet charity, carrying the cook in any manner at all, Frenchy waved his long-lost sombrero at Buck, who stood in the door, and shouted, "Yu old son-of-a-gun, I'm proud to know yu!"

Buck smiled and snapped his watch shut. "Time to amble," he said.

CHAPTER XI

Holding the Claim

"OH, WE'RE that gang from th' O-Bar-O," hummed Waffles, sinking the branding iron in the flank of a calf. The scene was one of great activity and hilarity. Several fires were burning near the huge corral and in them half a dozen irons were getting hot. Three calves were being held down for the brand of the "Bar-20" and two more were being dragged up on their sides by the ropes of the cowboys, the proud cow ponies showing off their accomplishments at the expense of the calves' feelings. In the corral the dust arose in steady clouds as calf after calf was "cut out" by the ropers and dragged out to get "tagged." Angry cows fought valiantly for their terrorized offspring, but always to no avail, for the hated rope of some perspiring and dust-grimed rider sent them crashing to earth. Over the plain were herds of cattle and groups of madly riding cowboys, and two cook wagons were stalled a short distance from the corral. The roundup of the Bar-20 was taking place, and each of the two outfits tried to outdo the other and each individual strove for a prize. The man who cut out and dragged to the fire the most calves in three days could leave for the Black Hills at the expiration of that time, the rest to follow as soon as they could.

In this contest Hopalong Cassidy led his nearest rival, Red Connors, both of whom were Bar-20 men, by twenty cut-outs, and there remained but half an hour more in which to compete. As Red disappeared into the sea of tossing horns Hopalong dashed out with a whoop, dragging a calf at the end of his rope.

"Hi, yu trellis-built rack of bones, come along there! Whoop!" he yelled, turning the prisoner over to the squad by the fire. "Chalk up this here insignificant wart of cross-eyed perversity: an' how many?" he called as he galloped back to the corral.

"One ninety-eight," announced Buck, blowing the sand from the tally sheet. "That's shore goin' some," he remarked to himself.

When the calf sprang up it was filled with terror, rage and pain, and charged at Billy from the rear as that pessimistic soul was leaning over and poking his finger at a somber horned toad. "Wow!" he yelled as his feet took huge steps up in the air, each one strictly on its own course. "Woof!" he grunted in the hot sand as he arose on his hands and knees and spat alkali.

"What's s'matter?" he asked dazedly of Johnny Nelson. "*Ain't* it funny!" he yelled sarcastically as he beheld Johnny holding his sides with laughter. "*Ain't* it funny!" he repeated belligerently. "Of course that four-laigged, knock-kneed, wobblin' son-of-a-Piute had to cut *me* out. They wasn't *nobody* in sight but Billy! Why didn't yu *say* he was comin'? Think I can see four ways to once? Why *didn't*—" At this point

Red cantered up with a calf, and by a quick maneuver, drew the taut rope against the rear of Billy's knees, causing that unfortunate to sit down heavily. As he arose choking with broken-winded profanity Red dragged the animal to the fire, and Billy forgot his grievances in the press of labor.

"How many, Buck?" asked Red.

"One-eighty."

"How does she stand?"

"Yore eighteen to th' bad," replied the foreman.

"Th' son-of-a-gun!" marveled Red, riding off.

Another whoop interrupted them, and Billy quit watching out of the corner eye for pugnacious calves as he prepared for Hopalong.

"Hey, Buck, this here cuss was with a Barred-Horseshoe cow," he announced as he turned it over to the branding man. Buck made a tally in a separate column and released the animal. "Hullo, Red! Workin'?" asked Hopalong of his rival.

"Some, yu little cuss," answered Red with all the good nature in the world. Hopalong was his particular "side partner," and he could lose to him with the best of feelings.

"Yu looks so nice an' cool, an' clean, I didn't know," responded Hopalong, eyeing a streak of sweat and dust which ran from Red's eyes to his chin and then on down his neck.

"What yu been doin'? Plowin' with yore nose?" returned Red, smiling blandly at his friend's appearance.

"Yah!" snorted Hopalong, wheeling toward the corral. "Come on, yu pie-eatin' doodlebug; I'll beat yu to th' gate!"

The two ponies sent showers of sand all over Billy, who eyed them in pugnacious disgust. "Of all th' lo-

coed imps that ever made life miserable fer a man,
them's th' worst! Is there any piece of fool nonsense
they hain't harnessed me with?" he beseeched of
Buck. "Is there anything they hain't done to me?
They hides my liquor; they stuffs th' sweatband of
my hat with rope; they ties up my pants; they puts
water in my *boots* an' *toads* in my *bunk*—ain't they
never goin' to get sane?"

"Oh, they're only kids—they can't help it," offered
Buck. "Didn't they hobble my cayuse when I was on
him an' near bust my neck?"

Hopalong interrupted the conversation by bringing up another calf, and Buck, glancing at his watch,
declared the contest at an end.

"Yu wins," he remarked to the newcomer. "An'
now yu get scarce or Billy will shore straddle yore
nerves. He said as how he was goin' to get square
on yu tonight."

"I didn't, neither, Hoppy!" earnestly contradicted
Billy, who had visions of a night spent in torment as
a reprisal for such a threat. "Honest I didn't, did I,
Johnny?" he asked appealingly.

"Yu shore did," lied Johnny, winking at Red, who
had just ridden up.

"I don't know what yore talkin' about, but yu shore
did," replied Red.

"If yu did," grinned Hopalong, "I'll shore make yu
hard to find. Come on, fellows," he said; "grub's
ready. Where's Frenchy?"

"Over chewin' th' rag with Waffles about his hat—
he's lost it again," answered Red.

"He needs a guardian fer that bonnet. Th' Kid an'
Salvation has jammed it in th' corral fence an' Waffles has to stand fer it."

"Let's put it in th' grub wagon an' see him cuss cookie," suggested Hopalong.

"Shore," endorsed Johnny; "Cookie'll feed him bum grub for a week to get square."

Hopalong and Johnny ambled over to the corral and after some trouble located the missing sombrero, which they carried to the grub wagon and hid in the flour barrel. Then they went over by the excited owner and dropped a few remarks about how strange the cook was acting and how he was watching Frenchy.

Frenchy jumped at the bait and tore over to the wagon, where he and the cook spent some time in mutual recrimination. Hopalong nosed around and finally dug up the hat, white as new-fallen snow.

"Here's a hat—found it in th' dough barrel," he announced, handing it over to Frenchy, who received it in open-mouthed stupefaction.

"Yu pie-makin' pirate! *Yu* didn't know where my lid was, *did* yu! Yu cross-eyed lump of hypocrisy!" yelled Frenchy, dusting off the flour with one full-armed swing on the cook's face, driving it into that unfortunate's nose and eyes and mouth. "Yu white-washed pirate, yu—rub yore face with water an' yu've got pancakes."

"Hey! What you doin'!" yelled the cook, kicking the spot where he had last seen Frenchy. "Don't yu know better'n that!"

"Yu live close to yoreself or I'll throw yu so high th' sun'll duck," replied Frenchy, a smile illuminating his face.

"Hey, cookie," remarked Hopalong confidentially, "I know who put up this joke on yu. Yu ask Billy who hid th' hat," suggested the tease. "Here he comes now—see how queer he looks."

"Th' mournful Piute," ejaculated the cook. "I'll shore make him wish he'd kept on his own trail. I'll flavor his slush [coffee] with year-old dishrags!"

At this juncture Billy ambled up, keeping his weather eye peeled for trouble. "Who's a dishrag?" he queried. The cook mumbled something about crazy hens not knowing when to quit cackling and climbed up in his wagon. And that night Billy swore off drinking coffee.

When the dawn of the next day broke, Hopalong was riding toward the Black Hills, leaving Billy to untie himself as best he might.

The trip was uneventful and several days later he entered Red Dog, a rambling shantytown, one of those western mushrooms that sprang up in a night. He took up his stand at the Miner's Rest, and finally secured six claims at the cost of nine hundred hard-earned dollars, a fund subscribed by the outfits, as it was to be a partnership affair.

He rode out to a staked-off piece of hillside and surveyed his purchase, which consisted of a patch of ground, six holes, six piles of dirt and a log hut. The holes showed that the claims had been tried and found wanting.

He dumped his pack of tools and provisions, which he had bought on the way up, and lugged them into the cabin. After satisfying his curiosity he went outside and sat down for a smoke, figuring up in his mind how much gold he could carry on a horse. Then, as he realized that he could get a pack mule to carry the surplus, he became aware of a strange presence near at hand and looked up into the muzzle of a Sharp's rifle. He grasped the situation in a flash and calmly blew several heavy smoke rings around the frowning barrel.

"Well?" he asked slowly.

"Nice day, stranger," replied the man with the rifle, "but don't yu reckon yu've made a mistake?"

Hopalong glanced at the number burned on a nearby stake and carelessly blew another smoke ring. He was waiting for the gun to waver.

"No, I reckons not," he answered. "Why?"

"Well, I'll jest tell yu since yu asks. This yere claim's mine an' I'm a reg'lar terror, I am. That's why; an' seein' as it is, yu better amble some."

Hopalong glanced down the street and saw an interested group watching him, which only added to his rage for being in such a position. Then he started to say something, faltered and stared with horror at a point several feet behind his opponent. The "terror" sprang to one side in response to Hopalong's expression, as if fearing that a snake or some such danger threatened him. As he alighted in his new position he fell forward and Hopalong slid a smoking Colt in its holster.

Several men left the distant group and ran toward the claim. Hopalong reached his arm inside the door and brought forth his Sharp's rifle, with which he covered their advance.

"Anything yu want?" he shouted savagely.

The men stopped and two of them started to sidle in front of two others, but Hopalong was not there for the purpose of permitting a move that would screen any gunplay and he stopped the game with a warning shout. Then the two held up their hands and advanced.

"We wants to git Dan," called out one of them, nodding at the prostrate figure.

"Come ahead," replied Hopalong, substituting a Colt for the rifle.

They carried their badly wounded and insensible burden back to those whom they had left, and several curses were hurled at the cowboy, who only smiled grimly and entered the hut to place things ready for a siege, should one come. He had one hundred rounds of ammunition and provisions enough for two weeks, with the assurance of reinforcements long before that time would expire. He cut several rough loopholes and laid out his weapons for quick handling. He knew that he could stop any advance during the day and planned only for night attacks. How long he could go without sleep did not bother him, because he gave it no thought, as he was accustomed to short naps and could awaken at will or at the slightest sound.

As dusk merged into dark he crept forth and collected several handfuls of dry twigs, which he scattered around the hut, as the cracking of these would warn him of an approach. Then he went in and went to sleep.

He awoke at daylight after a good night's rest, and feasted on canned beans and peaches. Then he tossed the cans out of the door and shoved his hat out. Receiving no response he walked out and surveyed the town at his feet. A sheepish grin spread over his face as he realized that there was no danger. Several red-shirted men passed by him on their way to town, and one, a grizzled veteran of many gold camps, stopped and sauntered up to him.

"Mornin'," said Hopalong.

"Mornin'," replied the stranger. "I thought I'd drop in an' say that I saw that gunplay of yourn yesterday. Yu ain't got no reason to look for a rush. This camp is half decent men an' half bullies, an' th' decent men won't stand fer no play like that. Them fellers that jest passed are neighbors of yourn, an' they won't lay abed if yu needs them. But yu wants to look out fer th' joints in th' town. Guess this business is out of yore line," he finished as he sized Hopalong up.

"She shore is, but I'm here to stay. Got tired of punchin' an' reckoned I'd git rich." Here he smiled and glanced at the hole. "How're yu makin' out?" he asked.

" 'Bout five dollars a day apiece, but that ain't nothin' when grub's so high. Got reckless th' other day an' had a egg at fifty cents."

Hopalong whistled and glanced at the empty cans at his feet. "Any marshal in this burg?"

"Yep. But he's one of th' gang. No good, an' drunk half th' time an' half drunk th' rest. Better come down an' have something," invited the miner.

"I'd shore like to, but I can't let no gang get in that door," replied the puncher.

"Oh, that's all right; I'll call my pardner down to keep house till yu gits back. He can hold her all right. Hey, Jake!" he called to a man who was some hundred paces distant; "come down here an' keep house till we gits back, will yu?"

The man lumbered down to them and took possession as Hopalong and his newly found friend started for the town.

They entered the "Miner's Rest" and Hopalong fixed the room is his mind with one swift glance. Three men—and they looked like the crowd he had stopped before—were playing poker at a table near the window. Hopalong leaned with his back to the bar and talked, with the players always in sight.

Soon the door opened and a bewhiskered, heavy-set man tramped in, and walking up to Hopalong, looked him over.

"Huh," he sneered, "yu are th' gent with th' festive guns that plugged Dan, ain't yu?"

Hopalong looked at him in the eyes and quietly replied: "An' who th' hell are yu?"

The stranger's eyes blazed and his face wrinkled with rage as he aggressively shoved his jaw close to Hopalong's face.

"Yu runt, I'm a better man than yu even if yu do wear hair pants," referring to Hopalong's chaps. "Yu cow-wrastlers make me tired, an' I'm goin' to show yu that this town is too good for you. Yu can say it right now that yu are a ornery, game-leg——"

Hopalong, blind with rage, smashed his insulter squarely between the eyes with all the power of his sinewy body behind the blow, knocking him in a heap under the table. Then he quickly glanced at the cardplayers and saw a hostile movement. His gun was out in a flash and he covered the trio as he walked up to them. Never in all his life had he felt such a desire to kill. His eyes were diamond points of accumulated fury, and those whom he faced quailed before him.

"Yu scum of th' earth! Draw, please draw! Pull yore guns an' gimme my chance! Three to one, an' I'll lay my guns here," he said, placing them on the bar and removing his hands. " 'Nearer My God to Thee' is purty appropriate fer yu just now! Yu seem to be a-scared of yore own guns. Git down on yore dirty knees an' say good an' loud that yu eats dirt! Shout out that yu are too currish to live with decent men," he said, even-toned and distinct, his voice vibrant with passion as he took up his Colts. "Get down!" he repeated, shoving the weapons forward and pulling back the hammers.

The trio glanced at each other, and all three dropped to their knees and repeated in venomous hatred the words Hopalong said for them.

"Now git! An' if I sees yu when I leaves I'll send yu after yore friend. I'll shoot on sight now. Git!" He escorted them to the door and kicked the last one out.

His miner friend still leaned against the bar and looked his approval.

"Well done, youngster! But yu wants to look out—that man," pointing to the now-groping victim of Hopalong's blow, "is th' marshal of this town. He or his pals will get yu if yu don't watch th' corners."

Hopalong walked over to the marshal, jerked him to his feet and slammed him against the bar. Then he tore the cheap badge from its place and threw it on the floor. Reaching down, he drew the marshal's revolver from its holster and shoved it in its owner's hand.

"Yore th' marshal of this place an' it's too good for me, but yore goin' to pick up that tin lie," pointed at the badge, "an' yore goin' to do it right now. Then yore goin' to get kicked out of that door, an' if yu stops runnin' while I can see yu I'll fill yu so full of holes yu'll catch cold. Yore a sumptious marshal, yu are! Yore th' snortingest ki-yi that ever stuck its tail atween its laigs, yu are. Yu wants to keep to yoreself or some papoose or I'll slide yu over th' Divide so fast yu won't have time to grease yore pants. Pick up that license-tag an' let me see you perculate so lively that yore back 'll look like a ten-cent piece in five seconds. Flit!"

The marshal, dazed and bewildered, stooped and

fumbled for the badge. Then he stood up and glanced at the gun in his hand and at the eager man before him. He slid the weapon in his belt and drew his hand across his fast-closing eyes. Cursing streaks of profanity, he staggered to the door and landed in a heap in the street from the force of Hopalong's kick. Struggling to his feet, he ran unsteadily down the block and disappeared around a corner.

The bartender, cool and unperturbed, pushed out three glasses on his treat: "I've seen yu afore, up in Cheyenne—'member? How's yore friend Red?" he asked as he filled the glasses with the best the house afforded.

"Well, shore 'nuff! Glad to see yu, Jimmy! What yu doin' away off here?" asked Hopalong, beginning to feel at home.

"Oh, jest filterin' round like. I'm awful glad to see yu—this yere wart of a town needs siftin' out. It was only last week I was wishin' one of yore bunch 'ud show up—that ornament yu jest buffaloed shore raised th' devil in here, an' I wished I had somebody to prospect his anatomy for a lead mine. But he's got a tough gang circulating with him. Ever hear of Dutch Shannon or Blinky Neary? They's with him."

"Dutch Shannon? Nope," he replied.

"Bad eggs, an' not a-carin' how they gits square. Th' feller yu' salted yesterday was a bosom friend of th' marshal's, an' he passed in his chips last night."

"So?"

"Yep. Bought a bottle of ready-made nerve an' went to his own funeral. Aristotle Smith was lookin' fer him up in Cheyenne last year. Aristotle said he'd give a century fer five minutes' palaver with him, but he shied th' town an' didn't come back. Yu know Aristotle, don't yu? He's th' geezer that made fame up to Poison Knob three years ago. He used to go to town ridin' astride a log on th' lumber flume. Made four miles in six minutes with th' promise of a ruction when he stopped. Once when he was loaded he tried to ride back th' same way he came, an' th' first thing he knowed he was three miles farther from his supper an' a-slippin' down that valley like he wanted to go somewhere. He swum out at Potter's Dam an' it took him a day to walk back. But he didn't make that play again, because he was frequently sober, an' when he wasn't he'd only stand off an' swear at th' slide."

"That's Aristotle, all hunk. He's th' chap that used to play checkers with Deacon Rawlins. They used empty an' loaded shells for men, an' when they got a king they'd lay one on its side. Sometimes they'd jar th' board an' they'd all be kings an' then they'd have a cussin' match," replied Hopalong, once more restored to good humor.

"Why," responded Jimmy, "he counted his wealth over twice by mistake an' shore raised a howl when he went to blow it—thought he'd been robbed, an' laid behind th' houses fer a week lookin' fer th' feller that done it."

"I've heard of that cuss—he shore was th' limit. What become of him?" asked the miner.

"He ambled up to Laramie an' stuck his head in th' window of that joint by th' plaza an' hollered 'Fire,' an' they did. He was shore a good feller, all th' same," answered the bartender.

Hopalong laughed and started for the door. Turning around he looked at his miner friend and asked: "Comin' along? I'm goin' back now."

"Nope. Reckon I'll hit th' tiger a whirl. I'll stop in when I passes."

"All right. So long," replied Hopalong, slipping out of the door and watching for trouble. There was no opposition shown him, and he arrived at his claim to find Jake in a heated argument with another of the gang.

"Here he comes now," he said as Hopalong walked up. "Tell him what yu said to me."

"I said yu made a mistake," said the other, turning to the cowboy in a half apologetic manner.

"An' what else?" insisted Jake.

"Why, ain't that all?" asked the claim-jumper's friend in feigned surprise, wishing that he had kept quiet.

"Well I reckons it is if yu can't back up yore words," responded Jake in open contempt.

Hopalong grabbed the intruder by the collar of his shirt and hauled him off the claim. "Yu keep off this, understand? I just kicked yore marshal out in th' street, an' I'll pay yu th' next call. If yu rambles in range of my guns yu'll shore get in th' way of a slug. Yu an' yore gang wants to browse on th' far side of th' range or yu'll miss a sunrise some mornin'. Scoot!"

Hopalong turned to his companion and smiled. "What 'd he say?" he asked genially.

"Oh, he jest shot off his mouth a little. They's all no good. I've collided with lots of them all over this country. They can't face a good man an' keep their nerve. What'd yu say to th' marshal?"

"I told him what he was an' threw him outen th' street," replied Hopalong. "In about two weeks we'll have a new marshal an' he'll shore be a dandy."

"Yes? Why don't yu take th' job yoreself? We're with yu."

"Better man comin'. Ever hear of Buck Peters or Red Connors of th' Bar-20, Texas?"

"Buck Peters? Seems to me I have. Did he punch fer th' Tin-Cup up in Montana, 'bout twenty years back?"

"Shore! Him and Frenchy McAllister punched all over that country an' they used to paint Cheyenne, too," replied Hopalong, eagerly.

"I knows him, then. I used to know Frenchy, too. Are they comin' up here?"

"Yes," responded Hopalong, struggling with another can while waiting for the fire to catch up. "Better have some grub with me—don't like to eat alone," invited the cowboy, the reaction of his late rage swinging him to the other extreme.

When their tobacco had got well started at the close of the meal and content had taken possession of them Hopalong laughed quietly and finally spoke:

"Did yu ever know Aristotle Smith when yu was up in Montana?"

"Did I! Well, me an' Aristotle prospected all through that country till he got so locoed I had to watch him fer fear he'd blow us both up. He greased th' fryin' pan with dynamite one night, an' we shore had to eat jerked meat an' canned stuff all th' rest of that trip. What made yu ask? Is he comin' up too?"

"No, I reckons not. Jimmy, th' bartender, said that he cashed in up at Laramie. Wasn't he th' cuss that built that boat out there on th' Arizona desert because he was scared that a flood might come? Th' sun shore warped that punt till it wasn't even good for a hencoop."

"Nope. That was Sister-Annie Tompkins. He was purty near as bad as Aristotle, though. He roped a puma up on th' Sacramentos, an' didn't punch no more fer three weeks. Well, here comes my pardner an' I reckons I'll amble right along. If yu needs any referee or a side pardner in any ruction yu has only got to warble up my way. So long."

The next ten days passed quietly and on the afternoon of the eleventh Hopalong's miner friend paid him a visit.

"Jake recommends yore peaches," he laughed as he shook Hopalong's hand. "He says yu boosted another of that crowd. That bein' so I thought I would drop in an' say that they're comin' after yu tonight, shore. Just heard of it from yore friend Jimmy. Yu can count on us when th' rush comes. But why didn't yu say yu was a pard of Buck Peters'? Me an' him used to shoot up Laramie together. From what yore friend James says, yu can handle this gang by yore lonesome, but if yu needs any encouragement yu make some sign an' we'll help th' event along some. They's eight of us that'll be waitin' up to get th' returns an' we're shore goin' to be in range."

"Gee, it's nice to run across a friend of Buck's! Ain't he a son-of-a-gun?" asked Hopalong, delighted at the news. Then, without waiting for a reply, he went on: "Yore shore square, all right, an' I hates to refuse yore offer, but I got eighteen friends comin' up an' they ought to get here by tomorrow. Yu tell Jimmy to head them this way when they shows up an' I'll have th' claim for them. There ain't no use of yu fellers gettin' mixed up in this. Th' bunch that's comin' can clean out any gang this side of sunup, an' I expects they'll shore be anxious to begin when they finds me eatin' peaches an' wastin' my time shootin' bums. Yu pass th' word along to yore friends, an' tell them to lay low an' see th' Arory Boerallis hit this town with its tail up. Tell Jimmy to do it up good when he speaks about me holdin' th' claim—I likes to see Buck an' Red fight when they're good an' mad."

The miner laughed and slapped Hopalong on the shoulder. "Yore all right, youngster! Yore just like Buck was at yore age. Say now, I reckons he wasn't a reg'lar terror on wheels! Why, I've seen him do more foolish things than any man I knows of, an' I calculate that if Buck pals with yu there ain't no water in yore sand. My name's Tom Halloway," he suggested.

"An' mine's Hopalong Cassidy," was the reply. "I've heard Buck speak of yu."

"Has yu? Well, don't it beat all how little this world is? Somebody allus turnin' up that knows somebody yu knows. I'll just amble along, Mr. Cassidy, an' don't yu be none bashful about callin' if yu needs me. Any pal of Buck's is my friend. Well, so long," said the visitor as he strode off. Then he stopped and turned around. "Hey, mister!" he called. "They are goin' to roll a fire barrel down agin yu from behind," indicating by an outstretched arm the point from where it would start. "If it burns yu out I'm goin' to take a hand from up there," pointing to a cluster of rocks well to the rear of where the crowd would work from, "an' I don't care whether yu likes it or not," he added to himself.

Hopalong scratched his head and then laughed. Taking up a pick and shovel, he went out behind the cabin and dug a trench parallel with and about twenty paces away from the rear wall. Heaping the excavated dirt up on the near side of the cut, he stepped back and surveyed his labor with open satisfaction. "Roll yore fire barrel an' be damn," he muttered. "Mebby she won't make a bully light for potshots, though," he added, grinning at the execution he would do.

Taking up his tools, he went up to the place from where the gang would roll the barrel, and made half a dozen mounds of twigs, being careful to make them very flimsy. Then he covered them with earth and packed them gently. The mounds looked very tempting from the viewpoint of a marksman in search of cover, and appeared capable of stopping any rifle ball that could be fired against them. Hopalong looked them over critically and stepped back.

"I'd like to see th' look on th' face of th' son-of-a-gun that uses them for cover—won't he be surprised?" and he grinned gleefully as he pictured his shots boring through them. Then he placed in the center of each a chip or a pebble or something that he thought would show up well in the firelight.

Returning to the cabin, he banked it up well with dirt and gravel, and tossed a few shovelfuls up on the roof as a safety valve to his exuberance. When he entered the door he had another idea, and fell to work scooping out a shallow cellar, deep enough to shelter him when lying at full length. Then he stuck his head out of the window and grinned at the false covers with their prominent bull's-eyes.

"When that prize-winnin' gang of ossified idiots runs up agin' these fortifications they shore will be disgusted. I'll bet four dollars an' seven cents they'll think their medicine man's no good. I hopes that puff-eyed marshal will pick out that hump with th' chip on it," and he hugged himself in anticipation.

He then cut down a sapling and fastened it to the roof and on it he tied his neckerchief, which fluttered valiantly and with defiance in the light breeze.

"I shore hopes they appreciates that," he remarked whimsically, as he went inside the hut and closed the door.

The early part of the evening passed in peace, and Hopalong, tired of watching in vain, wished for action. Midnight came, and it was not until half an hour before dawn that he was attacked. Then a noise sent him to a loophole, where he fired two shots at skulking figures some distance off. A fusillade of bullets replied; one of them ripped through the door at a weak spot and drilled a hole in a can of the everlasting peaches. Hopalong set the can in the frying pan and then flitted from loophole to loophole, shooting quick and straight. Several curses told him that he had not missed, and he scooped up a finger of peach juice. Shots thudded into the walls of his fort in an unceasing stream, and, as it grew lighter, several whizzed through the loopholes. He kept close to the earth and waited for the rush, and when it came sent it back, minus two of its members.

As he reloaded his Colts a bullet passed through his shirtsleeve and he promptly nailed the marksman. He looked out of a crack in the rear wall and saw the top of an adjoining hill crowned with spectators, all of whom were armed. Some time later he repulsed another attack and heard a faint cheer from his friends on the hill. Then he saw a barrel, blazing from end to end, roll out from the place he had so carefully covered with mounds. It gathered speed and bounded over the rough ground, flashed between two rocks and leaped into the trench, where it crackled and roared in vain.

"Now," said Hopalong, blazing at the mounds as

fast as he could load and fire his Sharp's, "we'll just see what yu thinks of yore nice little covers."

Yells of consternation and pain rang out in a swelling chorus, and legs and arms jerked and flopped, one man, in his astonishment at the shot that tore open his cheek, sitting up in plain sight of the marksman. Roars of rage floated up from the main body of the besiegers, and the discomfited remnant of barrel-rollers broke for real cover.

Then he stopped another rush from the front, made upon the supposition that he was thinking only of the second detachment. A hearty cheer arose from Tom Halloway and his friends, ensconced in their rocky position, and it was taken up by those on the hill, who danced and yelled their delight at the battle, to them more humorous than otherwise.

This recognition of his prowess from men of the caliber of his audience made him feel good, and he grinned: "Gee, I'll bet Halloway an' his friends is shore itchin' to get in this," he murmured, firing at a head that was shown for an instant. "Wonder what Red 'll say when Jimmy tells him—bet he'll plow dust like a cyclone," and Hopalong laughed, picturing to himself the satiation of Red's anger. "Old redheaded son-of-a-gun," murmured the cowboy affectionately, "he shore can fight."

As he squinted over the sights of his rifle his eye caught sight of a moving body of men as they cantered over the flats about two miles away. In his eagerness he forgot to shoot and carefully counted them. "Nine," he grumbled. "Wonder what's th' matter?"—fearing that they were not his friends. Then a second body numbering eight cantered into sight and followed the first.

"Whoop! There's th' Redhead!" he shouted, dancing in his joy. "Now," he shouted at the peach can joyously, "yu wait about thirty minutes an' yu'll shore reckon Hades has busted loose!"

He grabbed up his Colts, which he kept loaded for repelling rushes, and recklessly emptied them into the bushes and between the rocks and trees, searching every likely place for a human target. Then he slipped his rifle in a loophole and waited for good shots, having worked off the dangerous pressure of his exuberance.

Soon he heard a yell from the direction of the "Miner's Rest," and fell to jamming cartridges into his revolvers so that he could sally out and join in the fray by the side of Red.

The thunder of madly pounding hoofs rolled up the trail, and soon a horse and rider shot around the corner and headed for the copse. Three more raced close behind and then a bunch of six, followed by the rest, spread out and searched for trouble.

Red, a Colt in each hand and hatless, stood up in his stirrups and sent shot after shot into the fleeing mob, which he could not follow on account of the nature of the ground. Buck wheeled and dashed down the trail again with Red a close second, the others packed in a solid mass and after them. At the first level stretch the newcomers swept down and hit their enemies, going through them like a knife through cheese. Hopalong danced up and down with rage when he could not find his horse, and had to stand and yell, a spectator.

The fight drifted in among the buildings, where it became a series of isolated duels, and soon Hopalong saw panic-stricken horses carrying their riders out of the other side of the town. Then he went gunning for the man who had rustled his horse. He was unsuccessful and returned to his peaches.

Soon the riders came up, and when they saw Hopalong shove a peach into his powder-grimed mouth they yelled their delight.

"Yu old maverick! Eatin' peaches like yu was afraid we'd git some!" shouted Red indignantly, leaping down and running up to his pal as though to thrash him.

Hopalong grinned pleasantly and fired a peach against Red's eye. "I was savin' that one for yu, Reddie," he remarked, as he avoided Buck's playful kick. "Yu fellers git to work an' dig up some wealth—I'm hungry." Then he turned to Buck: "Yore th' marshal of this town, an' any son-of-a-gun what don't like it had better write. Oh, yes, here comes Tom Halloway—'member him?"

Buck turned and faced the miner and his hand went out with a jerk.

"Well, I'll be locoed if I didn't punch with yu on th' Tin-Cup!" he said.

"Yu shore did an' yu was purty devilish, but that there Cassidy of yourn beats anything I ever seen."

"He's a good kid," replied Buck, glancing to where Red and Hopalong were quarreling as to who had eaten the most pie in a contest held some years before.

Johnny, nosing around, came upon the perforated and partially scattered piles of earth and twigs, and vented his disgust of them by kicking them to pieces. "Hey! Hoppy! Oh, Hoppy!" he called, "what are these things?"

Hopalong jammed Red's hat over that person's

eyes and replied: "Oh, them's some loaded dice I fixed for them."

"Yu son-of-a-gun!" sputtered Red, as he wrestled with his friend in the exuberance of his pride. "Yu son-of-a-gun! Yu shore ought to be ashamed to treat 'em that way!"

"Shore," replied Hopalong. "But I ain't!"

CHAPTER XII

The Hospitality of Travennes

Mr. Buck Peters rode into Alkaline one bright September morning and sought refreshment at the Emporium. Mr. Peters had just finished some business for his employer and felt the satisfaction that comes with the knowledge of work well done. He expected to remain in Alkaline for several days, where he was to be joined by two of his friends and punchers, Mr. Hopalong Cassidy and Mr. Red Connors, both of whom were at Cactus Springs, seventy miles to the east. Mr. Cassidy and his friends had just finished a nocturnal tour of Santa Fé and felt somewhat peevish and dull in consequence, not to mention the sadness occasioned by the expenditure of the greater part of their combined capital on such foolishness as faro, roulette and wet-goods.

Mr. Peters and his friends had sought wealth in the Black Hills, where they had enthusiastically disfigured the earth in the fond expectation of uncovering vast stores of virgin gold. Their hopes were of

an optimistic brand and had existed until the last
canister of cornmeal flour had been emptied by Mr.
Cassidy's burro, which waited not upon its master's
pleasure nor upon the ethics of the case. When Mr.
Cassidy had returned from exercising the animal and
himself over two miles of rocky hillside in the vain
endeavor to give it his opinion of burros and sundry
chastisements, he was requested, as owner of the
beast, to give his counsel as to the best way of se-
curing eighteen breakfasts. Remembering that the
animal was headed north when he last saw it and
that it was too old to eat, anyway, he suggested a
plan which had worked successfully at other times
for other ends, namely, poker. Mr. McAllister, an expert at the great American game, volunteered his
service in accordance with the spirit of the occasion
and, half an hour later, he and Mr. Cassidy drifted
into Pell's poker parlors, which were located in the
rear of a Chinese laundry, where they gathered unto
themselves the wherewithal for the required breakfasts. An hour spent in the card room of the "Hur-
rah" convinced its proprietor that they had wasted
their talents for the past six weeks in digging for
gold. The proof of this permitted the departure of
the outfits with their customary éclat.

At Santa Fé the various individuals had gone their
respective ways, to reassemble at the ranch in the
near future, and for several days they had been drift-
ing south in groups of twos and threes and, like chaff
upon a stream, had eddied into Alkaline, where Mr.
Peters had found them arduously engaged in post-
poning the final journey. After he had gladdened
their hearts and soothed their throats by making several pithy remarks to the bartender, with whom he
established their credit, he cautioned them against

letting anyone harm them and, smiling at the humor of his warning, left abruptly.

Cactus Springs was burdened with a zealous and initiative organization known as vigilantes, whose duty it was to extend the courtesies of the land to cattle thieves and the like. This organization boasted of the name of Travennes' Terrors and of a muster roll of twenty. There was also a boast that no one had ever escaped them which, if true, was in many cases unfortunate. Mr. Slim Travennes, with whom Mr. Cassidy had participated in an extemporaneous exchange of Colt's courtesies in Santa Fé the year before, was the head of the organization and was also chairman of the committee on arrivals, and the two gentlemen of the Bar-20 had not been in town an hour before he knew of it. Being anxious to show the strangers every attention and having a keen recollection of the brand of gunplay commanded by Mr. Cassidy, he planned a smoother method of procedure and one calculated to permit him to enjoy the pleasures of a good old age. Mr. Travennes knew that horse thieves were regarded as social enemies, that the necessary proof of their guilt was the finding of stolen animals in their possession, that death was the penalty and that every man, whether directly concerned or not, regarded himself as judge, jury and executioner. He had several acquaintances who were bound to him by his knowledge of crimes they had committed and who could not refuse his slightest wish. Even if they had been free agents they were not above causing the death of an innocent man. Mr. Travennes, feeling very self-satisfied at his cleverness, arranged to have the proof placed where it would do the most harm and intended to take care of the rest by himself.

Mr. Connors, feeling much refreshed and very hungry, arose at daylight the next morning, and dressing quickly, started off to feed and water the horses. After having several tilts with the landlord about the bucket he took his departure toward the corral at the rear. Peering through the gate, he could hardly believe his eyes. He climbed over it and inspected the animals at close range, and found that those which he and his friend had ridden for the last two months were not to be seen, but in their places were two better animals, which concerned him greatly. Being fair and square himself, he could not understand the change and sought enlightenment of his more imaginative and suspicious friend.

"Hey, Hopalong!" he called, "come out here an' see what th' devil has happened!"

Mr. Cassidy stuck his auburn head out of the wounded shutter and complacently surveyed his companion. Then he saw the horses and looked hard.

"Quit yore foolin', yu old cuss," he remarked pleasantly, as he groped around behind him with his feet, searching for his boots. "Anybody would think yu was a little boy with yore fool jokes. Ain't yu ever goin' to grow up?"

"They've got our bronchs," replied Mr. Connors in an injured tone. "Honest, I ain't kiddin' yu," he added for the sake of peace.

"Who has?" came from the window, followed immediately by, "Yu've got my boots!"

"I ain't—they're under th' bunk," contradicted and explained Mr. Connors. Then, turning to the matter in his mind he replied, "I don't know who's got them. If I did do yu think I'd be holdin' hands with myself?"

"Nobody'd accuse yu of anything like that," came from the window, accompanied by an overdone snicker.

Mr. Connors flushed under his accumulated tan as he remembered the varied pleasures of Santa Fé, and he regarded the bronchos in anything but a pleasant state of mind.

Mr. Cassidy slid through the window and approached his friend, looking as serious as he could.

"Any tracks?" he inquired, as he glanced quickly over the ground to see for himself.

"Not after that wind we had last night. They might have growed there for all I can see," growled Mr. Connors.

"I reckon we better hold a powwow with th' foreman of this shack an' find out what he knows," suggested Mr. Cassidy. "This looks too good to be a swap."

Mr. Connors looked his disgust at the idea and then a light broke in upon him. "Mebby they was hard pushed an' wanted fresh cayuses," he said. "A whole lot of people get hard pushed in this country. Anyhow, we'll prospect th' boss."

They found the proprietor in his stocking feet, getting the breakfast, and Mr. Cassidy regarded the preparations with open approval. He counted the tin plates and found only three, and, thinking that there would be more plates if there were others to feed, glanced into the landlord's room. Not finding signs of other guests, on whom to lay the blame for the loss of his horse, he began to ask questions.

"Much trade?" he inquired solicitously.

"Yep," replied the landlord.

Mr. Cassidy looked at the three tins and wondered if there had ever been any more with which to supply his trade. "Been out this morning?" he pursued.

"Nope."

"Talks purty nigh as much as Buck," thought Mr. Cassidy, and then said aloud, "Anybody else here?"

"Nope."

Mr. Cassidy lapsed into a painful and disgusted silence and his friend tried his hand.

"Who owns a mosaic bronch, Chinee flag on th' near side, Skillet brand?" asked Mr. Connors.

"Quien sabe?"

"Gosh, he can nearly keep still in two lingoes," thought Mr. Cassidy.

"Who owns a bobtailed pinto, saddle-galled, cast in th' near eye, Star Diamond brand, white stockin' on th' off front prop, with a habit of scratchin' itself every other minute?" went on Mr. Connors.

"Slim Travennes," replied the proprietor, flopping a flapjack.

Mr. Cassidy reflectively scratched the back of his hand and looked innocent, but his mind was working overtime.

"Who's Slim Travennes?" asked Mr. Connors, never having heard of that person, owing to the reticence of his friend.

"Captain of th' vigilantes."

"What does he look like on th' general run?" blandly inquired Mr. Cassidy, wishing to verify his suspicions. He thought of the trouble he had with Mr. Travennes up in Santa Fé and of the reputation that gentleman possessed. Then the fact that Mr. Travennes was the leader of the local vigilantes came to his assistance and he was sure that the captain had a hand in the change. All these points existed in misty groups in his mind, but the next remark of the landlord caused them to rush together and reveal the plot.

"Good," said the landlord, flopping another flapjack, "and a warnin' to hoss thieves."

"Ahem," coughed Mr. Cassidy and then continued,

"is he a tall, lanky, yaller-headed son-of-a-gun, with a big nose an' lots of ears?"

"Mebby so," answered the host.

"Um, slopping over into bad Sioux," thought Mr. Cassidy, and then said aloud, "How long has he hung around this here layout?" at the same time passing a warning glance at his companion.

The landlord straightened up. "Look here, stranger, if yu hankers after his pedigree so all-fired hard yu had best pump him."

"I told yu this here feller wasn't a man what would give away all he knowed," lied Mr. Connors, turning to his friend and indicating the host. "He ain't got time for that. Anybody can see that he is a powerful busy man. An' then he ain't no child."

Mr. Cassidy thought that the landlord could tell all he knew in about five minutes and then not break any speed records for conversation, but he looked properly awed and impressed. "Well, yu needn't go an' get mad about it! I didn't know, did I?"

"Who's gettin' mad?" pugnaciously asked Mr. Connors. After his injured feelings had been soothed by Mr. Cassidy's sullen silence he again turned to the landlord.

"What did this Travennes look like when yu saw him last?" coaxed Mr. Connors.

"Th' same as he does now, as yu can see by lookin' out of th' window. That's him down th' street," enlightened the host, thawing to the pleasant Mr. Connors.

Mr. Cassidy adopted the suggestion and frowned. Mr. Travennes and two companions were walking toward the corral and Mr. Cassidy once again slid out of the window, his friend going by the door.

CHAPTER XIII

Travennes' Discomfiture

WHEN MR. Travennes looked over the corral fence he was much chagrined to see a man and a Colt's .45, both paying strict attention to his nose.

"Mornin', Duke," said the man with the gun. "Lose anything?"

Mr. Travennes looked back at his friends and saw Mr. Connors sitting on a rock holding two guns. Mr. Travennes' right and left wings were the targets and they pitted their frowns against Mr. Connors' smile.

"Not that I knows of," replied Mr. Travennes, shifting his feet uneasily.

"Find anything?" came from Mr. Cassidy as he sidled out of the gate.

"Nope," replied the captain of the Terrors, eyeing the Colt.

"Are yu in th' habit of payin' early mornin' calls to this here corral?" persisted Mr. Cassidy, playing with the gun.

"Ya-as. That's my business—I'm th' captain of th' vigilantes."

"That's too bad," sympathized Mr. Cassidy, moving forward a step.

Mr. Travennes looked put out and backed off. "What yu mean, stickin' me up thisaway?" he asked indignantly.

"Yu needn't go an' get mad," responded Mr. Cassidy. "Just business. Yore cayuse an' another shore climbed this corral fence last night an' ate up our bronchs, an' I just nachurlly want to know about it."

Mr. Travennes looked his surprise and incredulity and craned his neck to see for himself. When he saw his horse peacefully scratching itself he swore and looked angrily up the street. Mr. Connors, behind the shack, was hidden to the view of those on the street, and when two men ran up at a signal from Mr. Travennes, intending to insert themselves in the misunderstanding, they were promptly lined up with the first two by the man on the rock.

"Sit down," invited Mr. Connors, pushing a chunk of air out of the way with his guns. The last two felt a desire to talk and to argue the case on its merits, but refrained as the black holes in Mr. Connors' guns hinted at eruption. "Every time yu opens yore mouths yu get closer to th' Great Divide," enlightened that person, and they were childlike in their belief.

Mr. Travennes acted as though he would like to scratch his thigh where his Colt's chafed him, but postponed the event and listened to Mr. Cassidy, who was asking questions.

"Where's our cayuses, General?"

Mr. Travennes replied that he didn't know. He was

worried, for he feared that his captor didn't have a
secure hold on the hammer of the ubiquitous Colt's.

"Where's *my* cayuse?" persisted Mr. Cassidy.

"I don't know, but I wants to ask yu how yu got
mine," replied Mr. Travennes.

"Yu tell me how mine got out an' I'll tell yu how
yourn got in," countered Mr. Cassidy.

Mr. Connors added another to his collection before the captain replied.

"Out in this country people get in trouble when
they're found with other folks' cayuses," Mr. Travennes suggested.

Mr. Cassidy looked interested and replied: "Yu
shore ought to borrow some experience, an' there's
lots floating around. More than one man has smoked
in a powder mill, an' th' number of them planted
who looked in th' muzzle of a empty gun is scandalous. If my remarks don't perculate right smart I'll
explain."

Mr. Travennes looked down the street again, saw
number five added to the lineup, and coughed up
chunks of broken profanity, grieving his host by his
lack of courtesy.

"Time," announced Mr. Cassidy, interrupting the
round. "I wants them cayuses an' I wants 'em right
now. Yu an' me will amble off an' get 'em. I won't
bore yu with tellin' yu what'll happen if yu gets skit-
tish. Slope along an' don't be scared; I'm with yu,"
assured Mr. Cassidy as he looked over at Mr. Connors, whose ascetic soul pined for the flapjacks of
which his olfactories caught intermittent whiffs.

"Well, Red, I reckons yu has got plenty of room
out here for all yu may corral; anyhow there ain't a
whole lot more. My friend Slim an' I are shore going
to have a devil of a time if we can't find them cussed

bronchs. Whew, them flapjacks smell like a plain trail to payday. Just think of th' nice maple juice we used to get up to Cheyenne on them frosty mornings."

"Get out of here an' lemme alone! What do yu allus want to go an' make a feller unhappy for? Can't yu keep still about grub when yu knows I ain't had my morning's feed yet?" asked Mr. Connors, much aggrieved.

"Well, I'll be back directly an' I'll have them cayuses. Yu tend to business an' watch th' herd. That shorthorn yearling at th' end of th' line"—pointing to a young man who looked capable of taking risks—"he looks like he might take a chance an' gamble with yu," remarked Mr. Cassidy, placing Mr. Travennes in front of him and pushing back his own sombrero. "Don't put too much maple juice on them flapjacks, Red," he warned as he poked his captive in the back of the neck as a hint to get along. Fortunately Mr. Connors' closing remarks are lost to history.

Observing that Mr. Travennes headed south on the quest, Mr. Cassidy reasoned that the missing bronchos ought to be somewhere in the north, and he postponed the southern trip until such time when they would have more leisure at their disposal. Mr. Travennes showed a strong inclination to shy at this arrangement, but quieted down under persuasion, and they started off toward where Mr. Cassidy firmly believed the North Pole and the cayuses to be.

"Yu has got quite a metropolis here," pleasantly remarked Mr. Cassidy as under his direction they made for a distant corral. "I can see four different types of architecture, two of 'em on one residence," he continued as they passed a wood and adobe hut. "No doubt the railroad will put a branch down here someday an' then yu can hire their old cars for yore public buildings. Then when yu gets a post office yu will shore make Chicago hustle some to keep her end up. Let's assay that hollow for horsehide; it looks promisin'."

The hollow was investigated but showed nothing other than cactus and baked alkali. The corral came next, and there too was emptiness. For an hour the search was unavailing, but at the end of that time Mr. Cassidy began to notice signs of nervousness on the part of his guest, which grew less as they proceeded. Then Mr. Cassidy retraced their steps to the place where the nervousness first developed and tried another way and once more returned to the starting point.

"Yu seems to hanker for this fool exercise," quoth Mr. Travennes with much sarcasm. "If yu reckons I'm fond of this locoed ramblin' yu shore needs enlightenment."

"Sometimes I do get these fits," confessed Mr. Cassidy, "an' when I do I'm dead sore on objections. Let's peek in that there hut," he suggested.

"Huh; yore ideas of cayuses are mighty peculiar. Why don't you look for 'em up on those cactuses or behind that mesquite? *I* wouldn't be a heap surprised if they was roostin' on th' roof. They are mighty knowing animals, cayuses. I once saw one that could figger like a schoolmarm," remarked Mr. Travennes, beginning sarcastically and toning it down as he proceeded, out of respect for his companion's gun.

"Well, they might be in th' shack," replied Mr. Cassidy. "Cayuses know so much that it takes a month to unlearn them. I wouldn't like to bet they ain't in that hut, though."

Mr. Travennes snickered in a manner decidedly

uncomplimentary and began to whistle, softly at first.
The gentleman from the Bar-20 noticed that his companion was a musician; that when he came to a
strong part he increased the tones until they bid to
be heard at several hundred yards. When Mr. Travennes had reached a most passionate part in "Juan-
ita" and was expanding his lungs to do it justice he
was rudely stopped by the insistent pressure of his
guard's Colt's on the most ticklish part of his ear.

"I shore wish yu wouldn't strain yoreself thataway," said Mr. Cassidy, thinking that Mr. Travennes
might be endeavoring to call assistance. "I went an'
promised my mother on her deathbed that I wouldn't
let nobody whistle out loud like that, an' th' opery is
hereby stopped. Besides, somebody might hear them
mournful tones an' think that something is th' matter, which it ain't."

Mr. Travennes substituted heartfelt cursing, all of
which was heavily accented.

As they approached the hut Mr. Cassidy again tick-
led his prisoner and insisted that he be very quiet,
as his cayuse was very sensitive to noise and it might
be there. Mr. Cassidy still thought Mr. Travennes
might have friends in the hut and wouldn't for the
world disturb them, as he would present a splendid
target as he approached the building.

CHAPTER XIV

The Tale of a Cigarette

THE OPEN door revealed three men asleep on the earthen floor, two of whom were Mexicans. Mr. Cassidy then for the first time felt called upon to relieve his companion of the Colt's which so sorely itched that gentleman's thigh and then disarmed the sleeping guards.

In the far corner of the room were two bronchos, one of which tried in vain to kick Mr. Cassidy, not realizing that he was ten feet away. The noise awakened the sleepers, who sat up and then sprang to their feet, their hands instinctively streaking to their thighs for the weapons which peeked contentedly from the bosom of Mr. Cassidy's open shirt. One of the Mexicans made a lightning-like grab for the back of his neck for the knife which lay along his spine and was shot in the front of his neck for his trouble. The shot spoiled his aim, as the knife flashed past Mr. Cassidy's arm, wide by two feet, and thudded into the door frame, where it hummed angrily.

"Th' only man who could do that right was th' man who invented it, Mr. Bowie, of Texas," explained Mr. Cassidy to the other Mexican. Then he glanced at the broncho, that was squealing in rage and fear at the shot, which sounded like a cannon in the small room, and laughed.

"That's my cayuse all right, an' he wasn't up no cactus nor roostin' on th' roof, neither. He's th' most affectionate beast I ever saw. It took me nigh onto six months afore I could ride him without fighting him to a standstill," said Mr. Cassidy to his guest. Then he turned to the horse and looked it over. "Come here! What d'yu mean, acting thataway? Yu ragged end of nothin' wobbling in space! Yu wall-eyed, ornery, locoed guide to Hades! Yu won't be so frisky when yu've made them seventy hot miles between here an' Alkaline in five hours," he promised, as he made his way toward the animal.

Mr. Travennes walked over to the opposite wall and took down a pouch of tobacco which hung from a peg. He did this in a manner suggesting ownership, and after he had deftly rolled a cigarette with one hand he put the pouch in his pocket and, lighting up, inhaled deeply and with much satisfaction. Mr. Cassidy turned around and glanced the group over, wondering if the tobacco had been left in the hut on a former call.

"Did yu find yore makings?" he asked, with a note of congratulation in his voice.

"Yep. Want one?" asked Mr. Travennes.

Mr. Cassidy ignored the offer and turned to the guard whom he had found asleep.

"Is that his tobacco?" he asked, and the guard, anxious to make everything run smoothly, told the truth and answered: "Shore. He left it here last night," whereupon Mr. Travennes swore and Mr. Cassidy smiled grimly.

"Then yu knows how yore cayuse got in an' how mine got out," said the latter. "I wish yu would explain," he added, fondling his Colt's.

Mr. Travennes frowned and remained silent.

"I can tell yu, anyhow," continued Mr. Cassidy, still smiling, but his eyes and jaw belied the smile. "Yu took them cayuses out because yu wanted yourn to be found in their places. Yu remembered Santa Fé an' it rankled in yu. Not being man enough to notify me that yu'd shoot on sight an' being afraid my friends would get yu if yu plugged me on th' sly, yu tried to make out that me an' Red rustled yore cayuses. That meant a lynching with me an' Red in th' places of honor. Yu never saw Red afore, but yu didn't care if he went with me. Yu don't deserve fair play, but I'm going to give it to yu because I don't want anybody to say that any of th' Bar-20 ever murdered a man, not even a skunk like yu. My friends have treated me too square for that. Yu can take this gun an' yu can do one of three things with it, which are: walk out in th' open a hundred paces an' then turn an' walk toward me—after you face me yu can set it a-going whenever yu want to; th' second is, put it under yore hat an' I'll put mine an' th' others back by th' cayuses. Then we'll toss up an' th' lucky man gets it to use as he wants. Th' third is, shoot yourself."

Mr. Cassidy punctuated the close of his ultimatum by handing over the weapon, muzzle first, and, because the other might be an adept at "twirling," he kept its recipient covered during the operation. Then, placing his second Colt's with the captured weapons, he threw them through the door, being very careful not to lose the drop on his now-armed prisoner.

Mr. Travennes looked around and wiped the sweat from his forehead, and being an observant gentleman, took the proffered weapon and walked to the east, directly toward the sun, which at this time was halfway to the meridian. The glare of its straight rays and those reflected from the shining sand would, in a measure, bother Mr. Cassidy and interfere with the accuracy of his aim, and he was always thankful for small favors.

Mr. Travennes was the possessor of accurate knowledge regarding the lay of the land, and the thought came to him that there was a small but deep hole out toward the east and that it was about the required distance away. This had been dug by a man who had labored all day in the burning sun to make an oven so that he could cook mesquite root in the manner he had seen the Apaches cook it. Mr. Travennes blessed hobbies, specific and general, stumbled thoughtlessly and disappeared from sight as the surprised Mr. Cassidy started forward to offer his assistance. Upon emphatic notification from the man in the hole that his help was not needed, Mr. Cassidy wheeled around and in great haste covered the distance separating him from the hut, whereupon Mr. Travennes swore in self-congratulation and regret. Mr. Cassidy's shots barked a cactus which leaned near Mr. Travennes' head and flecked several clouds of alkali near that person's nose, causing him to sneeze, duck, and grin.

"It's his own gun," grumbled Mr. Cassidy as a bullet passed through his sombrero, having in mind the fact that his opponent had a whole belt full of .41's. If it had been Mr. Cassidy's gun that had been handed over he would have enjoyed the joke on Mr. Travennes, who would have had five cartridges between himself and the promised eternity, as he would have been unable to use the .41's in Mr. Cassidy's .45, while the latter would have gladly consented to the change, having as he did an extra .45. Never before had Mr. Cassidy looked with reproach upon his .45-caliber Colt's, and he sighed as he used it to notify Mr. Travennes that arbitration was not to be considered, which that person endorsed, said endorsement passing so close to Mr. Cassidy's ear that he felt the breeze made by it.

"He's been practicin' since I plugged him up in Santa Fé," thought Mr. Cassidy, as he retired around the hut to formulate a plan of campaign.

Mr. Travennes sang "Hi-le, hi-lo," and other selections, principally others, and wondered how Mr. Cassidy could hoist him out. The slack of his belt informed him that he was in the middle of a fast, and suggested starvation as the derrick that his honorable and disgusted adversary might employ.

Mr. Cassidy, while figuring out his method of procedure, absentmindedly jabbed a finger in his eye, and the ensuing tears floated an idea to him. He had always had great respect for ricochet shots since his friend Skinny Thompson had proved their worth on the hides of Sioux. If he could disturb the sand and convey several grains of it to Mr. Travennes' eyes the game would be much simplified. While planning for the proposed excavation, *à la* Colt's, he noticed several stones lying near at hand, and a new and better scheme presented itself for his consideration. If Mr. Travennes could be persuaded to get out of— well, it was worth trying.

Mr. Cassidy lined up his gloomy collection and

tersely ordered them to turn their backs to him and
to stay in that position, the suggestion being that if
they looked around they wouldn't be able to dodge
quickly enough. He then slipped bits of his lariat over
their wrists and ankles, tying wrists to ankles and
each man to his neighbor. That finished to his satisfaction, he dragged them in the hut to save them
from the burning rays of the sun. Having performed
this act of kindness, he crept along the hot sand,
taking advantage of every bit of cover afforded, and
at last he reached a point within a hundred feet of
the besieged. During the trip Mr. Travennes sang to
his heart's content, some of the words being improvised for the occasion and were not calculated to
increase Mr. Cassidy's respect for his own wisdom if
he should hear them. Mr. Cassidy heard, however,
and several fragments so forcibly intruded on his
peace of mind that he determined to put on the last
verse himself and to suit himself.

Suddenly Mr. Travennes poked his head up and
glanced at the hut. He was down again so quickly
that there was no chance for a shot at him and he
believed that his enemy was still sojourning in the
rear of the building, which caused him to fear that
he was expected to live on nothing as long as he
could and then give himself up. Just to show his defiance he stretched himself out on his back and sang
with all his might, his sombrero over his face to keep
the glare of the sun out of his eyes. He was interrupted, however, forgot to finish a verse as he had
intended, and jumped to one side as a stone bounced
off his leg. Looking up, he saw another missile curve
into his patch of sky and swiftly bear down on him.
He avoided it by a hair's breadth and wondered what
had happened. Then what Mr. Travennes thought

was a balloon, being unsophisticated in matters pertaining to aerial navigation, swooped down upon him and smote him on the shoulder and also bounced off. Mr. Travennes hastily laid music aside and took up elocution as he dodged another stone and wished that the mesquite-loving crank had put on a roof. In evading the projectile he let his sombrero appear on a level with the desert, and the hum of a bullet as it passed through his headgear and into the opposite wall made him wish that there had been constructed a cellar, also.

"Hi-le, hi-lo" intruded upon his ear, as Mr. Cassidy got rid of the surplus of his heart's joy. Another stone the size of a man's foot shaved Mr. Travennes' ear and he hugged the side of the hole nearest his enemy.

"Hibernate, blank yu!" derisively shouted the human catapult as he released a chunk of sandstone the size of a quail. "Draw in yore laigs an' buck," was his God-speed to the missile.

"Hey, yu!" indignantly yowled Mr. Travennes from his defective storm cellar. "Don't yu know any better'n to heave things thataway?"

"Hi-le, hi-lo," sang Mr. Cassidy, as another stone soared aloft in the direction of the complainant. Then he stood erect and awaited results with a Colt's in his hand leveled at the rim of the hole. A hat waved and an excited voice bit off chunks of expostulation and asked for an armistice. Then two hands shot up and Mr. Travennes, sore and disgusted and desperate, popped his head up and blinked at Mr. Cassidy's gun.

"Yu was fillin' th' hole up," remarked Mr. Travennes in an accusing tone, hiding the real reason for his evacuation. "In a little while I'd a been th' top of a pile instead of th' bottom of a hole," he announced, crawling out and rubbing his head.

Mr. Cassidy grinned and ordered his prisoner to one side while he secured the weapon which lay in the hole. Having obtained it as quickly as possible he slid it in his open shirt and clambered out again.

"Yu remind me of a feller I used to know," remarked Mr. Travennes, as he led the way to the hut, trying not to limp. "Only he throwed dynamite. That was th' way he cleared off chaparral—blowed it off. He got so used to heaving away everything he lit that he spoiled three pipes in two days."

Mr. Cassidy laughed at the fiction and then became grave as he pictured Mr. Connors sitting on the rock and facing down a line of men, any one of whom was capable of his destruction if given the interval of a second.

When they arrived at the hut Mr. Cassidy observed that the prisoners had moved considerably. There was a cleanly swept trail four yards long where they had dragged themselves, and they sat in the end nearer the guns. Mr. Cassidy smiled and fired close to the Mexican's ear, who lost in one frightened jump a little of what he had so laboriously gained.

"Yu'll wear out yore pants," said Mr. Cassidy, and then added grimly, "an' my patience."

Mr. Travennes smiled and thought of the man who had so ably seconded Mr. Cassidy's efforts and who was probably shot by this time. The outfit of the Bar-20 was so well known throughout the land that he was aware the name of the other was Red Connors. An unreasoning streak of sarcasm swept over him and he could not resist the opportunity to get in a stab at his captor.

"Mebby yore pard has wore out somebody's patience, too," said Mr. Travennes, suggestively and with venom.

His captor wheeled toward him, his face white with passion, and Mr. Travennes shrank back and regretted the words.

"I ain't shootin' dogs this here trip," said Mr. Cassidy, trembling with scorn and anger, "so yu can pull yourself together. I'll give yu another chance, but yu wants to hope almighty hard that Red is O.K. If he ain't, I'll blow yu so many ways at once that if yu sprouts yu'll make a good acre of weeds. If he *is* all right yu'd better vamoose this range, for there won't be no hole for yu to crawl into next time. What friends yu have left will have to tote yu off an' plant yu," he finished with emphasis. He drove the horses outside, and, after severing the bonds on his prisoners, lined them up.

"Yu," he began, indicating all but Mr. Travennes, "yu amble right smart toward Canada," pointing to the north. "Keep a-going till yu gets far enough away so a Colt's won't find yu." Here he grinned with delight as he saw his Sharp's rifle in its sheath on his saddle and, drawing it forth, he put away his Colt's and glanced at the trio, who were already industriously plodding northward. "Hey!" he shouted, and when they sullenly turned to see what new idea he had found he gleefully waved his rifle at them and warned them farther: "This is a Sharp's an' it's good for half a mile, so don't stop none too soon."

Having sent them directly away from their friends so they could not have him "potted" on the way back, he mounted his broncho and indicated to Mr. Travennes that he, too, was to ride, watching that that person did not make use of the Winchester which Mr. Connors was foolish enough to carry around on his saddle. Winchesters were Mr. Cassidy's pet aversion and Mr. Connors' most prized possession, this difference of opinion having upon many occasions caused hasty words between them. Mr. Connors, being better with his Winchester than Mr. Cassidy was with his Sharp's, had frequently proved that his choice was the wiser, but Mr. Cassidy was loyal to the Sharp's and refused to be convinced. Now, however, the Winchester became pregnant with possibilities and, therefore, Mr. Travennes rode a few yards to the left and in advance, where the rifle was in plain sight, hanging as it did on the right of Mr. Connors' saddle, which Mr. Travennes graced so well.

The journey back to town was made in good time and when they came to the buildings Mr. Cassidy dismounted and bade his companion do likewise, there being too many corners that a fleeing rider could take advantage of. Mr. Travennes felt of his bumps and did so, wishing hard things about Mr. Cassidy.

CHAPTER XV

The Penalty

WHILE MR. TRAVENNES had been entertained in the manner narrated, Mr. Connors had passed the time by relating stale jokes to the uproarious laughter of his extremely bored audience, who had heard the aged efforts many times since they had first seen the light of day, and most of whom earnestly longed for a drink. The landlord, hearing the hilarity, had taken advantage of the opportunity offered to see a free show. Not being able to see what the occasion was for the mirth, he had pulled on his boots and made his way to the show with a flapjack in the skillet, which, in his haste, he had forgotten to put down. He felt sure that he would be entertained, and he was not disappointed. He rounded the corner and was enthusiastically welcomed by the hungry Mr. Connors, whose ubiquitous guns coaxed from the skillet its dyspeptic wad.

"Th' saints be praised!" ejaculated Mr. Connors as a matter of form, not having a very clear idea of just what saints were, but he knew what flapjacks were and greedily overcame the heroic resistance of the one provided by chance and his own guns. As he rolled his eyes in ecstatic content the very man Mr. Cassidy had warned him against suddenly arose and in great haste disappeared around the corner of the corral, from which point of vantage he vented his displeasure at the treatment he had received by wasting six shots at the mortified Mr. Connors.

"Steady!" sang out that gentleman as the lineup wavered. "He's a precedent to hell for yu fellers! Don't yu get ambitious, none whatever." Then he wondered how long it would take the fugitive to secure a rifle and return to release the others by drilling him at long range.

His thoughts were interrupted by the vision of a red head that climbed into view over a rise a short distance off and he grinned his delight as Mr. Cassidy loomed up, jaunty and triumphant. Mr. Cassidy was executing calisthenics with a Colt's in the rear of Mr. Travennes' neck and was leading the horses.

Mr. Connors waved the skillet and his friend grinned his congratulation at what the token signified.

"I see yu got some more," said Mr. Cassidy, as he went down the lineup from the rear and collected nineteen revolvers of various makes and conditions, this number being explained by the fact that all but one of the prisoners wore two. Then he added the five that had kicked against his ribs ever since he had left the hut, and carefully threaded the end of his lariat through the trigger guards.

"Looks like we stuck up a government supply mule, Red," he remarked, as he fastened the whole collection to his saddle. "Fourteen Colt's, six Steven's, three Remington's an' one puzzle," he added, examining the "puzzle." " 'Made in Germany,' it says, an' it shore looks like it. It's got little pins stickin' out of th' cylinder, like yu had to swat it with a hammer or a rock, or something. It's real dangerous—warranted to go off, but mostly by itself, I reckon. It looks more like a cactus than a six-shooter—gosh, it's an eight-shooter! I allus said them Dutchmen were bloody-minded cusses—think of being able to shoot yoreself eight times before th' blamed thing stops!" Then, looking at the lineup for the owner of the weapon, he laughed at the woeful countenances displayed. "Did they sidle in by companies or squads?" he asked.

"By twos, mostly. Then they parade-rested an' got discharged from duty. I had eleven, but one got homesick, or disgusted, or something, an' deserted. It was that cussed flapjack," confessed and explained Mr. Connors.

"What!" said Mr. Cassidy in a loud voice. "Got away! Well, we'll have to make our getaway plumb sudden or we'll never go."

At this instant the escaped man again began his bombardment from the corner of the corral and Mr. Cassidy paused, indignant at the fusillade which tore up the dust at his feet. He looked reproachfully at Mr. Connors and then circled out on the plain until he caught a glimpse of a fleeing cowpuncher, whose back rapidly grew smaller in the fast-increasing distance.

"That's yore friend, Red," said Mr. Cassidy as he returned from his reconnaissance. "He's that shorthorn yearling. Mebby he'll come back again," he added hopefully. "Anyhow, we've got to move. He'll collect reinforcements an' mebby they all won't shoot like him. Get up on yore Clarinda an' hold th' fort for me," he ordered, pushing the farther horse over to his friend. Mr. Connors proved that an agile man can mount a restless horse and not lose the drop, and backed off three hundred yards, deftly substituting his Winchester for the Colt's. Then Mr. Cassidy likewise mounted with his attention riveted elsewhere and backed off to the side of his companion.

The bombardment commenced again from the corral, but this time Mr. Connors' rifle slid around in his lap and exploded twice. The bellicose gentleman of the corral yelled in pain and surprise and vanished.

"Purty good for a Winchester," said Mr. Cassidy in doubtful congratulation.

"That why I got him," snapped Mr. Connors in brief reply, and then he laughed. "Is them th' vigilantes what never let a man get away?" he scornfully asked, backing down the street and patting his Winchester.

"Well, Red, they wasn't all there. They was only twelve all told," excused Mr. Cassidy. "An' then we was two," he explained, as he wished the collection of six-shooters was on Mr. Connors' horse so they wouldn't bark his shin.

"An' we still are," corrected Mr. Connors, as they wheeled and galloped for Alkaline.

As the sun sank low on the horizon Mr. Peters finished ordering provisions at the general store, the only one Alkaline boasted, and sauntered to the saloon where he had left his men. He found them a few dollars richer, as they had borrowed ten dollars from the bartender on their reputations as poker players and had used the money to stake Mr. McAllister in a game against the local poker champion.

"Has Hopalong an' Red showed up yet?" asked Mr. Peters, frowning at the delay already caused.

"Nope," replied Johnny Nelson, as he paused from tormenting Billy Williams.

At that minute the doorway was darkened and Mr. Cassidy and Mr. Connors entered and called for refreshments. Mr. Cassidy dropped a huge bundle of six-shooters on the floor, making caustic remarks regarding their utility.

"What's th' matter?" inquired Mr. Peters of Mr. Cassidy. "Yu looks mad an' anxious. An *where in hell did yu corral them guns*?"

Mr. Cassidy drank deep and then reported with much heat what had occurred at Cactus Springs and added that he wanted to go back and wipe out the town, said desire being luridly endorsed by Mr. Connors.

"Why, shore," said Mr. Peters, "we'll *all* go. Such doings must be stopped instanter." Then he turned to the assembled outfits and asked for a vote, which was unanimous for war.

Shortly afterward eighteen angry cowpunchers rode to the east, two red-haired gentlemen well in front and urging speed. It was 8 P.M. when they left Alkaline, and the cool of the night was so delightful that the feeling of ease which came upon them made them lax and they lost three hours in straying from the dim trail. At eight o'clock the next morning they came in sight of their destination and separated into two squads, Mr. Cassidy leading the northern division and Mr. Connors the one which circled to the south. The intention was to attack from two directions, thus taking the town from front and rear.

Cactus Springs lay gasping in the excessive heat and the vigilantes who had toed Mr. Connors' line the day before were lounging in the shade of the "Palace" saloon, telling what they would do if they ever faced the same man again. Half a dozen sympathizers offered gratuitous condolence and advice and all were positive that they knew where Mr. Cassidy and Mr. Connors would go when they died.

The rolling thunder of madly pounding hoofs disturbed their postmortem and they arose in a body to flee from half their number, who, guns in hands, charged down upon them through clouds of sickly white smoke. Travennes' Terrors were minus many weapons and they could not be expected to give a glorious account of themselves. Windows rattled and fell in and doors and walls gave off peculiar sounds as they grew full of holes. Above the riot rattled the incessant crack of Colt's and Winchester, emphasized at close intervals by the assertive roar of .60-caliber buffalo guns. Off to the south came another rumble of hoofs and Mr. Connors, leading the second squad, arrived to participate in the payment of the debt.

Smoke spurted from windows and other points of vantage and hung wavering in the heated air. The shattering of woodwork told of .60 calibers finding their rest, and the whines that grew and diminished in the air sang the course of .45's.

While the fight raged hottest Mr. Nelson sprang from his horse and ran to the "Palace," where he collected and piled a heap of tinderlike wood, and soon the building burst out in flames, which, spreading, swept the town from end to end.

Mr. Cassidy fired slowly and seemed to be waiting for something. Mr. Connors laid aside his hot Winchester and devoted his attention to his Colt's. A spurt of flame and smoke leaped from the window of a 'dobe hut and Mr. Connors sat down, firing as he went. A howl from the window informed him that he had made a hit, and Mr. Cassidy ran out and dragged him to the shelter of a nearby boulder and asked how much he was hurt.

"Not much—in th' calf," grunted Mr. Connors. "He was a bad shot—must have been the cuss that got away yesterday," speculated the injured man as he slowly arose to his feet. Mr. Cassidy dissented from force of habit and returned to his station.

Mr. Travennes, who was sleeping late that morning, coughed and fought for air in his sleep, awakened in smoke, rubbed his eyes to make sure and, scorning trousers and shirt, ran clad in his red woolen undergarments to the corral, where he mounted his scared horse and rode for the desert and safety.

Mr. Cassidy, swearing at the marksmanship of a man who fired at his head and perforated his sombrero, saw a crimson rider sweep down upon him, said rider being heralded by a blazing .41.

"Gosh!" ejaculated Mr. Cassidy, scarcely believing his eyes. "Oh, it's my friend Slim going to hell," he remarked to himself in audible and relieved explanation. Mr. Cassidy's Colt's cracked a protest and then he joined Mr. Peters and the others and with them fought his way out of the flame-swept town of Cactus Springs.

An hour later Mr. Connors glanced behind him at the smoke silhouetted on the horizon and pushed his way to where Mr. Cassidy rode in silence. Mr. Connors grinned at his friend of the red hair, who responded in the same manner.

"Did yu see Slim?" casually inquired Mr. Connors, looking off to the south.

Mr. Cassidy sat upright in his saddle and felt of his Colt's. "Yes," he replied, "I saw him."

Mr. Connors thereupon galloped on in silence.

CHAPTER XVI

Rustlers on the Range

THE AFFAIR at Cactus Springs had more effect on the life at the Bar-20 than was realized by the foreman. News travels rapidly, and certain men, whose attributes were not of the sweetest, heard of it and swore vengeance, for Slim Travennes had many friends, and the result of his passing began to show itself. Outlaws have as their strongest defense the fear which they inspire, and little time was lost in making reprisals, and these caused Buck Peters to ride into Buckskin one bright October morning and then out the other side of the town. Coming to himself with a start he looked around shamefacedly and retraced his course. He was very much troubled, for, as foreman of the Bar-20, he had many responsibilities, and when things ceased to go aright he was expected not only to find the cause of the evil, but also the remedy. That was what he was paid seventy dollars a month for and that was what he had been endeavoring to do. As yet, however, he had only accomplished what the meanest cook's assistant had done. He knew the cause of his present woes to be rustlers (cattle thieves), and that was all.

Riding down the wide, quiet street, he stopped and dismounted before the ever-open door of a ramshackle one-story frame building. Tossing the reins over the flattened ears of his vicious pinto he strode into the building and leaned easily against the bar, where he drummed with his fingers and sank into a reverie.

A shining bald pate, bowed over an open box, turned around and revealed a florid face, set with two small, twinkling blue eyes, as the proprietor, wiping his hands on his trousers, made his way to Buck's end of the bar.

"Mornin', Buck. How's things?"

The foreman, lost in his reverie, continued to stare out the door.

"Mornin'," repeated the man behind the bar. "How's things?"

"Oh!" ejaculated the foreman, smiling, "purty cussed."

"Anything new?"

"Th' C-80 lost another herd last night."

His companion swore and placed a bottle at the foreman's elbow, but the latter shook his head. "Not this mornin'—I'll try one of them vile cigars, however."

"Them cigars are th' very best that—" began the proprietor, executing the order.

"Oh, hell!" exclaimed Buck with weary disgust. "Yu don't have to palaver none: I shore knows all that by heart."

"Them cigars—" repeated the proprietor.

"Yas, yas; them cigars—I know all about them cigars. Yu gets them for twenty dollars a thousand an' hypnotizes us into payin' yu a hundred," replied the foreman, biting off the end of his weed. Then he stared moodily and frowned. "I wonder why it is?" he asked. "We punchers like good stuff an' we pays good prices with good money. What do we get? Why, cabbage leaves an' leather for our smokin' an' alcohol an' extract for our drink. Now, up in Kansas City we goes to a sumptious layout, pays less an' gets bang-up stuff. If yu smelled one of them K. C. cigars yu'd shore have to ask what it was, an' as for th' liquor, why, yu'd think St. Peter asked yu to have one with him. It's shore wrong somewhere."

"They have more trade in K. C.," suggested the proprietor.

"An' help, an' taxes, an' a license, an' rent, an' brass, cut glass, mahogany an' French mirrors," countered the foreman.

"They have more trade," reiterated the man with the cigars.

"Forty men spend thirty dollars apiece with yu every month."

The proprietor busied himself under the bar. "Yu'll feel better tomorrow. Anyway, what do yu care, yu won't lose yore job," he said, emerging.

Buck looked at him and frowned, holding back the words which formed in anger. What was the use, he thought, when every man judged the world in his own way.

"Have yu seen any of th' boys?" he asked, smiling again.

"Nary a boy. Who do yu reckon's doin' all this rustlin'?"

"I'm reckonin', not shoutin'," responded the foreman.

The proprietor looked out the window and grinned: "Here comes one of yourn now."

The newcomer stopped his horse in a cloud of dust, playfully kicked the animal in the ribs and entered, dusting the alkali from him with a huge sombrero. Then he straightened up and sniffed: "What's burnin'?" he asked, simulating alarm. Then he noticed the cigar between the teeth of his foreman and grinned: "Gee, but yore a brave man, Buck."

"Hullo, Hopalong," said the foreman. "Want a smoke?" waving his hand toward the box on the bar.

Mr. Hopalong Cassidy side-stepped and began to roll a cigarette: "Shore, but I'll burn my own—I know what it is."

"What was yu doin' to my cayuse afore yu come in?" asked Buck.

"Nothin'," replied the newcomer. "That was mine what I kicked in th' corrugations."

"How is it yore ridin' th' calico?" asked the foreman. "I thought yu was dead stuck on that piebald."

"That piebald's a goat; he's been livin' off my pants lately," responded Hopalong. "Every time I looks th' other way he ambles over and takes a bite at me. Yu just wait 'til this rustler business is roped, an' branded, an' yu'll see me eddicate that blessed scrapheap into eatin' grass again. He swiped Billy's shirt th' other day—took it right off th' corral wall, where Billy'd left it to dry." Then, seeing Buck raise his eyebrows, he explained: "Shore, he washed it again. That makes three times since last fall."

The proprietor laughed and pushed out the everready bottle, but Hopalong shoved it aside and told the reason: "Ever since I was up to K. C. I've been spoiled. I'm drinkin' water an' slush."

"For Gawd's sake, has any more of yu fellers been up to K. C.?" queried the proprietor in alarm.

"Shore; Red an' Billy was up there, too," responded Hopalong. "Red's got a few remarks to shout to yu about yore painkiller. Yu better send for some decent stuff afore he comes to town," he warned.

Buck swung away from the bar and looked at his dead cigar. Then he turned to Hopalong. "What did you find?" he asked.

"Same old story: nice wide trail up to th' Staked Plain—then nothin'."

"It shore beats me," soliloquized the foreman. "It shore beats me."

"Think it was Tamale José's old gang?" asked Hopalong.

"If it was they took th' wrong trail home—that ain't th' way to Mexico."

Hopalong tossed aside his half-smoked cigarette. "Well, come on home; what's th' use stewin' over it? It'll come out all O.K. in th' wash." Then he laughed: "There won't be no piebald waitin' for it."

Evading Buck's playful blow he led the way to the door, and soon they were a cloud of dust on the plain. The proprietor, despairing of customers under the circumstances, absentmindedly wiped off the bar, and sought his chair for a nap, grumbling about the way his trade had fallen off, for there were few customers, and those who did call were heavy with loss of sleep, and with anxiety, and only paused long enough to toss off their drink. On the ranges there were occurrences which tried men's souls.

For several weeks cattle had been disappearing from the ranges and the losses had long since passed the magnitude of those suffered when Tamale José

and his men had crossed the Rio Grande and repeatedly levied heavy toll on the sleek herds of the
Pecos Valley. Tamale José had raided once too often, and prosperity and plenty had followed on the
ranches and the losses had been forgotten until the
fall roundups clearly showed that rustlers were again
at work.

Despite the ingenuity of the ranch owners and the
unceasing vigilance and night rides of the cowpunchers, the losses steadily increased until there
was promised a shortage which would permit no
drive to the western terminals of the railroad that
year. For two weeks the banks of the Rio Grande
had been patrolled and sharp-eyed men searched
daily for trails leading southward, for it was not
strange to think that the old raiders were again at
work, notwithstanding the fact that they had paid
dearly for their former depredations. The patrols
failed to discover anything out of the ordinary and
the searchers found no trails. Then it was that the
owners and foremen of the four central ranches met
in Cowan's saloon and sat closeted together for all
of one hot afternoon.

The conference resulted in riders being dispatched
from all the ranches represented, and one of the
couriers, Mr. Red Connors, rode north, his destination being faraway Montana. All the ranches within
a radius of a hundred miles received letters and
blanks and one week later the Pecos Valley Cattle-
Thief Elimination Association was organized and
working, with Buck as Chief Ranger.

One of the outcomes of Buck's appointment was a
sudden and marked immigration into the affected
territory. Mr. Connors returned from Montana with
Mr. Frenchy McAllister, the foreman of the Tin-Cup,

who was accompanied by six of his best and most trusted men. Mr. McAllister and party were followed by Mr. You-bet Somes, foreman of the Two-X-Two of Arizona, and five of his punchers, and later on the same day Mr. Pie Willis, accompanied by Mr. Billy Jordan and his two brothers, arrived from the Panhandle. The O-Bar-O, situated close to the town of Muddy Wells, increased its payroll by the addition of nine men, each of whom bore the written recommendation of the foreman of the Bar-20. The C-80, Double Arrow and the Three Triangle also received heavy reinforcements, and even Carter, owner of the Barred Horseshoe, far removed from the zone of the depredations, increased his outfits by half their regular strength. Buck believed that if a thing was worth doing at all that it was worth doing very well, and his acquaintances were numerous and loyal. The collection of individuals that responded to the call were noteworthy examples of "gunplay" and their aggregate value was at par with twice their numbers in cavalry.

Each ranch had one large ranch house and numerous line-houses scattered along the boundaries. These latter, while intended as camps for the outriders, had been erected in the days, none too remote, when Apaches, Arrapahoes, Sioux and even Cheyennes raided southward, and they had been constructed with the idea of defense paramount. Upon more than one occasion a solitary line-rider had retreated within their adobe walls and had successfully resisted all the cunning and ferocity of a score of paint-bedaubed warriors and, when his outfit had rescued him, emerged none the worse for his ordeal.

On the Bar-20, Buck placed these houses in condition to withstand seige. Twin barrels of water stood

in opposite corners, provisions were stored on the
hanging shelves and the bunks once again reveled
in untidiness. Spare rifles, in pattern ranging from
long-range Sharp's and buffalo guns to repeating car-
bines, leaned against the walls, and unbroken boxes
of cartridges were piled above the bunks. Instead of
the lonesome outrider, he placed four men to each
house, two of whom were to remain at home and
hold the house while their companions rode side by
side on their multi-mile beat. There were six of these
houses and, instead of returning each night to the
same line-house, the outriders kept on and made the
circuit, thus keeping everyone well informed and
breaking the monotony. These measures were expected to cause the rustling operations to cease at
once, but the effect was to shift the losses to the
Double Arrow, the line-houses of which boasted only
one puncher each. Unreasonable economy usually
defeats its object.

The Double Arrow was restricted on the north by
the Staked Plain, which in itself was considered a
superb defense. The White Sand Hills formed its
eastern boundary and were thought to be second
only to the northern protection. The only reason that
could be given for the hitherto comparative immu-
nity from the attacks of the rustlers was that its cattle clung to the southern confines where there were
numerous springs, thus making imperative the crossing of its territory to gain the herds.

It was in line-house No. 3, most remote of all, that
Johnny Redmond fought his last fight and was found
facedown in the half-ruined house with a hole in the
back of his head, which proved that one man was
incapable of watching all the loopholes in four walls
at once. There must have been some casualities on

the other side, for Johnny was reputed to be very painstaking in his "gunplay," and the empty shells which lay scattered on the floor did not stand for as many ciphers, of that his foreman was positive. He was buried the day he was found, and the news of his death ran quickly from ranch to ranch and made more than one careless puncher arise and pace the floor in anger. More men came to the Double Arrow and its sentries were doubled. The depredations continued, however, and one night a week later Frank Swift reeled into the ranch house and fell exhausted across the supper table. Rolling hoofbeats echoed flatly and died away on the plain, but the men who pursued them returned empty-handed. The wounds of the unfortunate were roughly dressed and in his delirium he recounted the fight. His companion was found literally shot to pieces twenty paces from the door. One wall was found blown in, and this episode, when coupled with the use of dynamite, was more than could be tolerated.

When Buck had been informed of this he called to him Hopalong Cassidy, Red Connors and Frenchy McAllister, and the next day the three men rode north and the contingents of the ranches represented in the Association were divided into two squads, one of which was to remain at home and guard the ranches; the other, to sleep fully dressed and armed and never to stray far from their ranch houses and horses. These latter would be called upon to ride swiftly and far when the word came.

CHAPTER XVII

Mr. Trendley Assumes Added Importance

THAT THE rustlers were working under a well-organized system was evident. That they were directed by a master of the game was ceaselessly beaten into the consciousness of the Association by the diversity, dash and success of their raids. No one, save the three men whom they had destroyed, had ever seen them. But, like Tamale José, they had raided once too often.

Mr. Trendley, more familiarly known to men as "Slippery," was the possessor of a biased conscience, if any at all. Tall, gaunt and weather-beaten and with coal-black eyes set deep beneath hairless eyebrows, he was sinister and forbidding. Into his forty-five years of existence he had crowded a century of experience, and unsavory rumors about him existed in all parts of the great West. From Canada to Mexico and from Sacramento to Westport his name stood for brigandage. His operations had been conducted with such consummate cleverness that in all the ac-

cusations there was lacking proof. Only once had he
erred, and then in the spirit of pure deviltry and in
the days of youthful folly, and his mistake was a
written note. He was even thought by some to have
been concerned in the Mountain Meadow Massacre;
others thought him to have been the leader of the
band of outlaws that had plundered along the Santa
Fé Trail in the late '60's. In Montana and Wyoming
he was held responsible for the outrages of the band
that had descended from the Holes-in-the-Wall territory and for over a hundred miles carried murder
and theft that shamed as being weak the most assid-
uous efforts of zealous Cheyennes. It was in this last
raid that he had made the mistake and it was in this
raid that Frenchy McAllister had lost his wife.

When Frenchy had first been approached by Buck
as to his going in search of the rustlers he had asked
to go alone. This had been denied by the foreman
of the Bar-20 because the men whom he had selected to accompany the scout were of such caliber
that their presence could not possibly form a hin-
drance. Besides being his most trusted friends they
were regarded by him as being the two best expo-
nents of "gunplay" that the West afforded. Each was
a specialist: Hopalong, expert beyond belief with his
Colt's six-shooters, was only approached by Red,
whose Winchester was renowned for its accuracy.
The three made a perfect combination, as the rash-
ness of the two younger men would be under the
controlling influence of a man who could retain his
coolness of mind under all circumstances.

When Buck and Frenchy looked into each other's
eyes there sprang into the mind of each the same
name—Slippery Trendley. Both had spent the greater
part of a year in fruitless search for that person, the

foreman of the Tin-Cup in vengeance for the murder of his wife, the blasting of his prospects and the loss of his herds; Buck, out of sympathy for his friend and also because they had been partners in the Double Y. Now that the years had passed and the long-sought-for opportunity was believed to be at hand, there was promised either a cessation of the outrages or that Buck would never again see his friends.

When the three mounted and came to him for final instructions Buck forced himself to be almost repellent in order to be capable of coherent speech. Hopalong glanced sharply at him and then understood, Red was all attention and eagerness and remarked nothing but the words.

"Have yu ever heard of Slippery Trendley?" harshly inquired the foreman.

They nodded, and on the faces of the younger men a glint of hatred showed itself, but Frenchy wore his poker countenance.

Buck continued: "Th' reason I asked yu was because I don't want yu to think yore goin' on no picnic. I ain't shore it's him, but I've had some hopeful information. Besides, he is th' only man I knows of who's capable of th' plays that have been made. It's hardly necessary for me to tell yu to sleep with one eye open and never to get away from yore guns. Now I'm goin' to tell yu th' hardest part: yu are goin' to search th' Staked Plain from one end to th' other, an' that's what no white man's ever done to my knowledge.

"Now, listen to this an' don't forget it: Twenty miles north from Last Stand Rock is a spring; ten miles south of that bend in Hell Arroyo is another. If yu gets lost within two days from th' time yu enters th' Plain, put yore left hand on a cactus sometime between sunup an' noon, move around until yu are over its shadow an' then ride straight ahead—that's south. If you goes loco beyond Last Stand Rock, follow th' shadows made before noon—that's th' quickest way to th' Pecos. Yu all knows what to do in a sandstorm, so I won't bore yu with that. Repeat all I've told yu," he ordered and they complied.

"I'm tellin' yu this," continued the foreman, indicating the two auxiliaries, "because yu might get separated from Frenchy. Now I suggests that yu look around near th' Devil's Rocks: I've heard that there are several water holes among them, an' besides, they might be turned into fair corrals. Mind yu, I know what I've said sounds damned idiotic for anybody that has had as much experience with th' Staked Plain as I have, but I've had every other place searched for miles around. Th' men of all th' ranches have been scoutin' an' th' Plain is th' only place left. Them rustlers has got to be found if we have to dig to hell for them. They've taken th' pot so many times that they reckons they owns it, an' we've got to at least make a bluff at drawin' cards. Mebby they're at th' bottom of th' Pecos," here he smiled faintly, "but wherever they are, we've *got* to find them. I want to holler 'Keno.'

"If yu finds where they hangs out come away instanter," here his face hardened and his eyes narrowed, "for it'll take more than yu three to deal with them th' way I'm a-hankerin' for. Come right back to th' Double Arrow, send me word by one of their punchers an' get all the rest yu can afore I gets there. It'll take me a day to get th' men together an' to reach yu. I'm goin' to use smoke signals to call th' other ranches, so there won't be no time lost. Carry all th' water yu can pack when yu leaves th' Double

Arrow an' don't depend none on cactus juice. Yu better take a packhorse to carry it, an' yore grub— yu can shoot it if yu have to hit th' trail real hard."

The three riders felt of their accouterments, said "So long," and cantered off for the packhorse and extra ammunition. Then they rode toward the Double Arrow, stopping at Cowan's long enough to spend some money, and reached the Double Arrow at nightfall. Early the next morning they passed the last line-house and, with the profane well-wishes of its occupants ringing in their ears, passed onto one of Nature's worst blunders—the Staked Plain.

CHAPTER XVIII

The Search Begins

As THE sun arose it revealed three punchers riding away from civilization. On all sides, stretching to the evil-appearing horizon, lay vast blotches of dirty-white and faded yellow alkali and sand. Occasionally a dwarfed mesquite raised its prickly leaves and rustled mournfully. With the exception of the riders and an occasional Gila monster, no life was discernible. Cacti of all shapes and sizes reared aloft their forbidding spines or spread out along the sand. All was dead, ghastly; all was oppressive, startlingly repellent in its sinister promise; all was the vastness of desolation.

Hopalong knew this portion of the desert for ten miles inward—he had rescued straying cattle along its southern rim—but once beyond that limit they would have to trust to chance and their own abilities. There were water holes on this skillet, but nine out of ten were death traps, reeking with mineral poisons, colored and alkaline. The two mentioned by

Buck could not be depended on, for they came and went, and more than one luckless wanderer had depended on them to allay his thirst, and had died for his trust. So the scouts rode on in silence, noting the half-buried skeletons of cattle which were strewn plentifully on all sides. Nearly three percent of the cattle belonging to the Double Arrow yearly found death on this tableland, and the herds of that ranch numbered many thousand heads. It was this which made the Double Arrow the poorest of the ranches, and it was this which allowed insufficient sentries in its line-houses. The skeletons were not all of cattle, for at rare intervals lay the sand-worn frames of men.

On the morning of the second day the oppression increased with the wind and Red heaved a sigh of restlessness. The sand began to skip across the plain in grains at first and hardly noticeable. Hopalong turned in his saddle and regarded the desert with apprehension. As he looked he saw that where grains had shifted handfuls were now moving. His mount evinced signs of uneasiness and was hard to control. A gust of wind, stronger than the others, pricked his face and grains of sand rolled down his neck. The leather of his saddle emitted strange noises as if a fairy tattoo was being beaten upon it and he raised his hand and pointed off toward the east. The others looked and saw what appeared to be a fog rise out of the desert and intervene between them and the sun. As far as eye could reach small whirlwinds formed and broke and one swept down and covered them with stinging sand. The day became darkened and their horses whinnied in terror and the clumps of mesquite twisted and turned to the gusts.

Each man knew what was to come upon them and they dismounted, hobbled their horses and threw them bodily to the earth, wrapping a blanket around the head of each. A rustling as of paper rubbing together became noticeable and they threw themselves flat upon the earth, their heads wrapped in their coats and buried in the necks of their mounts. For an hour they endured the tortures of hell and then, when the storm had passed, raised their heads and cursed Creation. Their bodies burned as though they had been shot with fine needles and their clothes were meshes where once was tough cloth. Even their shoes were perforated and the throat of each ached with thirst.

Hopalong fumbled at the canteen resting on his hip and gargled his mouth and throat, washing down the sand which wouldn't come up. His friends did likewise and then looked around. After some time had elapsed the loss of their packhorse was noticed and they swore again. Hopalong took the lead in getting his horse ready for service and then rode around in a circle half a mile in diameter, but returned empty-handed. The horse was gone and with it went their main supply of food and drink.

Frenchy scowled at the shadow of a cactus and slowly rode toward the northeast, followed closely by his friends. His hand reached for his depleted canteen, but refrained—water was to be saved until the last minute.

"I'm goin' to build a shack out here an' live in it, *I* am!" exploded Hopalong in withering irony as he dug the sand out of his ears and also from his six-shooter. "I just nachurally dotes on this, *I* do!"

The others were too miserable to even grunt and he neatly severed the head of a Gila monster from its scaly body as it opened its venomous jaws in rage at this invasion of its territory. "Lovely place!" he sneered.

"Yu better save them cartridges, Hoppy," interposed Red as his companion fired again, feeling that he must say something.

"An' what for?" blazed his friend. "To plug sandstorms? Anybody what we find on this godforsaken layout won't have to be shot—they will commit suicide an' think it's fun! Tell yu what, if them rustlers hangs out on this sand range they're better men than I reckons they are. Anybody what hides up here shore earns all he steals." Hopalong grumbled from force of habit and because no one else would. His companions understood this and paid no attention to him, which increased his disgust.

"What are we up here for?" he asked, belligerently. "Why, because them Double Arrow idiots can't even watch a desert! We have to do their work for them an' they hangs around home an' gets slaughtered! Yes, sir!" he shouted, "they can't even take care of themselves when they're in line-houses what are forts. Why, that time we cleaned out them an' th' C-80 over at Buckskin they couldn't help runnin' into singin' lead!"

"Yas," drawled Red, whose recollection of that fight was vivid. "Yas, an' why?" he asked, and then replied to his own question. "Because yu sat up in a barn behind them, Buck played his gun on th' side window, Pete an' Skinny lay behind a rock to one side of Buck, me an' Lanky was across th' street in front of them, an' Billy an' Johnny was in th' arroyo on th' other side. Cowan laid on his stummick on th' roof of his place with a .60-caliber buffalo gun, an' th' whole blamed town was agin them. There wasn't five seconds passed that lead wasn't rippin' through th' walls of their shack. Th' Houston House wasn't made for no fort, an' besides, they wasn't like th' gang that's punchin' now. That's why."

Hopalong became cheerful again, for here was a chance to differ from his friend. The two loved each other the better the more they squabbled.

"Yas!" responded Hopalong with sarcasm. "Yas!" he reiterated, drawling it out. "Yu was in front of them, an' with what? Why, an' old, white-haired, interfering Winchester, that's what! Me an' my Sharp's——"

"Yu and yore Sharp's!" exploded Red, whose dislike for that rifle was very pronounced. "Yu and yore Sharp's——"

"Me an' my Sharp's, as I was palaverin' before bein' interrupted," continued Hopalong, "did more damage in five min——"

"Played hell!" snapped Red with heat. "All yu an yore Sharp's could do was to cut yore initials in th' back door of their shack an'——"

"Did more damage in five minutes," continued Hopalong, "than all th' blasted Winchesters in th' whole damned town. Why——"

"An' then they was cut blamed poor. Every time that cannon of yourn exploded I shore thought th'——"

"Why, Cowan an' his buffalo did more damage (Cowan was reputed to be a very poor shot) than yu an'——"

"I thought th' artillery was comin' into th' disturbance. I could see yore red head——"

"MY red head!" exclaimed Hopalong, sizing up the crimson warlock of his companion. "MY red head!" he repeated, and then turned to Frenchy: "Hey, Frenchy, whose got th' reddest hair, me or Red?"

Frenchy slowly turned in his saddle and gravely scrutinized them. Being strictly impartial and truthful, he gave up the effort of differentiating and smiled. "Why, if th' tops of yore heads were poked through two holes in a board an' I didn't know which was which, I'd shore make a mistake if I tried to name 'em."

Thereupon the discussion was directed at the judge, and the forenoon passed very pleasantly, Frenchy even smiling in his misery.

CHAPTER XIX

Hopalong's Decision

SHORTLY AFTER noon, Hopalong, who had ridden with his head bowed low in meditation, looked up and slapped his thigh. Then he looked at Red and grinned.

"Look ahere, Red," he began, "there ain't no rustlers with their headquarters on this godforsaken sand heap, an' there never was. They have to have water an' lots of it, too, an' th' nearest of any account is th' Pecos, or some of them streams over in th' Panhandle. Th' Panhandle is th' best place. There are lots of streams an' lakes over there an' they're right in a good grass country. Why, an army could hide over there an' never be found unless it was hunted for blamed good. Then, again, it's close to th' railroad. Up north aways is th' south branch of th' Santa Fé Trail an' it's far enough away not to bother anybody in th' middle Panhandle. Then there's Fort Worth purty near, an' other trails. Didn't Buck say he had all th' rest of th' country searched? He meant

th' Pecos Valley an' th' Davis Mountains country. All
th' rustlers would have to do if they were in th' Panhandle would be to cross th' Canadian an' th' Cimar-
ron an' hit th' trail for th' railroad. Good fords, good
grass an' water all th' way, cattle fat when they are
delivered an' plenty of room. Th' more I thinks about
it th' more I cottons to the Panhandle."

"Well, it shore does sound good," replied Red, reflectively. "Do yu mean th' Cunningham Lake region
or farther north?"

"Just th' other side of this blasted desert: anywhere where there's water," responded Hopalong,
enthusiastically. "I've been doin' some hot reckonin'
for th' last two hours an' this is th' way it looks to
me: they drives th' cows up on this skillet for a ways,
then turns east an' hits th' trail for home an' water.
They can get around th' cañon near Thatcher's Lake
by a swing of th' north. I tell yu that's th' only way
out'n this. Who could tell where they turned with th'
wind raisin' th' devil with th' trail? Didn't we follow
a trail for a ways, an' then what? Why, there wasn't
none to follow. We can ride north 'till we walk behind ourselves an' never get a peek at them. I am in
favor of headin' for th' Sulphur Spring Creek district.
We can spend a couple of weeks, if we has to, an'
prospect that whole region without havin' to cut our
water down to a smell an' a taste an' live on jerked
beef. If we investigates that country we'll find something else than sandstorms, poisoned water holes an'
blisters."

"Ain't th' Panhandle full of nesters (farmers)?"
inquired Red, doubtfully.

"Along th' Canadian an' th' edges, yas; in th' middle, no," explained Hopalong. "They hang close together on account of th' Indians, an' they like th'

trails purty well because of there allus bein' somebody passin'."

"Buck ought to send some of th' Panhandle boys
up there," suggested Red. "There's Pie Willis an' th'
Jordans—they knows th' Panhandle like yu knows
poker."

Frenchy had paid no apparent attention to the
conversation up to this point, but now he declared
himself. "Yu heard what Buck said, didn't yu?" he
asked. "We were told to search th' Staked Plains from
one end to th' other an' I'm goin' to do it if I can
hold out long enough. I ain't goin' to palaver with
yu because what yu say can't be denied as far as
wisdom is concerned. Yu may have hit it plumb center, but I knows what I was ordered to do, an' yu
can't get me to go over there if you shouts all night.
When Buck says anything, she goes. He wants to
know where th' cards are stacked an' why he can't
holler 'Keno,' an' I'm goin' to find out if I can. Yu
can go to Patagonia if yu wants to, but yu go alone
as far as I am concerned."

"Well, it's better if yu don't go with us," replied
Hopalong, taking it for granted that Red would accompany him. "Yu can prospect this end of th' game
an' we'll be takin' care of th' other. It's two chances
now where we only had one afore."

"Yu go east an' I'll hunt around as ordered," responded Frenchy.

"East nothin'," replied Hopalong. "Yu don't get me
to wallow in hot alkali an' lose time ridin' in ankle-
deep sand when I can hit th' south trail, skirt th'
White Sand Hills an' be in God's country again. I ain't
goin' to wrastle with no cañon this here trip, none
whatever. I'm goin' to travel in style, get to Big
Spring by ridin' two miles to where I could only make

one on this stove. Then I'll head north along Sulphur Spring Creek an' have water an' grass all th' way, barrin' a few stretches. While you are bein' fricassed I'll be streakin' through cottonwood groves an' ridin' in th' creek."

"Yu'll have to go alone, then," said Red, resolutely. "Frenchy ain't a-goin' to die of lonesomeness on this desert if I knows what I'm about, an' I reckon I do, some. Me an' him'll follow out what Buck said, hunt around for a while an' then Frenchy can go back to th' ranch to tell Buck what's up an' I'll take th' trail yu are a-scared of an' meet yu at th' east end of Cunningham Lake three days from now."

"Yu better come with me," coaxed Hopalong, not liking what his friend had said about being afraid of the trail past the cañon and wishing to have someone with whom to talk on his trip. "I'm goin' to have a nice long swim tomorrow night," he added, trying bribery.

"An' I'm goin' to try to keep from hittin' my blisters," responded Red. "I don't want to go swimmin' in no creek full of moccasins—I'd rather sleep with rattlers or copperheads. Every time I sees a cottonmouth I feels like I had just sit down on one."

"I'll flip a coin to see whether yu comes or not," proposed Hopalong.

"If yu wants to gamble so bad I'll flip yu to see who draws our pay next month, but not for what yu said," responded Red, choking down the desire to try his luck.

Hopalong grinned and turned toward the south. "If I sees Buck afore yu do, I'll tell him yu an' Frenchy are growin' watermelons up near Last Stand Rock an' are waitin' for rain. Well, so long," he said.

"Yu tell Buck we're obeyin' orders!" shouted Red, sorry that he was not going with his bunkie.

Frenchy and Red rode on in silence, the latter feeling strangely lonesome, for he and the departed man had seldom been separated when journeys like this were to be taken. And when in search of pleasure they were nearly always together. Frenchy, while being very friendly with Hopalong, a friendship that would have placed them side by side against any odds, was not accustomed to his company and did not notice his absence.

Red looked off toward the south for the tenth time and for the tenth time thought that his friend might return. "He's a son-of-a-gun," he soliloquized.

His companion looked up: "He shore is, an' he's right about this rustler business, too. But we'll look around for a day or so an' then yu raise dust for th' lake. I'll go back to th' ranch an' get things primed, so there'll be no time lost when we get th' word."

"I'm sorry I went an' said what I did about me takin' th' trail he was a-scared of," confessed Red, after a pause. "Why, he ain't a-scared of nothin'."

"He got back at yu about them watermelons, so what's th' difference?" asked Frenchy. "He don't owe yu nothin'."

An hour later they searched the Devil's Rocks, but found no rustlers. Filling their canteens at a tiny spring and allowing their mounts to drink the remainder of the water, they turned toward Hell Arroyo, which they reached at nightfall. Here, also, their search availed them nothing and they paused in indecision. Then Frenchy turned toward his companion and advised him to ride toward the lake in the night when it was comparatively cool.

Red considered and then decided that the advice

was good. He rolled a cigarette, wheeled and faced the east and spurred forward: "So long," he called.

"So long," replied Frenchy, who turned toward the south and departed for the ranch.

The foreman of the Bar-20 was cleaning his rifle when he heard the hoofbeats of a galloping horse and he ran around the corner of the house to meet the newcomer, whom he thought to be a courier from the Double Arrow. Frenchy dismounted and explained why he returned alone.

Buck listened to the report and then, noting the fire which gleamed in his friend's eyes, nodded his approval to the course. "I reckon it's Trendley, Frenchy—I've heard a few things since yu left. An' yu can bet that if Hopalong an' Red have gone for him he'll be found. I expect action any time now, so we'll light th' signal fire." Then he hesitated; "Yu light it—yu've been waiting a long time for this."

The balls of smoke which rolled upward were replied to by other balls at different points on the plain, and the Bar-20 prepared to feed the numbers of hungry punchers who would arrive within the next twenty-four hours.

Two hours had not passed when eleven men rode up from the Three Triangle, followed eight hours later by ten from the O-Bar-O. The outfits of the Star Circle and the Barred Horseshoe, eighteen in all, came next and had scarcely dismounted when those of the C-80 and the Double Arrow, fretting at the delay, rode up. With the sixteen from the Bar-20 the force numbered seventy-five resolute and pugnacious cowpunchers, all aching to wipe out the indignities suffered.

CHAPTER XX

A Problem Solved

HOPALONG WORRIED his way out of the desert on a straight line, thus cutting in half the distance he had traveled when going into it. He camped that night on the sand and early the next morning took up his journey. It was noon when he began to notice familiar sights, and an hour later he passed within a mile of line-house No. 3, Double Arrow. Half an hour later he espied a cowpuncher riding like mad. Thinking that an investigation would not be out of place, he rode after the rider and overtook him, when that person paused and retraced his course.

"Hullo, Hopalong!" shouted the puncher, and he came near enough to recognize his pursuer. "Thought yu was farmin' up on th' Staked Plain?"

"Hullo, Pie," replied Hopalong, recognizing Pie Willis. "What was yu chasin' so hard?"

"Coyote—damn 'em, but can't they go some? They're gettin' so thick we'll shore have to try strichnine an' thin 'em out."

"I thought anybody that had been raised in th' Panhandle would know better'n to chase greased lightnin'," rebuked Hopalong. "Yu has got about as much show catchin' one of them as a tenderfoot has of bustin' an outlawed cayuse."

"Shore; I know it," responded Pie, grinning. "But it's fun seein' them hunt th' horizon. What are yu doin' down here an' where are yore pardners?"

Thereupon Hopalong enlightened his inquisitive companion as to what had occurred and as to his reasons for riding south. Pie immediately became enthusiastic and announced his intention of accompanying Hopalong on his quest, which intention struck that gentleman as highly proper and wise. Then Pie hastily turned and played at chasing coyotes in the direction of the line-house, where he announced that his absence would be accounted for by the fact that he and Hopalong were going on a journey of investigation into the Panhandle. Billy Jordan, who shared with Pie the accommodations of the house, objected and showed, very clearly, why he was eminently better qualified to take up the proposed labors than his companion. The suggestions were fast getting tangled up with the remarks, when Pie, grabbing a chunk of jerked beef, leaped into his saddle and absolutely refused to heed the calls of his former companion and return. He rode to where Hopalong was awaiting him as if he were afraid he wasn't going to live long enough to get there. Confiding to his companion that Billy was a "locoed sage hen," he led the way along the base of the White Sand Hills and asked many questions. Then they turned toward the east and galloped hard.

It had been Hopalong's intention to carry out what he had told Red and to go to Big Spring first and thence north along Sulphur Spring Creek, but to this his guide strongly dissented. There was a shortcut, or several of them for that matter, was Pie's contention, and any one of them would save a day's hard riding. Hopalong made no objection to allowing his companion to lead the way over any trail he saw fit, for he knew that Pie had been born and brought up in the Panhandle, the Cunningham Lake district having been his backyard, as it were. So they followed the shortcut having the most water and grass, and pounded out a lively tattoo as they raced over the stretches of sand which seemed to slide beneath them.

"What do yu know about this here business?" inquired Pie, as they raced past a chaparral and onto the edge of a grassy plain.

"Nothin' more'n yu do, only Buck said he thought Slippery Trendley is at th' bottom of it."

"What!" ejaculated Pie in surprise. "Him!"

"Yore on. An' between yu an' me an' th' Devil, I wouldn't be a heap surprised if Deacon Rankin is with him, neither."

Pie whistled: "Are him an' th' Deacon pals?"

"Shore," replied Hopalong, buttoning up his vest and rolling a cigarette. "Didn't they allus hang out together! One watched that th' other didn't get plugged from behind. It was a sort of yu-scratch-my-back-an'-I'll-scratch-yourn arrangement."

"Well, if they still hangs out together, I know where to hunt for our cows," responded Pie. "Th' Deacon used to range along th' headwaters of th' Colorado—it ain't far from Cunningham Lake. Thunderation!" he shouted, "I knows th' very ground they're on—I can take yu to th' very shack!" Then to himself he muttered: "An' that doodlebug Billy

Jordan thinkin' he knowed more about th' Panhandle than me!"

Hopalong showed his elation in an appropriate manner and his companion drank deeply from the proffered flask. Thereupon they treated their mounts to liberal doses of strap-oil and covered the ground with great speed.

They camped early, for Hopalong was almost worn out from the exertions of the past few days and the loss of sleep he had sustained. Pie, too excited to sleep and having had unbroken rest for a long period, volunteered to keep guard, and his companion eagerly consented.

Early the next morning they broke camp and the evening of the same day found them fording Sulphur Spring Creek, and their quarry lay only an hour beyond, according to Pie. Then they forded one of the streams which form the headwaters of the Colorado, and two hours later they dismounted in a cottonwood grove. Picketing their horses they carefully made their way through the timber, which was heavily grown with brush, and, after half an hour's maneuvering, came within sight of the further edge. Dropping down on all fours, they crawled to the last line of brush and looked out over an extensive bottoms. At their feet lay a small river, and in a clearing on the farther side was a rough camp, consisting of about a dozen lean-to shacks and log cabins in the main collection, and a few scattered cabins along the edge. A huge fire was blazing before the main collection of huts, and to the rear of these was an indistinct black mass, which they knew to be the corral.

At a rude table before the fire more than a score of men were eating supper and others could be heard moving about and talking at different points in the background. While the two scouts were learning the lay of the land, they saw Mr. Trendley and Deacon Rankin walk out of the cabin most distant from the fire, and the latter limped. Then they saw two men lying on rude cots, and they wore bandages. Evidently Johnny Redmond had scored in his fight.

The odor of burning cowhide came from the corral, accompanied by the squeals of cattle, and informed them that brands were being blotted out. Hopalong longed to charge down and do some blotting out of another kind, but a heavy hand was placed on his shoulder and he silently wormed his way after Pie as that person led the way back to the horses. Mounting, they picked their way out of the grove and rode over the plain at a walk. When far enough away to insure that the noise made by their horses would not reach the ears of those in the camp they cantered toward the ford they had taken on the way up.

After emerging from the waters of the last forded stream, Pie raised his hand and pointed off toward the northwest, telling his companion to take that course to reach Cunningham Lake. He himself would ride south, taking, for the saving of time, a yet shorter trail to the Double Arrow, from where he would ride to Buck. He and the others would meet Hopalong and Red at the split rock they had noticed on their way up.

Hopalong shook hands with his guide and watched him disappear into the night. He imagined he could still catch whiffs of burning cowhide and again the picture of the camp came to his mind. Glancing again at the point where Pie had disappeared, he stuffed his sombrero under a strap on his saddle and slowly rode toward the lake. A coyote slunk past him on a time-destroying lope and an owl hooted at the foolishness of men. He camped at the base of a cottonwood and at daylight took up his journey after a scanty breakfast from his saddlebags.

Shortly before noon he came in sight of the lake and looked for his friend. He had just ridden around a clump of cottonwoods when he was hit on the back with something large and soft. Turning in his saddle, with his Colt's ready, he saw Red sitting on a stump, a huge grin extending over his features. He replaced the weapon, said something about fools and dismounted, kicking aside the bundle of grass his friend had thrown.

"Yore shore easy," remarked Red, tossing aside his cold cigarette. "Suppose I was Trendley, where would yu be now?"

"Diggin' a hole to put yu in," pleasantly replied Hopalong. "If I didn't know he wasn't around this part of the country I wouldn't a rode as I did."

The man on the stump laughed and rolled a fresh cigarette. Lighting it, he inquired where Mr. Trendley was, intimating by his words that the rustler had not been found.

"About thirty miles to th' southeast," responded the other. "He's figurin' up how much dust he'll have when he gets our cows on th' market. Deacon Rankin is with him, too."

"Th' devil!" exclaimed Red, in profound astonishment.

"Yore right," replied his companion. Then he explained all the arrangements and told of the camp.

Red was for riding to the rendezvous at once, but his friend thought otherwise and proposed a swim, which met with approval. After enjoying themselves in the lake they dressed and rode along the trail Hopalong had made in coming for his companion, it being the intention of the former to learn more thoroughly the lay of the land immediately surrounding the camp. Red was pleased with this, and while they rode he narrated all that had taken place since the separation on the Plain, adding that he had found the trail left by the rustlers after they had quitted the desert and that he had followed it for the last two hours of his journey. It was well beaten and an eighth of a mile wide.

At dark they came within sight of the grove and picketed their horses at the place used by Pie and Hopalong. Then they moved forward and the same sight greeted their eyes that had been seen the night before. Keeping well within the edge of the grove and looking carefully for sentries, they went entirely around the camp and picked out several places which would be of strategic value later on. They noticed that the cabin used by Slippery Trendley was a hundred paces from the main collection of huts and that the woods came to within a tenth part of that distance of its door. It was heavily built, had no windows and faced the wrong direction.

Moving on, they discovered the storehouse of the enemy, another tempting place. It was just possible, if a siege became necessary, for several of the attacking force to slip up to it and either destroy it by fire or take it and hold it against all comers. This suggested a look at the enemy's water supply, which was the river. A hundred paces separated it from the nearest cabin and any rustler who could cross that zone under the fire of the besiegers would be welcome to his drink.

It was very evident that the rustlers had no thought

of defense, thinking, perhaps, that they were immune from attack with such a well-covered trail between them and their foes. Hopalong mentally accused them of harboring suicidal inclinations and returned with his companion to the horses. They mounted and sat quietly for a while, and then rode slowly away and at dawn reached the split rock, where they awaited the arrival of their friends, one sleeping while the other kept guard. Then they drew a rough map of the camp, using the sand for paper, and laid out the plan of attack.

As the evening of the next day came on they saw Pie, followed by many punchers, ride over a rise a mile to the south and they rode out to meet him.

When the force arrived at the camp of the two scouts they were shown the plan prepared for them. Buck made a few changes in the disposition of the men and then each member was shown where he was to go and was told why. Weapons were put in a high state of efficiency, canteens were refilled and haversacks were somewhat depleted. Then the newcomers turned in and slept while Hopalong and Red kept guard.

CHAPTER XXI

The Call

AT THREE o'clock the next morning a long line of men slowly filed into the cottonwood grove, being silently swallowed up by the dark. Dismounting, they left their horses in the care of three of their number and disappeared into the brush. Ten minutes later forty of the force were distributed along the edge of the grove fringing on the bank of the river and twenty more minutes gave ample time for a detachment of twenty to cross the stream and find concealment in the edge of the woods which ran from the river to where the corral made an effective barrier on the south. Eight crept down on the western side of the camp and worked their way close to Mr. Trendley's cabin door, and the seven who followed this detachment continued and took up their positions at the rear of the corral, where, it was hoped, some of the rustlers would endeavor to escape into the woods by working their way through the cattle in the corral and then scaling the stockade wall.

These seven were from the Three Triangle and the Double Arrow, and they were positive that any such attempt would not be a success from the viewpoint of the rustlers.

Two of those who awaited the pleasure of Mr. Trendley crept forward, and a rope swished through the air and settled over the stump which lay most convenient on the other side of the cabin door. Then the slack moved toward the woods, raised from the ground as it grew taut and, with the stump for its axis, swung toward the door, where it rubbed gently against the rough logs. It was made of braided horse-hair, was half an inch in diameter and was stretched eight inches above the ground.

As it touched the door, Lanky Smith, Hopalong and Red stepped out of the shelter of the woods and took up their positions behind the cabin, Lanky behind the northeast corner where he would be permitted to swing his right arm. In his gloved right hand he held the carefully arranged coils of a fifty-foot lariat, and should the chief of the rustlers escape tripping he would have to avoid the cast of the best roper in the southwest. The two others took the northwest corner and one of them leaned slightly forward and gently twitched the tripping-rope. The man at the other end felt the signal and whispered to a companion, who quietly disappeared in the direction of the river and shortly afterward the mournful cry of a whippoorwill dirged out on the early morning air. It had hardly died away when the quiet was broken by one terrific crash of rifles, and the two camp guards asleep at the fire awoke in another world.

Mr. Trendley, sleeping unusually well for the unjust, leaped from his bed to the middle of the floor

and alighted on his feet and wide-awake. Fearing
that a plot was being consummated to deprive him
of his leadership, he grasped the Winchester which
leaned at the head of his bed and, tearing open the
door, crashed headlong to the earth. As he touched
the ground, two shadows sped out from the shelter
of the cabin wall and pounced upon him. Men who
can rope, throw and tie a wild steer in thirty seconds
flat do not waste time in trussing operations, and
before a minute had elapsed he was being carried
into the woods, bound and helpless. Lanky sighed,
threw the rope over one shoulder and departed after
his friends.

When Mr. Trendley came to his senses he found
himself bound to a tree in the grove near the horses.
A man sat on a stump not far from him, three others
were seated around a small fire some distance to the
north, and four others, one of whom carried a rope,
made their way into the brush. He strained at his
bonds, decided that the effort was useless and
watched the man on the stump, who struck a match
and lit a pipe. The prisoner watched the light flicker
up and go out and there was left in his mind a picture that he could never forget. The face which had
been so cruelly, so grotesquely revealed was that of
Frenchy McAllister, and across his knees lay a heavy
caliber Winchester. A curse escaped from the lips of
the outlaw; the man on the stump spat at a firefly
and smiled.

From the south came the crack of rifles, incessant
and sharp. The reports rolled from one end of the
clearing to the other and seemed to sweep in waves
from the center of the line to the ends. Faintly in the
infrequent lulls in the firing came an occasional

report from the rear of the corral, where some desperate rustler paid for his venture.

Buck went along the line and spoke to the riflemen, and after some time had passed and the light had become stronger, he collected the men into groups of five and six. Taking one group and watching it closely, it could be seen that there was a world of meaning in this maneuver. One man started firing at a particular window in an opposite hut and then laid aside his empty gun and waited. When the muzzle of his enemy's gun came into sight and lowered until it had nearly gained its sight level, the rifles of the remainder of the group crashed out in a volley and usually one of the bullets, at least, found its intended billet. This volley firing became universal among the besiegers and the effect was marked.

Two men sprinted from the edge of the woods near Mr. Trendley's cabin and gained the shelter of the storehouse, which soon broke out in flames. The burning brands fell over the main collection of huts, where there was much confusion and swearing. The early hour at which the attack had been delivered at first led the besieged to believe that it was an Indian affair, but this impression was soon corrected by the volley firing, which turned hope into despair. It was no great matter to fight Indians, that they had done many times and found more or less enjoyment in it; but there was a vast difference between brave and puncher, and the chances of their salvation became very small. They surmised that it was the work of the cow-men on whom they had preyed and that vengeful punchers lay hidden behind that death-fringe of green willow and hazel.

Red, assisted by his inseparable companion, Hopalong, laboriously climbed up among the branches of a black walnut and hooked one leg over a convenient limb. Then he lowered his rope and drew up the Winchester which his accommodating friend fastened to it. Settling himself in a comfortable position and sheltering his body somewhat by the tree, he shaded his eyes by a hand and peered into the windows of the distant cabins.

"How is she, Red?" anxiously inquired the man on the ground.

"Bully: want to come up?"

"Nope. I'm goin' to catch yu when yu lets go," replied Hopalong with a grin.

"Which same I ain't goin' to," responded the man in the tree.

He swung his rifle out over a forked limb and let it settle in the crotch. Then he slewed his head around until he gained the bead he wished. Five minutes passed before he caught sight of his man and then he fired. Jerking out the empty shell he smiled and called out to his friend: "One."

Hopalong grinned and went off to tell Buck to put all the men in trees.

Night came on and still the firing continued. Then an explosion shook the woods. The storehouse had blown up and a sky full of burning timber fell on the cabins and soon three were half consumed, their occupants dropping as they gained the open air. One hundred paces makes fine potshooting, as Deacon Rankin discovered when evacuation was the choice necessary to avoid cremation. He never moved after he touched the ground and Red called out: "Two," not knowing that his companion had departed.

The morning of the next day found a wearied and hopeless garrison, and shortly before noon a soiled white shirt was flung from a window in the nearest cabin. Buck ran along the line and ordered the firing to cease and caused to be raised an answering flag of truce. A full minute passed and then the door slowly opened and a leg protruded, more slowly followed by the rest of the man, and Cheyenne Charley strode out to the bank of the river and sat down. His example was followed by several others and then an unexpected event occurred. Those in the cabins who preferred to die fighting, angered at this desertion, opened fire on their former comrades, who barely escaped by rolling down the slightly inclined bank into the river. Red fired again and laughed to himself. Then the fugitives swam down the river and landed under the guns of the last squad. They were taken to the rear and, after being bound, were placed under a guard. There were seven in the party and they looked worn out.

When the huts were burning the fiercest the uproar in the corral arose to such a pitch as to drown all other sounds. There were left within its walls a few hundred cattle whose brands had not yet been blotted out, and these, maddened to frenzy by the shooting and the flames, tore from one end of the enclosure to the other, crashing against the alternate walls with a noise which could be heard far out on the plain. Scores were trampled to death on each charge and finally the uproar subsided in sheer want of cattle left with energy enough to continue. When the corral was investigated the next day there were found the bodies of four rustlers, but recognition was impossible.

Several of the defenders were housed in cabins having windows in the rear walls, which the occupants considered fortunate. This opinion was revised, however, after several had endeavored to escape by these openings. The first thing that occurred when a man put his head out was the hum of a bullet, and in two cases the experimenters lost all need of escape.

The volley firing had the desired effect, and at dusk there remained only one cabin from which came opposition. Such a fire was concentrated on it that before an hour had passed the door fell in and the firing ceased. There was a rush from the side, and the Barred Horseshoe men who swarmed through the cabins emerged without firing a shot. The organization that had stirred up the Pecos Valley ranches had ceased to exist.

CHAPTER XXII

The Showdown

A FIRE burned briskly in front of Mr. Trendley's cabin that night and several punchers sat around it occupied in various ways. Two men leaned against the wall and sang softly of the joys of the trail and the range. One of them, Lefty Allen, of the O-Bar-O, sang in his sweet tenor, and other men gradually strolled up and seated themselves on the ground, where the fitful gleam of responsive pipes and cigarettes showed like fireflies. The songs followed one after another, first a lover's plea in soft Spanish and then a rollicking tale of the cowtowns and men. Supper had long since been enjoyed and all felt that life was, indeed, well worth living.

A shadow loomed against the cabin wall and a procession slowly made its way toward the open door. The leader, Hopalong, disappeared within and was followed by Mr. Trendley, bound and hobbled and tied to Red, the rear being brought up by Frenchy, whose rifle lolled easily in the crotch of his elbow. The singing went on uninterrupted and the hum of voices between the selections remained unchanged. Buck left the crowd around the fire and went into the cabin, where his voice was heard assenting to something. Hopalong emerged and took a seat at the fire, sending two punchers to take his place. He was joined by Frenchy and Red, the former very quiet.

In the center of a distant group were seven men who were not armed. Their belts, half full of cartridges, supported empty holsters. They sat and talked to the men around them, swapping notes and experiences, and in several instances found former friends and acquaintances. These men were not bound and were apparently members of Buck's force. Then one of them broke down, but quickly regained his nerve and proposed a game of cards. A fire was started and several games were immediately in progress. These seven men were to die at daybreak.

As the night grew older man after man rolled himself in his blanket and lay down where he sat, sinking off to sleep with a swiftness that bespoke tired muscles and weariness. All through the night, however, there were twelve men on guard, of whom three were in the cabin.

At daybreak a shot from one of the guards awakened every man within hearing, and soon they romped and scampered down to the river's edge to indulge in the luxury of a morning plunge. After an hour's horseplay they trooped back to the cabin and soon had breakfast out of the way.

Waffles, foreman of the O-Bar-O, and Youbet Somes strolled over to the seven unfortunates who had just completed a choking breakfast and nodded a hearty "Good morning." Then others came up and finally all moved off toward the river. Crossing it, they disappeared into the grove and all sounds of their advance grew into silence.

Mr. Trendley, escorted outside for the air, saw the procession as it became lost to sight in the brush. He sneered and asked for a smoke, which was granted. Then his guards were changed and the men began to straggle back from the grove.

Mr. Trendley, with his back to the cabin, scowled defiantly at the crowd that hemmed him in. The coolest, most damnable murderer in the West was not now going to beg for mercy. When he had taken up crime as a means of livelihood he had decided that if the price to be paid for his course was death, he would pay like a man. He glanced at the cottonwood grove, wherein were many ghastly secrets, and smiled. His hairless eyebrows looked like livid scars and his lips quivered in scorn and anger.

As he sneered at Buck there was a movement in the crowd before him and a pathway opened for Frenchy, who stepped forward slowly and deliberately, as if on his way to some bar for a drink. There was something different about the man who had searched the Staked Plain with Hopalong and Red: he was not the same puncher who had arrived from Montana three weeks before. There was lacking a certain air of carelessness and he chilled his friends, who looked upon him as if they had never really known him. He walked up to Mr. Trendley and gazed deeply into the evil eyes.

Twenty years before, Frenchy McAllister had changed his identity from a happy-go-lucky, devil-may-care cowpuncher and became a machine. The grief that had torn his soul was not of the kind which seeks its outlet in tears and wailing: it had turned and struck inward, and now his deliberate ferocity was icy and devilish. Only a glint in his eyes told of exultation, and his words were sharp and incisive; one could well imagine one heard the click of his teeth as they bit off the consonants: every letter was clear-cut, every syllable startling in its clearness.

"Twenty years and two months ago today," he began, "you arrived at the ranch house of the Double Y, up near the Montana-Wyoming line. Everything was quiet, except, perhaps, a woman's voice, singing. You entered, and before you left you pinned a note to that woman's dress. I found it, and it is due."

The air of carelessness disappeared from the members of the crowd and the silence became oppressive. Most of those present knew parts of Frenchy's story, and all were in hearty accord with anything he might do. He reached within his vest and brought forth a deerskin bag. Opening it, he drew out a package of oiled silk and from that he took a paper. Carefully replacing the silk and the bag, he slowly unfolded the sheet in his hand and handed it to Buck, whose face hardened. Two decades had passed since the foreman of the Bar-20 had seen that precious sheet, but the scene of its finding would never fade from his memory. He stood as if carved from stone, with a look on his face that made the crowd shift uneasily and glance at Trendley.

Frenchy turned to the rustler and regarded him evilly. "You are the hellish brute that wrote that note," pointing to the paper in the hand of his friend. Then, turning again, he spoke: "Buck, read that paper."

The foreman cleared his throat and read distinctly:

"McAllister: Yore wife is to damn good to live.

Trendley."

There was a shuffling sound, but Buck and Frenchy, silently backed up by Hopalong and Red, intervened, and the crowd fell back, where it surged in indecision.

"Gentlemen," said Frenchy, "I want you to vote on whether any man here has more right to do with Slippery Trendley as he sees fit than myself. Anyone who thinks so, or that he should be treated like the *others*, step forward. Majority rules."

There was no advance and he spoke again: "Is there anyone here who objects to this man dying?"

Hopalong and Red awkwardly bumped their knuckles against their guns and there was no response.

The prisoner was bound with cowhide to the wall of the cabin and four men sat near and facing him. The noonday meal was eaten in silence, and the punchers rode off to see about rounding up the cattle that grazed over the plain as far as eye could see. Suppertime came and passed, and busy men rode away in all directions. Others came and relieved the guards, and at midnight another squad took up the vigil.

Day broke and the thunder of hoofs as the punchers rounded up the cattle in herds of about five thousand each became very noticeable. One herd swept past toward the south, guarded and guided by fifteen men. Two hours later and another followed, taking a slightly different trail so as to avoid the close-cropped grass left by the first. At irregular intervals during the day other herds swept by, until six had passed and denuded the plain of cattle.

Buck, perspiring and dusty, accompanied by Hop-along and Red, rode up to where the guards smoked and joked. Frenchy came out of the cabin and smiled at his friends. Swinging in his left hand was a newly filled Colt's .45, which was recognized by his friends as the one found in the cabin and it bore a rough "T" gouged in the butt.

Buck looked around and cleared his throat: "We've got th' cows on th' home trail, Frenchy," he suggested.

"Yas?" inquired Frenchy. "Are there many?"

"Six drives of about five thousand to th' drive."

"All th' boys gone?" asked the man with the newly filled Colt's.

"Yas," replied Buck, waving his hand at the guards, ordering them to follow their friends. "It's a good deal for us: we've done right smart this hand. An' it's a good thing we've got so many punchers: thirty thousand's a big contract."

"About five times th' size of th' herd that blamed near made angels out'en me an' yu," responded Frenchy with a smile.

"I hope almighty hard that we don't have no stampedes on this here drive. Thirty thousand locoed cattle would just about wipe up this here territory. If th' last herds go wild they'll pick up th' others, an' then there'll be th' devil to pay."

Frenchy smiled again and shot a glance at where Mr. Trendley was bound to the cabin wall.

Buck looked steadily southward for some time and then flecked a foam-sud from the flank of his horse. "We are goin' south along th' Creek until we gets to Big Spring, where we'll turn right smart to th' west. We won't be able to make more'n twelve miles a day, 'though I'm goin' to drive them hard. How's yore grub?"

"Grub to burn."

"Got yore rope?" asked the foreman of the Bar-20, speaking as if the question had no especial meaning.

Frenchy smiled: "Yes."

Hopalong absentmindedly jabbed his spurs into his mount with the result that when the storm had subsided the spell was broken and he said "So long," and rode south, followed by Buck and Red. As they swept out of sight behind a grove Red turned in his saddle and waved his hat. Buck discussed with assiduity the prospects of a rainfall and was very cheerful about the recovery of the stolen cattle. Red could see a tall, broad-shouldered man standing with his feet spread far apart, swinging a Colt's .45, and Hopalong swore at everything under the sun. Dust arose in streaming clouds far to the south and they spurred forward to overtake the outfits.

Buck Peters, riding over the starlit plain, in his desire to reach the first herd, which slept somewhere to the west of him under the care of Waffles, thought of the events of the past few weeks and gradually became lost in the memories of twenty years before, which crowded up before his mind like the notes of a half-forgotten song. His nature, tempered by two decades of a harsh existence, softened as he lived again the years that had passed and as he thought of the things which had been. He was so completely lost in his reverie that he failed to hear the muffled hoofbeats of a horse that steadily gained upon him, and when Frenchy McAllister placed a friendly hand on his shoulder he started as if from a deep sleep.

The two looked at each other and their hands met. The question which sprang into Buck's eyes found a silent answer in those of his friend. They rode on side by side through the clear night and together drifted back to the days of the Double Y.

After an hour had passed, the foreman of the Bar-20 turned to his companion and then hesitated:

"Did, did—was he a cur?"

Frenchy looked off toward the south and, after an interval, replied: "Yas." Then, as an afterthought, he added, "Yu see, he never reckoned it would be that way."

Buck nodded, although he did not fully understand, and the subject was forever closed.

CHAPTER XXIII

Mr. Cassidy Meets a Woman

THE WORK of separating the cattle into herds of the different brands was a big contract, but with so many men it took but a comparatively short time, and in two weeks all signs of the rustlers had faded. It was then that good news went the rounds and the men looked forward to a week of pleasure, which was all the sharper accentuated by the grim mercilessness of the expedition into the Panhandle. Here was a chance for unlimited hilarity and a whole week in which to give strict attention to celebrating the recent victory.

So one day Mr. Hopalong Cassidy rode rapidly over the plain, thinking about the joys and excitement promised by the carnival to be held at Muddy Wells. With that rivalry so common to Western towns the inhabitants maintained that the carnival was to break all records, this because it was to be held in their town. Perry's Bend and Buckskin had each promoted a similar affair, and if this year's festivities were to be an improvement on those which had gone before, they would most certainly be worth riding miles to see. Perry's Bend had been unfortunate in being the first to hold a carnival, inasmuch as it only set a mark to be improved upon, and Buckskin had taken advantage of this and had added a brass band, and now in turn was to be eclipsed.

The events slated were numerous and varied, the most important being those which dealt directly with the everyday occupations of the inhabitants of that section of the country. Broncho-busting, steer-roping and tying, rifle and revolver shooting, trick riding and fancy roping made up the main features of the programme and were to be set off by horse and foot racing and other county fair necessities. Buckskin's brass band was to be on hand and the climax was to be capped by a scientific exhibition between two real roped-arena stars. Therefore Muddy Wells rubbed its hands and smiled in condescending egotism while the crowded gaming halls and the three-card-monte men on the street corners enriched themselves at the cost of know-it-all visitors.

Hopalong was firmly convinced that his day of hard riding was well worthwhile, for the Bar-20 was to be represented in strength. Probably a clearer insight into his idea of a carnival can be gained by his definition, grouchily expressed to Red Connors on the day following the last affair: "Raise Hell, go broke, wake up an' begin punching cows all over again." But that was the day after and the day after is always filled with remorse.

Hopalong and Red, having twice in succession won the revolver and rifle competitions, respectively, hoped to make it "three straight." Lanky Smith, the Bar-20 rope expert, had taken first prize in the only contest he had entered. Skinny Thompson had lost and drawn with Lefty Allen, of the O-Bar-O, in the broncho-busting event, but as Skinny had improved greatly in the interval, his friends confidently expected him to "yank first place" for the honor of his ranch. These expectations were backed with all the available Bar-20 money, and, if they were not realized, something in the nature of a calamity would swoop down upon and wrap that ranch in gloom. Since the O-Bar-O was aggressively optimistic the betting was at even money, hats and guns, and the losers would begin life anew so far as earthly possessions were concerned. No other competitors were considered in this event, as Skinny and Lefty had so far outclassed all others that the honor was believed to lie between these two.

Hopalong, blissfully figuring out the chances of the different contestants, galloped around a clump of mesquite only fifteen miles from Muddy Wells and stiffened in his saddle, for twenty rods ahead of him on the trail was a woman. As she heard him approach she turned and waited for him to overtake her, and when she smiled he raised his sombrero and bowed.

"Will you please tell me where I am?" she asked.

"Yu are fifteen miles southeast of Muddy Wells," he replied.

"But which is southeast?"

"Right behind yu," he answered. "Th' town lies right ahead."

"Are you going there?" she asked.

"Yes, ma'am."

"Then you will not care if I ride with you?" she asked. "I am a trifle frightened."

"Why, I'd be some pleased if yu do, 'though there ain't nothing out here to be afraid of now."

"I had no intention of getting lost," she assured him, "but I dismounted to pick flowers and cactus leaves and after a while I had no conception of where I was."

"How is it yu are out here?" he asked. "Yu shouldn't get so far from town."

"Why, papa is an invalid and doesn't like to leave his room, and the town is *so* dull, although the carnival is waking it up somewhat. Having nothing to do I procured a horse and determined to explore the country. Why, this is like Stanley and Livingstone, isn't it? You rescued the explorer!" and she laughed heartily. He wondered who in thunder Stanley and Livingstone were, but said nothing.

"I like the West, it is so big and free," she continued. "But it is very monotonous at times, especially when compared with New York. Papa swears dreadfully at the hotel and declares that the food will drive him insane, but I notice that he eats much more heartily than he did when in the city. And the service!—it is awful. But when one leaves the town behind it is splendid, and I can appreciate it because I had such a hard season in the city last winter—so many balls, parties and theaters that I simply wore myself out."

"I never hankered much for them things," Hopalong replied. "An' I don't like th' towns much, either. Once or twice a year I gets as far as Kansas City, but I soon tires of it an' hits th' back trail. Yu see, I don't like a fence country—I wants lots of room an' air."

She regarded him intently: "I know that you will think me very forward."

He smiled and slowly replied: "I think yu are all O.K."

"There do not appear to be many women in this country," she suggested.

"No, there ain't many," he replied, thinking of the kind to be found in all of the cowtowns. "They don't seem to hanker for this kind of life—they wants parties an' lots of dancin' an' them kind of things. I reckon there ain't a whole lot to tempt 'em to come."

"You evidently regard women as being very frivolous," she replied.

"Well, I'm speakin' from there not being any out here," he responded, "although I don't know much about them, to tell th' truth. Them what are out here can't be counted." Then he flushed and looked away.

She ignored the remark and placed her hand to her hair: "Goodness! My hair must look terrible!"

He turned and looked: "Yore hair is pretty—I allus did like brown hair."

She laughed and put back the straggling locks: "It is terrible! Just look at it! Isn't it awful?"

"Why, no: I reckons not," he replied critically. "It looks sort of free an' easy thataway."

"Well, it's no matter, it cannot be helped," she laughed. "Let's race!" she cried and was off like a shot.

He humored her until he saw that her mount was getting unmanageable, when he quietly overtook her and closed her pony's nostrils with his hand, the operation having a most gratifying effect.

"Joe hadn't oughter let yu had this cayuse," he said.

"Why, how do you know of whom I procured it?" she asked.

"By th' brand: it's a O-Bar-O, canceled, with J. H. over it. He buys all of his cayuses from th' O-Bar-O."

She found out his name, and, after an interval of silence, she turned to him with eyes full of inquiry: "What is that thorny shrub just ahead?" she asked.

"That's mesquite," he replied eagerly.

"Tell me all about it," she commanded.

"Why, there ain't much to tell," he replied, "only it's a valuable tree out here. Th' Apaches use it a whole lot of ways. They get honey from th' blossoms an' glue an' gum, an' they use th' bark for tannin' hide. Th' dried pods an' leaves are used to feed their cattle, an' th' wood makes corrals to keep 'em in. They use th' wood for making other things, too, an' it is of two colors. Th' sap makes a dye what won't wash out, an' th' beans make a bread what won't sour or get hard. Then it makes a barrier that shore is a dandy—coyotes an' men can't get through it, an' it protects a whole lot of birds an' things. Th' snakes hate it like poison, for th' thorns get under their scales an' whoops things up for 'em. It keeps th' sand from shiftin', too. Down South where there is plenty of water, it often grows forty feet high, but up here it squats close to th' ground so it can save th' moisture. In th' night th' temperature sometimes falls thirty degrees, an' that helps it, too."

"How can it live without water?" she asked.

"It gets all th' water it wants," he replied, smiling. "Th' taproots go straight down 'til they find it, sometimes fifty feet. That's why it don't shrivel up in th' sun. Then there are a lot of little roots under it an' they protects th' taproots. Th' shade it gives is th' coolest out here, for th' leaves turn with th' wind an' lets th' breeze through—they're hung on little stems."

"How splendid!" she exclaimed. "Oh! Look there!"

she cried, pointing ahead of them. A chaparral cock strutted from its decapitated enemy, a rattlesnake, and disappeared in the chaparral.

Hopalong laughed: "Mr. Scissors-bill Read-runner has great fun with snakes. He runs along th' sand— an' he *can* run, too—an' sees a snake takin' a siesta. Snip! goes his bill an' th' snake slides over th' Divide. Our fighting friend may stop some coyote's appetite before morning, though, unless he stays where he is."

Just then a gray wolf blundered in sight a few rods ahead of them, and Hopalong fired instantly. His companion shrunk from him and looked at him reproachfully.

"Why did you do that!" she demanded.

"Why, because they costs us big money every year," he replied. "There's a bounty on them because they pull down calves, an' sometimes full-grown cows. I'm shore wonderin' why he got so close—they're usually just out of range, where they stays."

"Promise me that you will shoot no more while I am with you."

"Why, shore: I didn't think yu'd care," he replied. "Yu are like that sky-pilot over to Las Cruces—he preached agin killin' things, which is all right for him, who didn't have no cows."

"Do you go to the missions?" she asked.

He replied that he did, sometimes, but forgot to add that it was usually for the purpose of hilarity, for he regarded sky pilots with humorous toleration.

"Tell me all about yourself—what you do for enjoyment and all about your work," she requested.

He explained in minute detail the art of punching cows, and told her more of the West in half an hour that she could have learned from a year's experience. She showed such keen interest in his words that it was a pleasure to talk to her, and he monopolized the conversation until the town intruded its sprawling collection of unpainted shacks and adobe huts in their field of vision.

CHAPTER XXIV

The Strategy of Mr. Peters

HOPALONG AND his companion rode into Muddy Wells at noon, and Red Connors, who leaned with Buck Peters against the side of Tom Lee's saloon, gasped his astonishment. Buck looked twice to be sure, and then muttered incredulously: "What th' hell!" Red repeated the phrase and retreated within the saloon, while Buck stood his ground, having had much experience with women, inasmuch as he had narrowly escaped marrying. He thought that he might as well get all the information possible, and waited for an introduction. It was in vain, however, for the two rode past without noticing him.

Buck watched them turn the corner and then called for Red to come out, but that person, fearing an ordeal, made no reply and the foreman went in after him. The timorous one was corraling bracers at the bar and nearly swallowed down the wrong channel when Buck placed a heavy hand on his broad shoulder.

"'G'way!" remarked Red. "I don't want no introduction, none whatever," he asserted. "G'way!" he repeated, backing off suspiciously.

"Better wait 'til yu are asked," suggested Buck. "Better wait 'til yu sees th' rope afore yu duck." Then he laughed: "Yu bashful fellers make me plumb disgusted. Why, I've seen yu face a bunch of guns an' never turn a hair, an' here yore all in because yu fear yu'll have to stand around an' hide yore hands. She won't bite yu. Anyway, from what I saw, Hopalong is due to be her grub—he never saw me at all, th' chump."

"He shore didn't see me, none," replied Red with distinct relief. "Are they gone?"

"Shore," answered Buck. "An' if they wasn't they wouldn't see us, not if we stood in front of them an' yelled. She's a hummer—stands two hands under him an' is a whole lot prettier than that picture Cowan has got over his bar. There's nothing th' matter with his eyesight, but he's plumb locoed, all th' same. He'll go an' get stuck on her an' then she'll hit th' trail for home an' mamma, an' he won't be worth his feed for a year." Then he paused in consternation: "Thunder, Red: he's got to shoot tomorrow!"

"Well, suppose he has?" responded Red. "I don't reckon she'll stampede his gunplay none."

"Yu don't reckon, eh?" queried Buck with much irony. "No, an' that's what's th' matter with yu. Why, do yu expect to see him tomorrow? Yu won't if I knows him an' I reckon I do. Nope, he'll be follerin' her all around."

"He's got sand to burn," remarked Red in awe. "Wonder how he got to know her?"

"Yu can gamble she did th' introducing part—he ain't got th' nerve to do it himself. He saved her life, or she thinks he did, or some romantic nonsense like that. So yu better go around an' get him away, an' keep him away, too."

"Who, *me*?" inquired Red in indignation. "*Me* go around an' tote him off? *I* ain't no wagon: yu go, or send Johnny."

"Johnny would say something real pert an' get knocked into th' middle of next week for it. He won't do, so I reckon yu better go yoreself," responded Buck, smiling broadly and moving off.

"Hey, yu! Wait a minute!" cried Red in consternation. Buck paused and Red groped for an excuse: "Why don't you send Billy?" he blurted in desperation.

The foreman's smile assumed alarming proportions and he slapped his thigh in joy: "Good boy!" he laughed. "Billy's th' man—good Lord, but won't he give Cupid cold feet! Rustle around an' send th' pessimistic soul to me."

Red, grinning and happy, rapidly visited door after door, shouted, "Hey, Billy!" and proceeded to the next one. He was getting pugnacious at his lack of success when he espied Mr. Billy Williams tacking along the accidental street as if he owned it. Mr. Williams was executing fancy steps and was trying to sing many songs at once.

Red stopped and grabbed his bibulous friend as that person veered to starboard: "Yore a peach of a life-preserver, yu are!" he exclaimed.

Billy balanced himself, swayed back and forth and frowned his displeasure at this unwarranted action: "I *ain't* no wife-deserter!" he shouted. "Unrope me an' give me th' trail! No tenderfoot can ride me!" Then he recognized his friend and grinned joyously: "Shore I will, but only one. Jus' one more, jus' one more. Yu see, m' friend, it was all Jimmy's fault. He—"

Red secured a chancery hold and dragged his wailing and remonstrating friend to Buck, who frowned his displeasure.

"This yere," said Red in belligerent disgust, "is th' dod-blasted hero what's a-goin' to save Hopalong from a mournful future. What are we a-goin' to do?"

Buck slipped the Colt's from Billy's holster and yanked the erring one to his feet: "Fill him full of sweet oil, souce him in th' trough, walk him around for awhile an' see what it does," he ordered.

Two hours later Billy walked up to his foreman and weakly asked what was wanted. He looked as though he had just been released from a six-months' stay in a hospital.

"Yu go over to th' hotel an' find Hopalong," said the foreman sternly. "Stay with him all th' time, for there is a plot on foot to wing him on th' sly. If yu ain't mighty spry he'll be dead by night."

Having delivered the above instructions and prevarications, Buck throttled the laugh which threatened to injure him and scowled at Red, who again fled into the saloon for fear of spoiling it all with revealed mirth.

The convalescent stared in open-mouthed astonishment:

"What's he doin' in th' hotel, an' who's goin' to plug him?" he asked.

"Yu leave that to me," replied Buck. "All yu has to do is to get on th' job with yore gun," handing the weapons to him, "an' freeze to him like a flea on a cow. Mebby there'll be a woman in th' game, but that ain't none of yore funeral—yu do what I said."

"Damn th' women!" exploded Billy, moving off. When he had entered the hotel Buck went in to Red.

"For God's sake!" moaned that person in senseless reiteration. "Th' Lord help Billy! Holy Mackinaw!" he shouted. "Gimme a drink an' let me tell th' boys."

The members of the outfit were told of the plot and they gave their uproarious sanction, all needing bracers to sustain them.

Billy found the clerk swapping lies with the bartender and, procuring the desired information, climbed the stairs and hunted for room No. 6. Discovering it, he dispensed with formality, pushed open the door and entered.

He found his friend engaged in conversation with a pretty young woman, and on a couch at the far side of the room lay an elderly, white-whiskered gentleman who was reading a magazine. Billy felt like a criminal for a few seconds and then there came to him the thought that his was a mission of great import and he braced himself to face any ordeal. "Anyway," he thought, "th' prettier they are th' more hell they can raise."

"What are *yu* doing here?" cried Hopalong in amazement.

"That's all right," averred the protector, confidentially.

"What's all right?"

"Why, everything," replied Billy, feeling uncomfortable.

The elderly man hastily sat up and dropped his magazine when he saw the armed intruder, his eyes as wide open as his mouth. He felt for his spectacles, but did not need them, for he could see nothing but the Colt's which Billy jabbed at him.

"None of that!" snapped Billy. " 'Nds up!" he ordered, and the hands went up so quick that when they stopped the jerk shook the room. Peering over the gentleman's leg, Billy saw the spectacles and backed to the wall as he apologized: "It's shore on me, Stranger—I reckoned yu was contemplatin' some gunplay."

Hopalong, blazing with wrath, arose and shoved Billy toward the hall, when Mr. Johnny Nelson, oozing fight and importance, intruded his person into the zone of action.

"Lord!" ejaculated the newcomer, staring at the vision of female loveliness which so suddenly greeted him. "Mamma," he added under his breath. Then he tore off his sombrero: "Come out of this, Billy, yu chump!" he exploded, backing toward the door, being followed by the protector.

Hopalong slammed the door and turned to his hostess, apologizing for the disturbance.

"Who are they?" palpitated Miss Deane.

"What the hell are they doing up here!" blazed her father.

Hopalong disclaimed any knowledge of them and just then Billy opened the door and looked in.

"There he is again!" cried Miss Deane, and her father gasped.

Hopalong ran out into the hall and narrowly missed kicking Billy into Kingdom Come as that person slid down the stairs, surprised and indignant.

Mr. Billy Williams, who sat at the top of the stairs, was feeling hungry and thirsty when he saw his friend, Mr. Pete Wilson, the slow-witted, approaching.

"Hey, Pete," he called, "come up here an' watch this door while I rustles some grub. Keep yore eyes open," he cautioned.

As Pete began to feel restless the door opened and a dignified gentleman with white whiskers came out into the hall and then retreated with great haste and no dignity. Pete got the drop on the door and waited. Hopalong yanked it open and kissed the muzzle of the weapon before he could stop, and Pete grinned.

"Coming to th' fight?" he loudly asked. "It's going to be a hell of a sumptious scrap—just th' kind yu allus like. Come on, th' boys are waitin' for yu."

"Keep quiet!" hissed Hopalong.

"What for?" asked Pete in surprise. "Didn't yu say yu shore wanted to see that scrap?"

"Shut yore face an' get scarce, or yu'll go home in cans!"

As Hopalong seated himself once more Red strolled up to the door and knocked. Hopalong ripped it open and Red, looking as fierce and worried as he could, asked Hopalong if he was all right. Upon being assured by smoking adjectives that he was, the caller looked relieved and turned thoughtfully away.

"Hey, yu! Come here!" called Hopalong.

Red waved his hand and said that he had to meet a man and clattered down the stairs. Hopalong thought that he, also, had to meet a man and, excusing himself, hastened after his friend and overtook him in the street, where he forced a confession. Returning to his hostess he told her of the whole outrage, and she was angry at first, but seeing the humorous side of it, she became convulsed with laughter. Her father re-read his paragraph for the thirteenth time and then, slamming the magazine on the floor, asked how many times he was expected to read ten lines before he knew what were in them, and went down to the bar.

Miss Deane regarded her companion with laughing eyes and then became suddenly sober as he came toward her.

"Go to your foreman and tell him that you will shoot tomorrow, for I will see that you do, and I will bring luck to the Bar-20. Be sure to call for me at one o'clock: I will be ready."

He hesitated, bowed, and slowly departed, making his way to Tom Lee's, where his entrance hushed the hilarity which had reigned. Striding to where Buck stood, he placed his hands on his hips and searched the foreman's eyes.

Buck smiled: "Yu ain't mad, are yu?" he asked.

Hopalong relaxed: "No, but damn near it."

Red and the others grabbed him from the rear, and when he had been "buffaloed" into good humor he threw them from him, laughed and waved his hand toward the bar:

"Come up, yu sons-of-guns. Yore a damned nuisance sometimes, but yore a bully gang all th' same."

CHAPTER XXV

Mr. Ewalt Draws Cards

TEX EWALT, cowpuncher, prospector, sometimes a rustler, but always a dude, rode from El Paso in deep disgust at his steady losses at faro and monte. The pecuniary side of these caused him no worry, for he was flush. This pleasing opulence was due to his business ability, for he had recently sold a claim for several thousand dollars. The first operation was simple, being known in Western phraseology as "jumping"; and the second, somewhat more complicated, was known as "salting."

The first of the money spent went for a complete new outfit, and he had parted with just three hundred and seventy dollars to feed his vanity. He desired something contrasty and he procured it. His sombrero, of gray felt a quarter of an inch thick, flaunted a band of black leather, on which was conspicuously displayed a solid silver buckle. His neck was protected by a crimson kerchief of the finest, heaviest silk. His shirt, in pattern the same as those commonly worn in the cow country, was of buckskin, soft as a baby's cheek and impervious to water, and the Angora goatskin chaps, with the long silken hair worn outside, were as white as snow. Around his waist ran loosely a broad, black leather belt supporting a heavy black holster, in which lay its walnut-handled burden, a .44-caliber Remington six-shooter; and fifty center-fire cartridges peeked from their loops, twenty-five on a side. His boots, the soles thin and narrow and the heels high, were black and of the finest leather. Huge spurs, having two-inch rowels, were held in place by buckskin straps, on which, also, were silver buckles. Protecting his hands were heavy buckskin gloves, also waterproof, having wide, black gauntlets.

Each dainty hock of his dainty eight-hundred-pound buckskin pony was black, and a black star graced its forehead. Well groomed, with flowing mane and tail, and with the brand on its flank being almost imperceptible, the animal was far different in appearance from most of the cow-ponies. Vicious and high-spirited, it cavorted just enough to show its lines to the best advantage.

The saddle, a famous Cheyenne and forty pounds in weight, was black, richly embossed, and decorated with bits of beaten silver which flashed back the sunlight. At the pommel hung a thirty-foot coil of braided horsehair rope, and at the rear was a Sharp's .50-caliber, breech-loading rifle, its owner having small use for any other make. The color of the bridle was the same as the saddle and it supported a heavy U bit which was capable of a leverage sufficient to break the animal's jaw.

Tex was proud of his outfit, but his face wore a frown—not there only on account of his losses, but also by reason of his mission, for under all his finery beat a heart as black as any in the cow country. For months he had smothered hot hatred and he was now on his way to ease himself of it.

He and Slim Travennes had once exchanged shots with Hopalong in Santa Fé, and the month which he had spent in bed was not pleasing, and from that encounter had sprung the hatred. That he had been in the wrong made no difference with him. Some months later he had learned of the death of Slim, and it was due to the same man. That Slim had again been in the wrong also made no difference, for he realized the fact and nothing else. Lately he had been told of the death of Slippery Trendley and Deacon Rankin, and he accepted their passing as a personal affront. That they had been caught red-handed in cattle stealing of huge proportions and received only what was customary under the conditions formed no excuse in his mind for their passing. He was now on his way to attend the carnival at Muddy Wells, knowing that his enemy would be sure to be there.

While passing through Las Cruces he met Porous Johnson and Silent Somes, who were thirsty and who proclaimed that fact, whereupon he relieved them of their torment and, looking forward to more treatment of a similar nature, they gladly accompanied him without asking why or where.

As they left the town in their rear Tex turned in his saddle and surveyed them with a cynical smile.

"Have yu heard anything of Trendley?" he asked.

They shook their heads.

"Him an' th' Deacon was killed over in th' Panhandle," he said.

"What!" chorused the pair.

"Jack Dorman, Shorty Danvers, Charley Teale,

Stiffhat Bailey, Billy Jackson, Terry Nolan an' Sailor Carson was lynched."

"What!" they shouted.

"Fish O'Brien, Pinochle Schmidt, Tom Wilkins, Apache Gordon, Charley of th' Bar Y, Penobscot Hughes an' about twenty others died fightin'."

Porous looked his astonishment: "Cavalry?"

"An' I'm going after th' —— who did it," he continued, ignoring the question. "Are yu with me?—yu used to pal with some of them, didn't yu?"

"We did, an' we're shore with yu!" cried Porous.

"Yore right," endorsed Silent. "But who done it?"

"That gang what's punchin' for th' Bar-20— Hopalong Cassidy is th' one I'm pining for. Yu fellers can take care of Peters an' Connors."

The two stiffened and exchanged glances of uncertainty and apprehension. The outfit of the Bar-20 was too well known to cause exuberant joy to spring from the idea of war with it, and well in the center of all the tales concerning it were the persons Tex had named. To deliberately set forth with the avowed intention of planting these was not at all calculated to induce sweet dreams.

Tex sneered his contempt.

"Yore shore uneasy: yu ain't a-scared, are yu?" he drawled.

Porous relaxed and made a show of subduing his horse: "I reckon I ain't scared plumb to death. Yu can deal me a hand," he asserted.

"I'll draw cards too," hastily announced Silent, buttoning his vest. "Tell us about that jamboree over in th' Panhandle."

Tex repeated the story as he had heard it from a bibulous member of the Barred Horseshoe, and then added a little of torture as a sauce to whet their appetites for revenge.

"How did Trendley cash in?" asked Porous.

"Nobody knows except that bum from th' Tin-Cup. I'll get him later. I'd a got Cassidy up in Santa Fé, too, if it wasn't for th' sun in my eyes. Me an' Slim loosened up on him in th' Plaza, but we couldn't see nothing with him a-standin' against th' sun."

"Where's Slim now?" asked Porous. "I ain't seen him for some time."

"Slim's with Trendley," replied Tex. "Cassidy handed him over to St. Pete at Cactus Springs. Him an' Connors sicked their outfit on him an' his vigilantes, bein' helped some by th' O-Bar-O. They wiped th' town plumb off th' earth, an' now I'm going to do some wipin' of my own account. I'll prune that gang of some of its blossoms afore long. It's cost me seventeen friends so far, an' I'm going to stop th' leak, or make another."

They entered Muddy Wells at sunrise on the day of the carnival and, eating a hearty breakfast, sallied forth to do their share toward making the festivities a success.

The first step considered necessary for the acquirement of ease and polish was begun at the nearest bar, and Tex, being the host, was so liberal that his friends had reached a most auspicious state when they followed him to Tom Lee's.

Tex was too wise to lose his head through drink and had taken only enough to make him careless of consequences. Porous was determined to sing "Annie Laurie," although he hung on the last word of the first line until out of breath and then began anew. Silent, not wishing to be outdone, bawled at the top of his lungs a medley of music-hall words to the air of a hymn.

Tex, walking as awkwardly as any cowpuncher, approached Tom Lee's, his two friends trailing erratically, arm in arm, in his rear. Swinging his arm he struck the door a resounding blow and entered, hand on gun, as it crashed back. Porous and Silent stood in the doorway and quarreled as to what each should drink and, compromising, lurched in and seated themselves on a table and resumed their vocal perpetrations.

Tex swaggered over to the bar and tossed a quarter upon it: "Corn juice," he laconically exclaimed. Tossing off the liquor and glancing at his howling friends, he shrugged his shoulders and strode out by the rear door, slamming it after him. Porous and Silent, recounting friends who had "cashed in" fell to weeping and they were thus occupied when Hopalong and Buck entered, closely followed by the rest of the outfit.

Buck walked to the bar and was followed by Hopalong, who declined his foreman's offer to treat. Tom Lee set a bottle at Buck's elbow and placed his hands against the bar.

"Friend of yourn just hit th' back trail," he remarked to Hopalong. "He was primed some for trouble, too," he added.

"Yaas?" drawled Hopalong with little interest.

The proprietor restacked the few glasses and wiped off the bar.

"Them's his pardners," he said, indicating the pair on the table.

Hopalong turned his head and gravely scrutinized them. Porous was bemoaning the death of Slim Travennes and Hopalong frowned.

"Don't reckon he's no relation of mine," he grunted.

"Well, he ain't yore sister," replied Tom Lee, grinning.

"What's his brand?" asked the puncher.

"I reckon he's a maverick, 'though yu put yore brand on him up to Santa Fé a couple of years back. Since he's throwed back on yore range I reckon he's yourn if yu wants him."

"I reckon Tex is some sore," remarked Hopalong, rolling a cigarette.

"I reckon he is," replied the proprietor, tossing Buck's quarter in the cash box. "But, say, you should oughter see his rig."

"Yaas?"

"He's shore a cowpunch dude—my, but he's some sumptious an' highfalutin'. An' bad? Why, he reckons th' Lord never brewed a more high-toned brand of cussedness than his'n. He shore reckons he's th' baddest man that ever simmered."

"How'd he look as th' leadin' man in a necktie festival?" blazed Johnny from across the room, feeling called upon to help with the conversation.

"He'd be a howlin' success, son," replied Skinny Thompson, "judgin' by his friends what we elevated over in th' Panhandle."

Lanky Smith leaned forward with his elbow on the table, resting his chin in the palm of his hand: "Is Ewalt still a-layin' for yu, Hopalong?" he asked.

Hopalong turned wearily and tossed his half-consumed cigarette into the box of sand which did duty as a cuspidore: "I reckon so; an' he shore can hatch whenever he gets good an' ready, too."

"He's probably a-broodin' over past grievances,"

offered Johnny, as he suddenly pushed Lanky's elbow from the table, nearly causing a catastrophe.

"Yu'll be broodin' over present grievances if yu don't look out, yu everlastin' nuisance yu," growled Lanky, planting his elbow in its former position with an emphasis which conveyed a warning.

"These bantams ruffle my feathers," remarked Red. "They go around braggin' about th' egg they're goin' to lay an' do enough cacklin' to furnish music for a dozen. Then when th' affair comes off yu'll generally find they's been settin' on a doorknob."

"Did yu ever see a hen leave th' walks of peace an' bugs an' rustle hell-bent across th' trail plumb in front of a cayuse?" asked Buck. "They'll leave off rustlin' grub an' become candidates for th' graveyard just for cussedness. Well, a whole lot of men are th' same way. How many times have I seen them swagger into a gin shop an' try to run things sudden an' hard, an' that with half a dozen better men in th' same room? There's shore a-plenty of trouble a-comin' to every man without rustlin' around for more."

" 'Member that time yu an' Frenchy tried to run th' little town of Frozen Nose, up in Montana?" asked Johnny, winking at the rest.

"An' we did run it, for a while," responded Buck. "But that only goes to show that most young men are chumps—we were just about yore age then."

Red laughed at the youngster's discomfiture: "That little squib of yourn shore touched her off—I reckon we irrigates on yu this time, don't we?"

"Th' more th' Kid talks, th' more money he needs," remarked Lanky, placing his glass on the bar. "He had to buy drinks for me an' Skinny twice last night."

"I got two more after yu left," added Skinny. "He shore oughter practice keeping still."

At one o'clock sharp Hopalong walked up to the clerk of the hotel and grinned. The clerk looked up:

"Hullo, Cassidy?" he exclaimed, genially. "What was all that fuss about this mornin' when I was away? I haven't seen you for a long time, have I? How are you?"

"That fuss was a fool joke of Buck's, an' I wish they had been throwed out," Hopalong replied. "What I want to know is if Miss Deane is in her room. Yu see, I have a date with her."

The clerk grinned:

"So she's roped you, too, has she?"

"What do yu mean?" asked Hopalong in surprise.

"Well, well," laughed the clerk. "You punchers are easy. Any third-rate actress that looks good to eat can rope you fellows, all right. Now look here, Laura, you keep shy of her corral, or you'll be broke so quick you won't believe you ever had a cent: that's straight. This is the third year that she's been here and I know what I'm talking about. How did you come to meet her?"

Hopalong explained the meeting and his friend laughed again:

"Why, she knows this country like a book. She can't get lost anywhere around here. But she's damned clever at catching punchers."

"Well, I reckon I'd better take her, go broke or not," replied Hopalong. "Is she in her room?"

"She is, but she is not alone," responded the clerk. "There is a dude puncher up there with her and she left word here that she was indisposed, which means that you are outlawed."

"Who is he?" asked Hopalong, having his suspicions.

"That friend of yours: Ewalt. He sported a wad this morning when she passed him, and she let him make her acquaintance. He's another easy mark. He'll be busted wide open tonight."

"I reckon I'll see Tex," suggested Hopalong, starting for the stairs.

"Come back, you chump!" cried the clerk. "I don't want any shooting here. What do you care about it? Let her have him, for it's an easy way out of it for you. Let him think he's cut you out, for he'll spend all the more freely. Get your crowd and enlighten them—it'll be better than a circus. This may sound like a steer, but it's straight."

Hopalong thought for a minute and then leaned on the cigar case:

"I reckon I'll take about a dozen of yore very best cigars, Charley. Got any real high-toned brands?"

"Cortez panatella—two for a dollar," Charley replied. "But, seein' that it's you, I'll throw off a dollar on a dozen. They're a fool notion of the old man, for we can't sell one in a month."

Hopalong dug up a handful and threw one on the counter, lighting another: "Yu light a Cortez panatella with me," he said, pocketing the remainder. "That's five dollars she didn't get. So long."

He journeyed to Tom Lee's and found his outfit making merry. Passing around his cigars he leaned against the bar and delighted in the first really good smoke he had since he came home from Kansas City.

Johnny Nelson blew a cloud of smoke at the ceiling and paused with a pleased expression on his face:

"This is a lalapoloosa of a cigar," he cried. "Where'd yu get it, an' how many's left?"

"I got it from Charley, an' there's more than yu can buy at fifty a shot."

"Well, I'll just take a few for luck," Johnny responded, running out into the street. Returning in five minutes with both hands full of cigars he passed them around and grinned: "They're birds, all right!"

Hopalong smiled, turned to Buck and related his conversation with Charley. "What do yu think of that?" he asked as he finished.

"I think Charley oughter be yore guardian," replied the foreman.

"He was," replied Hopalong.

"If we sees Tex we'll all grin hard," laughed Red, making for the door. "Come on to th' contests—Lanky's gone already."

Muddy Wells streamed to the carnival grounds and relieved itself of its enthusiasm and money at the booths on the way. Cowpunchers, Indians, Mexicans, and the few tourists that were present were delighted with the picturesque scene. The town was full of fakirs and before one of them stood a group of cowpunchers, apparently drinking in the words of a barker.

"Right this way, gents, and see the woman who don't eat. Lived for two years without food, gents. Right this way, gents. Only a quarter of a dollar. Get your tickets, gents, and see——"

Red pushed forward:

"What did yu say, Pard?" he asked. "I'm a little off in my near ear. What's that about eatin' a woman for two years?"

"The greatest wonder of the age, gents. The wom——"

"Any discount for th' gang?" asked Buck, gawking.

"Why don't yu quit smokin' an' buy th' lady a meal?" asked Johnny from the center of the group.

"Th' cane yu ring th' cane yu get!" came from the other side of the street and Hopalong purchased rings for the outfit. Twenty-four rings got one cane, and it was divided between them as they wended their way toward the grounds.

"That makes six wheels she didn't get," murmured Hopalong.

As they passed the snake charmer's booth they saw Tex and his companion ahead of them in the crowd, and they grinned broadly. "I like th' front row in th' balcony," remarked Johnny, who had been to Kansas City. "Don't cry in th' second act—it ain't real," laughed Red. "We'll hang John Brown on a sour apple-tree—in th' Panhandle," sang Skinny as they passed them.

Arriving at the grounds they hunted up the registration committee and entered in the contests. As Hopalong signed for the revolver competition he was rudely pushed aside and Tex wrote his name under that of his enemy. Hopalong was about to show quick resentment for the insult, but thought of what Charley had said, and he grinned sympathetically. The seats were filling rapidly, and the outfit went along the ground looking for friends. A bugle sounded and a hush swept over the crowd as the announcement was made for the first event.

"Broncho-busting.—Red Devil, never ridden: Frenchy McAllister, Tin-Cup, Montana; Meteor, killed his man: Skinny Thompson, Bar-20, Texas; Vixen, never ridden: Lefty Allen, O-Bar-O, Texas."

All eyes were focused on the plain where the horse was being led out for the first trial. After the usual preliminaries had been gone through Frenchy walked over to it, vaulted in the saddle and the bandage was torn from the animal's eyes. For ten minutes the onlookers were held spellbound by the fight before them, and then the horse kicked and galloped away and Frenchy was picked up and carried from the field.

"Too bad!" cried Buck, running from the outfit.

"Did yu see it?" asked Johnny excitedly. "Th' cinch busted."

Another horse was led out and Skinny Thompson vaulted to the saddle, and after a fight of half an hour rode the animal from the enclosure to the clamorous shouts of his friends. Lefty Allen also rode his mount from the same gate, but took ten minutes more in which to do it.

The announcer conferred with the timekeepers and then stepped forward: "First, Skinny Thompson, Bar-20, thirty minutes and ten seconds; second, Lefty Allen, O-Bar-O, forty minutes and seven seconds."

Skinny returned to his friends shamefacedly and did not look as if he had just won a championship. They made way for him, and Johnny, who could not restrain his enthusiasm, clapped him on the back and cried: "Yu old son-of-a-gun!"

The announcer again came forward and gave out the competitors for the next contest, steer-roping and tying. Lanky Smith arose and, coiling his rope carefully, disappeared into the crowd. The fun was not so great in this, but when he returned to his outfit with the phenomenal time of six minutes and eight seconds for his string of ten steers, with twenty-two seconds for one of them, they gave him vociferous greeting. Three of his steers had gotten up after he had leaped from his saddle to tie them, but his horse had taken care of that. His nearest rival was one minute over him and Lanky retained the championship.

Red Connors shot with such accuracy in the rifle contest as to run his points twenty per cent higher than Waffles, of the O-Bar-O, and won the new rifle.

The main interest centered in the revolver contest, for it was known that the present champion was to defend his title against an enemy and fears were expressed in the crowd that there would be an "accident." Buck Peters and Red stood just behind the firing line with their hands on hips, and Tex, seeing the precautions, smiled grimly as he advanced to the line.

Six bottles, with their necks an inch above a board, stood twenty paces from him, and he broke them all in as many shots, taking six seconds in which to do it. Hopalong followed him and tied the score. Three tin balls rolling erratically in a blanket supported by two men were sent flying into the air in four shots, Tex taking three seconds. His competitor sent them from the blanket in three shots and in the same time. In slow shooting from sights Tex passed his rival in points and stood to win. There was but one more event to be contested and in it Hopalong found his joy. Shooting from the hip when the draw is timed is not the sport of even good shots, and when Tex made sixty points out of a possible hundred, he felt that he had shot well. When Hopalong went to the line his friends knew that they would now see shooting such as would be almost unbelievable, that the best draw-and-shoot marksman in their State was the man who limped slightly as he advanced and who chewed reflectively on his fifty-cent cigar. He wore two guns and he stepped with confidence before the marshal of the town, who was also judge of the contest.

The tiny spherical bell which lay on the ground was small enough for the use of a rifle and could hardly be seen from the rear seats of the amphitheater. There was a word spoken by the timekeeper, and a gloved hand flashed down and up, and the bell danced and spun and leaped and rolled as shot after shot followed it with a precision and speed which brought the audience to a heavy silence. Taking the gun which Buck tossed to him and throwing it into the empty holster, he awaited the signal, and then smoke poured from his hips and the bell clanged continuously, once while it was in the air. Both guns emptied in the two-hand shooting, he wheeled and jerked loose the guns which the marshal wore, spinning around without a pause, the target hardly ceasing in its ringing. Under his arms he shot, backward and between his legs; leaping from side to side, ducking and dodging, following the bell wherever it went. Reloading his weapons quickly he twirled them on his fingers and enveloped himself in smoke out of which came vivid flashes as the bell gave notice that he shot well. His friends, and there were many in the crowd, torn from their affected nonchalance by shooting the like of which they had not attributed even to him, roared and shouted and danced in a frenzy of delight. Red also threw his guns to Hopalong, who caught them in the air and turning, faced Tex, who stood white of face and completely lost in the forgetfulness of admiration and amazement. The guns spun again on his fingers and a button flew from the buckskin shirt of his enemy; another tore a flower from his breast and another drove it into the ground at his feet as others stirred his hair and cut the buckle off his pretty sombrero. Tex, dazed, but wise enough to stand quiet, felt his belt tear loose and drop to his feet, felt a spur rip from its strap and saw his cigarette leap from his lips. Throwing the guns to Red, Hopalong laughed and abruptly turned and was lost in the crowd.

For several seconds there was silence, but when the dazed minds realized what their eyes had seen, there arose a roar which shook the houses in the town. Roar after roar thundered forth and was sent crashing back again by the distant walls, sweeping down on the discomfited dude and causing him to slink into the crowd to find a place less conspicuous. He was white yet and keen fear gripped his heart as he realized that he had come to the carnival with the expressed purpose of killing his enemy in fair combat. The whole town knew it, for he had taken pains to spread the news. The woman he had been with knew it from words which she had overheard while on her way to the grounds with him. His friends knew it and would laugh him into forgetfulness as the fool who boasted. Now he understood why he had lost so many friends: they had attempted what he had sworn to attempt. Look where he would he could see only a smoke-wrapped demon who moved and shot with a speed incredible. There was reason why Slim had died. There was reason why Porous and Silent had paled when they learned of their mission. He hated his conspicuous clothes and his pretty broncho, and the woman who had gotten him to squander his money, and who was doubtless convulsed with laughter at his expense. He worked himself into a passion which knew no fear and he ran for the streets of the town, there to make good his boast or to die. When he found his enemy he felt himself grasped with a grip of steel and Buck Peters swung him around and grinned maliciously in his face:

"Yu plaything!" hoarsely whispered the foreman. "Why don't yu get away while yu can? Why do yu want to throw yoreself against certain death? I don't want my pleasure marred by a murder, an' that is what it will be if yu makes a gunplay at Hopalong. He'll shoot yu as he did yore buttons. Take yore pretty clothes an' yore pretty cayuse an' go where this is not known, an' if ever again yu feels like killing Hopalong, get drunk an' forget it."

Turn the page
for an excerpt from
the exciting sequel to
Bar-20:

HOPALONG CASSIDY

coming soon
from
Tor Books

Antonio's Scheme

THE RAW and mighty West, the greatest stage in all the history of the world for so many deeds of daring which verged on the insane, was seared with grave-lined trails. In many localities the bad-man made history in a terse and business-like way, and also made the first law for the locality—that of the gun.

There were good bad-men and bad bad-men, the killer by necessity and the wanton murderer; and the shifting of these to their proper strata evolved the foundation for the law of to-day. The good bad-man, those in whose souls lived the germs of law and order and justice, gradually became arrayed against the other class, and stood up manfully for their principles, let the odds be what they might; and bitter, indeed, was the struggle, and great the price.

From the gold camps of the Rockies to the shriek-ing towns of the coast, where wantonness stalked unchecked; from the vast stretches of the cattle ranges to the ever-advancing terminals of the persistent railroads, to the cow towns, boiling and seething in the loosed passions of men who brooked no restraint in their revels, no one section of country ever boasted of such numbers of genuine bad-men of both classes as the great, semi-arid Southwest. Here was one of the worst collections of raw humanity ever broadcast in one locality; it was a word and a shot, a shot and a laugh or a curse.

In this red setting was stuck a town which we will call Eagle, the riffle which caught all the dregs of passing humanity. Unmapped, known only to those who had visited it, reared its flimsy buildings in the face of God and rioted day and night with no thought of reckoning; mad, insane with hellishness unlimited.

Late in the afternoon rode Antonio, "bronchobuster" for the H2, a man of little courage, much avarice, and great capacity for hatred. Crafty, filled with cunning of the coyote kind, shifty-eyed, gloomy, taciturn, and scowling, he was well fitted for the part he had elected to play in the range dispute between his ranch and the Bar-20. He was absolutely without mercy or conscience; indeed, one might aptly say that his conscience, if he had ever known one, had been pulled out by the roots and its place filled with viciousness. Cold-blooded in his ferocity, easily angered and quick to commit murder if the risk were small, he embraced within his husk of soul the putrescence of all that was evil.

In Eagle he had friends who were only a shade less evil than himself; but they had what he lacked and because of it were entitled to a forced respect of small weight—they had courage, that spontaneous, initiative, heedless courage which toned the atmosphere of the whole West to a magnificent crimson. Were it not for the reason that they had

drifted to his social level they would have spurned
his acquaintance and shot him for a buzzard; but,
while they secretly held him in great contempt for
his cowardice, they admired his criminal cunning,
and profited by it. He was too wise to show himself
in the true light to his foreman and the outfit, knowing full well that death would be the response, and
so lived a lie until he met his friends of the town,
when he threw off his cloak and became himself, and
where he plotted against the man who treated him
fairly.

Riding into the town, he stopped before a saloon
and slouched in to the bar, where the proprietor was
placing a new stock of liquors on the shelves.

"Where's Benito, an' th' rest?" he asked.

"Back there," replied the other, nodding toward a
rear room.

"Who's in there?"

"Benito, Hall, Archer an' Frisco."

"Where's Shaw?"

"Him an' Clausen an' Cavalry went out 'bout ten
minutes ago."

"I want to see 'em when they come in," Antonio
remarked, headed towards the door, where he listened, and then went in.

In the small room four men were grouped around
a table, drinking and talking, and at his entry they
looked up and nodded. He nodded in reply and
seated himself apart from them, where he soon became wrapped in thought.

Benito arose and went to the door. *"Mescal,
pronto,"* he said to the man outside.

"Damned *pronto*, too," growled Antonio. "A man
would die of alkali in this place before he's waited
on."

The proprietor brought a bottle and filled the glasses, giving Antonio his drink first, and silently withdrew.

The broncho-buster tossed off the fiery stuff and then turned his shifty eyes on the group. "Where's Shaw?"

"Don't know—back soon," replied Benito.

"Why didn't he wait, when he knowed I was comin' in?"

Hall leaned back from the table and replied, keenly watching the inquisitor, "Because he don't give a damn."

"You—!" Antonio shouted, half rising, but the others interfered and he sank back again, content to let it pass. But not so Hall, whose Colt was half drawn.

"I'll kill you some day," he gritted, but before anything could come of it Shaw and his companions entered the room and the trouble was quelled.

Soon the group was deep in discussion over the merits of a scheme which Antonio unfolded to them, and the more it was weighed the better it appeared. Finally Shaw leaned back and filled his pipe. "You've got th' brains of th' devil,' 'Tony."

"Eet ees not'ing," replied Antonio.

"Oh, drop that lingo an' talk straight—you ain't on th' H2 now," growled Hall.

"Benito, you know this country like a book," Shaw continued. "Where's a good place for us to work from, or ain't there no choice?"

"Thunder Mesa."

"Well, what of it?"

"On the edge of the desert, high, big. The walls are stone, an' so very smooth. Nobody can get up."

"How can we get up then?"

"There's a trail at one end," replied Antonio,

crossing his legs and preparing to roll a cigarette. "It's too steep for cayuses, an' too narrow; but we can crawl up. An' once up, all hell can't follow as long as our cartridges hold out."

"Water?" inquired Frisco.

"At th' bottom of th' trail, an' th' spring is on top," Antonio replied. "Not much, but enough."

"Can you work yore end all right?" asked Shaw.

"Yes," laughed the other. "I am 'that fool, Antonio,' on th' ranch. But they're th' fools. We can steal them blind an' if they find it out—well," here he shrugged his shoulders, "th' Bar-20 can take th' blame. I'll fix that, all right. This trouble about th' line is just what I've been waitin' for, an' I'll help it along. If we can get 'em fightin' we'll run off with th' bone *we* want. That'll be easy."

"But can you get 'em fightin'?" asked Cavalry, so called because he had spent several years in that branch of the Government service, and deserted because of the discipline.

Antonio laughed and ordered more *mescal* and for some time took no part in the discussion which went on about him. He was dreaming of success and plenty and a ranch of his own which he would start in Old Mexico, in a place far removed from the border, and where no questions would be asked. He would be a rich man, according to the standards of that locality, and what he said would be law among the peons. He liked to day-dream, for everything came out just as he wished; there was no discordant note. He was so certain of success, so conceited as not to ask himself if any of the Bar-20 or H2 outfits were not his equal or superior in intelligence. It was only a matter of time, he told himself, for he could easily get the two ranches embroiled in a range war, and once embroiled, his plan would succeed and he would be safe.

"What do you want for your share, 'Tony?" suddenly asked Shaw.

"Half."

"What! *Half?*"

"*Si.*"

"You're loco!" cried the other. "Do you reckon we're going to buck up agin th' biggest an' hardest fightin' outfit in this country an' take all sorts of chances for a measly half, to be divided up among seven of us!" He brought his fist down on the table with a resounding thump. "You an' yore game can go to hell first!" he shouted.

"I like a hog, all right," sneered Clausen, angrily.

"I thought it out an' I got to look after th' worst an' most important part of it, an' take three chances to you fellers' one," replied Antonio, frowning. "I said half, an' it goes."

"Run all th' ends, an' keep it all," exclaimed Hall. "An', by God, we've got a hand in it, now. If you try to hog it we'll drop a word where it'll do th' most good, an' don't you forget it, neither."

"Antonio is right," asserted Benito, excitedly. "It's risky for him."

"Keep yore yaller mouth shut," growled Cavalry. "Who gave you any say in this?"

"Half," said Antonio, shrugging his shoulders.

"Look here, you," cried Shaw, who was, in reality, the leader of the crowd, inasmuch as he controlled all the others with the exception of Benito and Antonio, and these at times by the judicious use of flattery. "We'll admit that you've got a right to th' biggest share, but not to no half. You have a chance to get away, because you can watch 'em, but how about us, out there on th' edge of hell? If they come for us we won't know nothing about it till we're surrounded. Now we want to play square with you, and we'll give you twice as much as any one of th' rest of us. That'll make nine shares an' give you two of 'em. What more do you want, when you've got to have us to run th' game at all?"

Antonio laughed ironically. "Yes. I'm where I can watch, an' get killed first. You can hold th' mesa for a month. I ain't as easy as I look. It's my game, not yourn; an' if you don't like what I ask, stay out."

"We will!" cried Hall, arising, followed by the others. His hand rested on the butt of his revolver and trouble seemed imminent. Benito wavered and then slid nearer to Antonio. "You can run yore game all by yore lonesome, as *long* as you *can*!" Hall shouted. "I know a feller what knows Cassidy, an' I'll spoil yore little play right now. You'll look nice at th' end of a rope, won't you? It's this: share like Shaw said or get out of here, and look out for trouble aplenty to-morrow morning. I've put up with yore gall an' swallered yore insultin' actions just as long as I'm going to, and I've got a powerful notion to fix you right here and now!"

"No fightin', you fools!" cried the proprietor, grabbing his Colt and running to the door of the room. "It's up to you fellers to stick together!"

"I'll be damned if I'll stand—" began Frisco.

"They want too much," interrupted Antonio, angrily, keeping close watch over Hall.

"We want a fair share, an' that's all!" retorted Shaw. "Sit down, all of you. We can wrastle this out without no gunplay."

"You-all been yappin' like a set of fools," said the proprietor. "I've heard every word you-all said. If you got a mite of sense you'll be some tender how you shout about it. It's shore risky enough without tellin' everybody this side of sun-up."

"I mean just what I said," asserted Hall. "It's Shaw's offer, or nothin'. We ain't playing fool."

"Here! Here!" cried Shaw, pushing Hall into a seat. "If you two have got anything to settle, wait till some other time."

"That's more like it," growled the proprietor, shuffling back to the bar.

"Good Lord, 'Tony," cried Shaw in a low voice. "That's fair enough; we've got a right to something, ain't we? Don't let a good thing fall through just because you want th' whole earth. Better have a little than none."

"Well, gimme a third, then."

"I'll give you a slug in th' eye, you hog!" promised Hall, starting to rise again, but Shaw held him back. "Sit down, you fool!" he ordered, angrily. Then he turned to Antonio. "Third don't go; take my offer or leave it."

"Gimme a fourth; that's fair enough."

Shaw thought for a moment and then looked up. "Well, that's more like it. What do you say, fellers?"

"No!" cried Hall. "Two-ninths, or nothin'!"

"A fourth is two-eighths, only a little more," Shaw replied.

"Well, all right," muttered Hall, sullenly.

"That's very good," laughed Benito, glad that things were clearing.

The others gave their consent to the division and Shaw smiled. "Well, that's more like it. Now we'll go into this thing an' sift it out. Keep mum about it— there's twenty men in town that would want to join us if they knowed."

"I'm goin' to be boss; what I say goes," spoke up Antonio. "It's my game an' I'm takin' th' most risky end."

"You ain't got sand enough to be boss of anything," sneered Hall. "Yore sand is chalk."

"You'll say too much someday," retorted Antonio, glaring.

"Oh, not to *you*, I reckon," rejoined Hall, easily.

"Shut up, both of you!" snapped Shaw. "You can be boss, 'Tony," he said, winking at Hall. "You've got more brains for a thing like this than any of us. I don't see how you can figger it out like you do."

Antonio laughed but he remembered one thing, and swore to take payment if the plan leaked out; the proprietor had confessed hearing every word, which was not at all to his liking. If Quinn should tell, well, Quinn would die; he would see to that, he and Benito.

Mary Meeker Rides North

MARY MEEKER, daughter of the H2 owner and fore-man, found pleasure in riding on little tours of investigation. She had given the southern portions her attention first and found, after the newness had worn off, that she did not care for the level, sandy stretches of half-desert land which lay so flat for miles. The prospect was always the same, always uninteresting and wearying and hot. Now she determined upon a step which she had wished to take for a long time, and her father's request that she should not take it grew less and less of a deterrent factor. He had given so much thought and worry to that mysterious valley, that she at last gave rein to her curiosity and made ready to see for herself. It was green and hilly, like the rugged Montana she had quitted to come down to the desert. There were hills of respectable size, for these she saw daily from the ranch house door, and she loved hills; anything would be better than the limitless sand.

She had known little of restraint; her corner of the world had been filled entirely by men and she had absorbed much of their better traits. Self-reliant as a cowgirl should be, expert with either Colt or Winchester, and at home in the saddle, she feared nothing the desert might hold, except thirst. She was not only expert with weapons, but she did not fear to use them against men, as she had proved on one occasion in wild Montana. So she would ride to the hills which called her so insistently and examine the valley.

One bright morning just before the roundup began she went to the corral and looked at her horse, a cross between Kentucky stock and cow-pony and having in a great degree the speed of the first and the hardiness of the last, and sighed to think that she could not ride it for days to come. Teuton was crippled and she must choose some other animal. She had overheard Doc Riley tell Ed Joyce that the piebald in the smaller corral was well broken, and this was the horse she would take. The truth of the matter was that the piebald was crafty and permitted the saddle to be fixed and himself ridden for varying periods of time before showing what he thought of such things. Doc, unprepared for the piebald's sudden change in demeanor, had taken a tumble, which made him anxious to have his wounded conceit soothed by seeing Ed Joyce receive the same treatment.

Mary found no trouble in mounting and riding the animal and she was glad that she had overheard Doc, for now she had two horses which were thoroughly reliable, although, of course, Teuton was the only really good horse on the range. She rode out of the corral and headed for the White Horse Hills, scarcely

twelve miles away. What if her father had warned
her not to ride near the lawless punchers who rode
the northern range? They were only men and she
was sure that to a woman they would prove to be
gentlemen.

The southern boundary of the Bar-20 ran along
the top of the hills and from them east to the river,
and it was being patrolled by three Bar-20 punchers,
Hopalong, Johnny, and Red, all on the lookout for
straying cattle of both ranches. Neither Hopalong nor
Red had ever seen Mary Meeker, but Johnny had
upon the occasion of his scout over the H2 range,
and he had felt eminently qualified to describe her.
He had finished his eulogistic monologue by assert-
ing that as soon as his more unfortunate friends saw
her they would lose sleep and sigh often, which
prophecy was received in various ways and called
forth widely differing comment. Red had snorted
outright and Pete swore to learn that a woman was
on the range; for Pete had been married, and his
wife preferred another man. Hopalong, remembering a former experience of his own, smiled in knowing cynicism when told that he again would fall
under the feminine spell.

Red was near the river and Johnny half-way to
the hills when Hopalong began the ascent of Long
Hill, wondering why it was that Meeker had made
no attempt to cross the boundary in force and bring
on a crisis; and from Meeker his mind turned to the
daughter.

"So there's a woman down here now," he muttered, riding down into an arroyo and up the other
bank. "This country is gettin' as bad as Kansas,
damned if it ain't. First thing we know it'll be nursin'

bottles an' school houses, an' hell loose all th' time instead of once in a while."

He heard hoofbeats and glanced up quickly, alert and ready for trouble, for who would be riding where he was but some H2 puncher?

"What th'—!" he exclaimed under his breath, for riding towards him at an angle was Mary Meeker; and Johnny was wrong in his description of her, but, he thought, the Kid had done as well as his limited vocabulary would allow. She *was* pretty, pretty as— she was more than pretty!

She had seen him at the same time and flashed a quick glance which embraced everything; and she was surprised, for he was not only passably good-looking, barring the red hair, but very different from the men her father had told her made up the outfit of the Bar-20. He removed his sombrero instantly and drew up to let her pass, a smile on his face. Yes, he thought, Johnny had wronged her, for no other woman could have such jet-black hair crowning such a face.

"By God!" he whispered, and went no farther, for that was the summing up of his whole opinion of her.

"He *is* a gentleman," she thought triumphantly, for he had proved that she was right in her surmise regarding the men of the northern ranch. She spurred to pass him and then her piebald took part in the proceedings. The prick of the spur awakened in him a sudden desire to assert his rights, and he promptly pitched to make up for his hitherto gentle behavior. So taken up with what the last minute had brought forth she was unprepared for the vicious bucking and when she opened her eyes her head was propped against Hopalong's knee and her face dripping with the contents of his canteen. "Damn yore ugly skin!" he was saying to the piebald, which stood quietly a short distance away, evidently enjoying the result of his activity. "Just you wait! I'll show you what's due to come yore way purty soon!" He turned again to the woman and saw that her eyes were closed as before. "By God, yore—yore beautiful!"

She moved slightly and color came into her cheeks with a sudden rush and he watched her anxiously. Soon she moved again and then, opening her eyes, struggled to gain her feet. He helped her up and held her until she drew away from him.

"What was it?" she asked.

"That ugly cayuse went an' pitched when you wasn't lookin' for it," he told her. "Are you hurt much?"

"No, just dizzy. I don't want to make you trouble," she replied.

"You ain't makin' me any trouble, not a bit," he assured her earnestly. "But I'd like to make some trouble for that ornery cayuse of yourn. Let me tone him down some."

"No; it was my fault. I should'a been lookin—I never rode him before."

"Well, you've got to take my cayuse to get home on," he said. "He's bad, but he's a regular angel when stacked up agin that bronc. I'll ride the festive piebald, an' we can trade when you get home." Under his breath he said: "Oh, just wait till I get on you, pinto! I'll give you what you need, all right!"

"Thank you, but I can ride him now that I know just what he is," she said, her eyes flashing with determination. "I've never let a bronc get th' best of me in th' long run, an' I ain't goin' to begin now. I came up here to look at th' hills an' th' valley, an' I'm not going back home till I've done it."

"That's the way to talk!" he cried in admiration. "I'll get him for you," he finished, swinging into his saddle. He loosened the lariat at the saddle horn while he rode towards the animal, which showed sudden renewed interest in the proceedings, but it tarried too long. Just as it wheeled and leaped forward the rope settled and the next thing it knew was that the sky had somehow slid under its stomach, for it had been thrown over backward and flat on its back. When it had struggled to its feet it found Hopalong astride it, spurring vigorously on the side farthest from Mary, and for five minutes the air was greatly disturbed. At the end of that time he dismounted and led a penitent pony to its mistress, who vaulted lightly into the saddle and waited for her companion to mount. When he had joined her they rode up the hill together side by side.

Johnny wished to smoke and felt for his tobacco pouch, which he found to be empty. He rode on for a short distance, angry with himself for his neglect, and then remembered that Hopalong had a plentiful supply. He could overtake the man on the hill much quicker than he could Red, who had said that he was going to ride south along the river to see if Jumping Bear Creek was dry. If it were, Meeker could be expected to become active in his aggression. Johnny wheeled and cantered back along the boundary trail, alertly watching for trespassing cattle.

It was not long before he came within sight of the thicket which stood a little east of the base of Long Hill, and he nearly fell from the saddle in astonishment, for his friend was on the ground, holding a woman's head on his knee! Johnny didn't care to intrude, and cautiously withdrew to the shelter of the small chaparral, where he waited impatiently.

Wishing to stretch his legs, he dismounted and picketed his horse and walked around the thicket until satisfied that he was out of sight of his friend.

Suddenly he fancied that he heard something suspicious and he crept back around the thicket, keeping close to its base. When he turned the corner he saw the head of a man on the other side of the chaparral which lay a little southwest of his position. It was Antonio, and he was intently watching the two on the slope of the hill, and entirely unaware that he was being watched in turn.

Johnny carefully drew his Colt and covered Antonio who he hated instinctively. He had seen the shifty-eyed broncho-buster on more than one occasion and never without struggling with himself to keep from shooting. Now his finger pressed gently against the trigger of the weapon and he wished for a passable excuse to send the other into eternity; but Antonio gave him no cause, only watching eagerly and intently, his face set in such an expression of malignancy as to cause Johnny's finger to tremble.

Johnny arose slightly until he could see Hopalong and his companion and he smothered an exclamation. "Gosh A'mighty!" he whispered, again watching Antonio. "That's Meeker's gal or I'm a liar! Th' son-of-a-gun, keeping quiet about it all this time. An' no wonder Antonio's on th' trail!"

It was not long before Johnny looked again for Hopalong and saw him riding up the hill with his companion. Then he crept forward, watching Antonio closely, his Colt ready for instant use. Antonio slowly drew down until he was lost to sight of the Bar-20 puncher, who ran slightly forward and gained the side of the other thicket, where he again crept forward, and around the chaparral. When he next caught sight of the broncho-buster the latter was walking towards his horse and his back was turned to Johnny.

"Hey, you!" called the Bar-20 puncher, arising and starting after the other.

Antonio wheeled, leaped to one side and half drew his revolver, but he was covered and he let the weapon slide back into the holster.

"What are you doing?"

Antonio's reply was a scowl and his inquisitor continued without waiting for words from the other.

"Never mind that, I saw what you was doing," Johnny said. "An' I shore knew what you wanted to do, because I came near doing it to you. Now it ain't a whole lot healthy for you to go snooping around this line like you was, for I'll plug you on suspicion next time. Get on that cayuse of yourn an' hit th' trail south—go on, make tracks!"

Antonio mounted and slowly wheeled. "You hab drop, now," he said significantly. "Nex' time, *quien sabe*?"

Johnny dropped his Colt into the holster and removed his hand from the butt. "You're a liar!" he shouted, savagely. "I ain't got th' drop. It's an even break, an' what are you going to do about it?"

Antonio shrugged his shoulders and rode on without replying, quite content to let things stand as they were. He had learned something which he might be able to use to advantage later on and he had strained the situation just a little more.

"Huh! Next time!" snorted Johnny in contempt as he turned to go back to his horse. "It'll allus be 'next' time' with him, 'less he gets a good pot shot at me, which he won't. He ain't got sand enough to put up a square fight. Now for Red; he'll shore be riding this way purty soon, an' that'll never do. Hoppy won't want anybody foolin' around th' hills for a while, lucky devil."

More than an hour had passed before he met Red and he forthwith told him that he had caught Antonio scouting on foot along the line.

"I ain't none surprised, Kid," Red replied, frowning. "You've seen how th' H2 cows are being driven north agin us an' that means we'll be tolerable busy purty soon. Th' Jumping Bear is dry as tinder, an' it won't be long before Meeker'll be driving to get in th' valley."

"Well, I'm some glad of that," Johnny replied, frankly. "It's been peaceful too blamed long down here. Come on, we'll ride east an' see if we can find any cows to turn. Hey! Look there!" he cried, spurring forward.

The Roundup

THE TEXAN sky seemed a huge mirror upon which were reflected the white fleecy clouds sailing northward; the warm spring air was full of that magnetism which calls forth from their earthy beds the gramma grass and the flowers; the scant vegetation had taken on new dress and traces of green now showed against the more sombre-colored stems; while in the distance, rippling in glistening patches where, disturbed by the wind, the river sparkled like a tinsel ribbon flung carelessly on the grays and greens of the plain. Birds winged their joyous way and filled the air with song; and far overhead a battalion of tardy geese flew, arrowlike, towards the cool lakes of the north, their faint honking pathetic and continuous. Skulking in the coulees or speeding across the skyline of some distant rise occasionally could be seen a coyote or gray wolf. The cattle, less gregarious than they had been in the colder months, made tentative sorties from the lessening herd, and began

to stray off in search of the tender green grass which
pushed up recklessly from the closely cropped, with-
ered tufts. Rattlesnakes slid out and uncoiled their
sinuous lengths in the warm sunlight, and copperheads raised their burnished armor from their winter
retreats. All nature had felt the magic touch of the
warm winds, and life in its multitudinous forms was
discernible on all sides. The gaunt tragedy of a hard
winter for that southern range had added its chilling
share to the horrors of the past and now the cattle
took heart and lost their weakness in the sunlight,
hungry but contented.

The winter had indeed been hard, one to be remembered for years to come, and many cattle had
died because of it; many skeletons, stripped clean by
coyotes and wolves, dotted the arroyos and coulees.
The cold weather had broken suddenly, and several
days of rain, followed by sleet, had drenched the
cattle thoroughly. Then from out of the north came
one of those unusual rages of nature, locally known
as a "Norther," freezing pitilessly; and the cattle,
weakened by cold and starvation, had dumbly suc-
cumbed to this last blow. Their backs were covered
with an icy shroud, and the deadly cold gripped their
vitals with a power not to be resisted. A glittering
sheet formed over the grasses as far as eye could
see, and the cattle, unlike the horses, not knowing
enough to stamp through it, nosed in vain at the
sustenance beneath, until weakness compelled them
to lie down in the driving snow, and once down,
they never arose. The storm had raged for the
greater part of a week, and then suddenly one morning the sun shown down on a velvety plain, blinding
in its whiteness; and when spring had sent the snow
mantle roaring through the arroyos and water

courses in a turmoil of yellow water and driftwood, and when the range riders rode forth to read the losses on the plain, the remaining cattle were staggering weakly in search of food. Skeletons in the coulees told the story of the hopeless fight, how the unfortunate cattle had drifted before the wind to what shelter they could find and how, huddled together for warmth, they had died one by one. The valley along Conroy Creek had provided a rough shelter with its scattered groves and these had stopped the cattle drift, so much dreaded by cowmen.

It had grieved Buck Peters and his men to the heart to see so many cattle swept away in one storm, but they had done all that courage and brains could do to save them. So now, when the plain was green again and the warm air made riding a joy, they were to hold the calf roundup. When Buck left his blanket after the first night spent in the roundup camp and rode off to the horse herd, he smiled from suppressed elation, and was glad that he was alive.

Peaceful as the scene appeared there was trouble brewing, and it was in expectation of this that Buck had begun the roundup earlier than usual. The unreasoning stubbornness of one man, and the cunning machinations of a natural rogue, threatened to bring about, from what should have been only a misunderstanding, as pretty a range war as the Southwest had seen. Those immediately involved were only a few when compared to the number which might eventually be brought into the strife, but if this had been pointed out to Jim Meeker he would have replied that he "didn't give a damn."

Jim Meeker was a Montana man who thought to carry out on the H2 range, of which he was foreman,

the same system of things which had served where
he had come from. This meant trouble right away,
for the Bar-20, already short in range, would not
stand idly by and see him encroach upon their land
for grass and water, more especially when he broke
a solemn compact as to range rights which had been
made by the former owners of the H2 with the Bar-
20. It meant not only the forcible use of Bar-20 range,
but also a great hardship upon the herds for which
Buck Peters was responsible.

Meeker's obstinacy was covertly prodded by Antonio for his own personal gains, but this the Bar-20
foreman did not know; if he had known it there
might have been much trouble averted.

Buck Peters was probably the only man of all of
them who realized just what such a war would mean,
to what an extent rustling would flourish while the
cowmen fought. His best efforts had been used to
avert trouble, so far successfully; but that he would
continue to do so was doubtful. He had an outfit
which, while meaning to obey him in all things and
to turn from any overt act of war, was not of the
kind to stand much forcing or personal abuse; their
nervous systems were constructed on the hair-trigger
plan, and their very loyalty might set the range
ablaze with war. However, on this most perfect of
mornings Meeker's persistent aggression did not
bother him, he was free from worry for the time.

Just north of Big Coulee, in which was a goodly
sized water hole, a group of blanket-swathed figures
lay about a fire near the chuck wagon, while the
sleepy cook prepared breakfast for his own outfit,
and for the eight men which the foreman of the C80
and the Double Arrow had insisted upon Buck taking. The sun had not yet risen, but the morning glow

showed gray over the plain, and it would not be long
before the increasing daylight broke suddenly. The
cook fires crackled and blazed steadily, the iron pots
hissing under their dancing and noisy lids, while the
coffee pots bubbled and sent up an aromatic steam,
and the odor of freshly baked biscuits swept forth as
the cook uncovered a pan. A pile of tin plates was
stacked on the tail-board of the wagon while a large
sheet-iron pail contained tin cups. The figures, feet
to the fire, looked like huge, grotesque cocoons, for
the men had rolled themselves in their blankets, their
heads resting on their saddles, and in many cases
folded sombreros next to the leather made softer pil-
lows.

Back of the chuck wagon the eastern sky grew
rapidly brighter, and suddenly daylight in all its
power dissipated the grayish light of the moment
before. As the rim of the golden sun arose above the
low sand hills to the east the foreman rode into
camp. Some distance behind him Harry Jones and
two other C80 men drove up the horse herd and
enclosed it in a flimsy corral quickly extemporized
from lariats; flimsy it was, but it sufficed for cow-
ponies that had learned the lesson of the rope.

"All ready, Buck," called Harry before his words
were literally true.

With assumed ferocity but real vociferation Buck
uttered a shout and watched the effect. The cocoons
became animated, stirred and rapidly unrolled, with
the exception of one, and the sleepers leaped to their
feet and folded the blankets. The exception stirred,
subsided, stirred again and then was quiet. Buck and
Red stepped forward while the others looked on
grinning to see the fun, grasped the free end of the
blanket and suddenly straightened up, their hands

going high above their heads. Johnny Nelson,
squawking, rolled over and over and, with a yell of
surprise, sat bolt upright and felt for his gun.

"Huh!" he snorted. "Reckon yo're smart, don't
you!"

"Purty near a shore 'nuf pin-wheel, Kid,' laughed
Red.

"Don't you care, Johnny; you can finish it tonight,"
consoled Frenchy McAllister, now one of Buck's outfit.

"Breakfast, Kid, breakfast!" sang out Hopalong as
he finished drying his face.

The breakfast was speedily out of the way, and
pipes were started for a short smoke as the punchers
walked over to the horse herd to make their selections. By exercising patience, profanity, and perse-
verance they roped their horses and began to saddle
up. Ed Porter, of the C80, and Skinny Thompson,
Bar-20, cast their ropes with a sweeping, preliminary
whirl over their heads, but the others used only a
quick flit and twist of the wrist. A few mildly exciting
struggles for the mastery took place between riders
and mounts, for some cow-ponies are not always
ready to accept their proper places in the scheme of
things.

"Slab-sided jumpin' jack!" yelled Rich Finn, a Double Arrow puncher, as he fought his horse. "Allus
raisin' th' devil afore I'm all awake!"

"Lemme hold her head, Rich," jeered Billy Williams.

"Her laigs, Billy, not her head," corrected Lanky
Smith, the Bar-20 rope expert, whose own horse had
just become sensible.

"Don't hurt him, bronc; we need him," cautioned
Red.

"Come on, fellers; gettin' late," called Buck.

Away they went, tearing across the plain, Buck in the lead. After some time had passed the foreman raised his arm and Pete Wilson stopped and filled his pipe anew, the west-end man of the cordon. Again Buck's arm went up and Skinny Thompson dropped out, and so on until the last man had been placed and the line completed. At a signal from Buck the whole line rode forward, gradually converging on a central point and driving the scattered cattle before it.

Hopalong, on the east end of the line, sharing with Billy the posts of honor, was now kept busy dashing here and there, wheeling, stopping, and maneuvering as certain strong-minded cattle, preferring the freedom of the range they had just quitted, tried to break through the cordon. All but branded steers and cows without calves had their labors in vain, although the escape of these often set examples for ambitious cows with calves. Here was where reckless and expert riding saved the day, for the cowponies, trained in the art of punching cows, entered into the game with zest and executed quick turns which more than once threatened a catastrophe to themselves and riders. Range cattle can run away from their domesticated kin, covering the ground with an awkward gait that is deceiving; but the ponies can run faster and turn as quickly.

Hopalong, determined to turn back one stubborn mother cow, pushed too hard, and she wheeled to attack him. Again the nimble pony had reasons to move quickly and Hopalong swore as he felt the horns touch his leg.

"On th' prod, hey! Well, stay on it!" he shouted, well knowing that she would. "Pig-headed old fool—

all right, Johnny; I'm comin'!" and he raced away to turn a handful of cows which were proving too much for his friend. *"Ki-yi-yeow-eow-eow-eow-eow!"* he yelled, imitating the coyote howl.

The cook had moved his wagon as soon as breakfast was over and journeyed southeast with the cavvieyh; and as the cordon neared its objectives the punchers could see his camp about half a mile from the level pasture where the herd would be held for the cutting-out and branding. Cookie regarded himself as the most important unit of the roundup and acted accordingly, and he was not far wrong.

"Hey, Hoppy!" called Johnny through the dust of the herd, "there's cookie. I was 'most scared he'd get lost."

"Can't you think of anythin' else but grub?" asked Billy Jordan from the rear.

"Can you tell me anything better to think of?"

There were from three to four hundred cattle in the herd when it neared the stopping point, and dust arose in low-hanging clouds above it. Its pattern of differing shades of brown, with yellow and black and white relieving it, constantly shifted like a kaleidoscope as the cattle changed positions; and the rattle of horns on horns and the muffled bellowing could be heard for some distance.

Gradually the cordon surrounded the herd and, when the destination was reached, the punchers rode before the front ranks of cattle and stopped them. There was a sudden tremor, a compactness in the herd, and the cattle in the rear crowded forward against those before; another tremor, and the herd was quiet. Cow-punchers took their places around it, and kept the cattle from breaking out and back to the range, while every second man, told off by the foreman, raced at top speed towards the camp, there to eat a hasty dinner and get a fresh horse from his *remuda*, as his string of from five to seven horses was called. Then he galloped back to the herd and relieved his nearest neighbor. When all had reassembled at the herd the work of cutting-out began.

Lanky Smith, Panhandle Lukins, and two more Bar-20 men rode some distance east of the herd, there to take care of the cow-and-calf cut as it grew by the cutting-out. Hopalong, Red, Johnny, and three others were assigned to the task of getting the mother cows and their calves out of the main herd and into the new one, while the other punchers held the herd and took care of the stray herd when they should be needed. Each of the cutters-out rode after some calf, and the victim, led by its mother, worked its way after her into the very heart of the mass; and in getting the pair out again care must be taken not to unduly excite the other cattle. Wiry, happy, and conceited cow-ponies unerringly and patiently followed mother and calf into the press, nipping the pursued when too slow and gradually forcing them to the outer edge of the herd; and when the mother tried to lead its offspring back into the herd to repeat the performance, she was in almost every case cleverly blocked and driven out on the plain where the other punchers took charge of her and added her to the cow-and-calf cut.

Johnny jammed his sombrero on his head with reckless strength and swore luridly as he wheeled to go back into the herd.

"What's th' matter, Kid?" laughingly asked Skinny as he turned his charges over to another man.

"None of yore damned business!" blazed Johnny. Under his breath he made a resolve. "If I get you two out here again I'll keep you here if I have to shoot you!"

"Are they slippery, Johnny?" jibed Red, whose guess was correct. Johnny refused to heed such asinine remarks and stood on his dignity.

As the cow-and-calf herd grew in size and the main herd dwindled, more punchers were shifted to hold it; and it was not long before the main herd was comprised entirely of cattle without calves, when it was driven off to freedom after being examined for other brands. As soon as the second herd became of any size it was not necessary to drive the cows and the calves to it when they were driven out of the first herd, as they made straight for it. The main herd, driven away, broke up as it would, while the guarded cows stood idly beside their resting offspring awaiting further indignities.

The drive had covered so much ground and taken so much time that approaching darkness warned Buck not to attempt the branding until the morrow, and he divided his force into three shifts. Two of these hastened to the camp, gulped down their supper, and rolling into their blankets, were soon sound asleep. The horse herd was driven off to where the grazing was better, and night soon fell over the plain.

The cook's fires gleamed through the darkness and piles of biscuits were heaped on the tail-board of the wagon, while pots of beef and coffee simmered over the fires, handy for the guards as they rode in during the night to awaken brother punchers, who would take their places while they slept. Soon the cocoons were quiet in the grotesque shadows caused by the fires and a deep silence reigned over the camp. Occasionally some puncher would awaken long enough to look at the sky to see if the weather had changed, and satisfied, return to sleep.

Over the plain sleepy cowboys rode slowly around the herd, glad to be relieved by some other member of the outfit, who always sang as he approached the cattle to reassure them and save a possible stampede. For cattle, if suddenly disturbed at night by anything, even the waving of a slicker in the hands of some careless rider, or a wind-blown paper, will rise in a body—all up at once, frightened and nervous. The sky was clear and the stars bright and when the moon rose it flooded the plain with a silvery light and made fairy patterns in the shadows.

Snatches of song floated down the gentle wind as the riders slowly circled the herd, for the human voice, no matter how discordant, was quieting. A low and plaintive "Don't let this par-ting grieve y-o-u" passed from hearing around the resting cows, soon to be followed by "When-n in thy dream-ing, nights like t-h-e-s-e shall come a-gain—" as another watcher made the circuit. The serene cows, trusting in the prowess and vigilance of these low-voiced centaurs to protect them from danger, dozed and chewed their cuds in peace and quiet, while the natural noises of the night relieved the silence in unobtruding harmony.

Far out on the plain a solitary rider watched the herd from cover and swore because it was guarded so closely. He glanced aloft to see if there was any hope of a storm and finding that there was not, muttered savagely and rode away. It was Antonio, wishing that he could start a stampede and so undo the work of the day and inflict heavy losses on the Bar-20. He did not dare to start a grass fire for at the first flicker of a light he would be charged by one or more of the night riders and if caught, death would be his reward.

While the third shift rode and sang the eastern sky became a dome of light reflected from below and the sunrise, majestic in all its fiery splendor, heralded the birth of another perfect day.

Through the early morning hours the branding continued, and the bleating of cattle told of the hot stamping irons indelibly burning the sign of the Bar-20 on the tender hides of calves. Mother cows fought and plunged and called in reply to the terrified bawling of their offspring, and sympathetically licked the burns when the frightened calves had been allowed to join them. Cowboys were deftly roping calves by their hind legs and dragging them to the fires of the branding men. Two men would hold a calf, one doubling the foreleg back on itself at the knee and the other, planting one booted foot against the calf's under hind leg close to its body, pulled back on the other leg while his companion, who held the foreleg, rested on the animal's head. The third man, drawing the hot iron from the fire, raised and held it suspended for a second over the calf's flank, and then there was an odor and a puff of smoke; and the calf was branded with a mark which neither water nor age would wipe out.

Pete Wilson came riding up dragging a calf at the end of his rope, and turned the captive over to Billy Williams and his two helpers, none of them paying any attention to the cow which followed a short distance behind him. Lanky seized the unfortunate calf and leaned over to secure the belly hold, when someone shouted a warning and he dropped the struggling animal and leaped back and to one side as the mother charged past. Wheeling to return the attack, the cow suddenly flopped over and struck the earth with a thud as Buck's rope went home. He dragged her away and then releasing her, chased her back into the herd.

"*Hi!* Get that little devil!" shouted Billy to Hopalong, pointing to the fleeing calf.

"Why didn't you watch for her," demanded the indignant Lanky of Pete. "Do you think this is a ten-pin alley!"

Hopalong came riding up with the calf, which swiftly became recorded property.

"Bar-20; tally one," sang out the monotonous voice of the tally man. "Why didn't you grab her when she went by, Lanky?" he asked, putting a new point on his pencil.

"Hope th' next one leads yore way!" retorted Lanky, grinning.

"Won't. I ain't abusin' th' kids."

"Bar-20; tally one," droned a voice at the next fire.

All was noise, laughter, dust, and a seeming confusion, but every man knew his work thoroughly and was doing it in a methodical way, and the confusion was confined to the victims and their mothers.

When the herd had been branded and allowed to return to the plain, the outfit moved on into a new territory and the work was repeated until the whole range, with the exception of the valley, had been covered. When the valley was worked it required more time in comparison with the amount of ground covered than had been heretofore spent on any part of the range; for the cattle were far more numerous, and it was no unusual thing to have a herd of great size before the roundup place had been reached. This heavy increase in the numbers of the cattle to be herded made a corresponding increase in the time and labor required for the cutting-out and branding. Five days were required in working the eastern and central parts of the valley and it took three more days to clean up around the White Horse Hills, where the ground was rougher and the riding harder. And at every cutting-out there was a large stray-herd made up of H2 and Three Triangle cattle. The H2 had been formerly the Three Triangle. Buck had been earnest in his instructions regarding the strays, for now was the opportunity to rid his range of Meeker's cattle without especial significance; once over the line it would be a comparatively easy matter to keep them there.

For taking care of this extra herd and also because Buck courted scrutiny during the branding, the foreman accepted the services of three H2 men. This addition to his forces made the work move somewhat more rapidly and when, at the end of each day's cutting-out, the stray herd was complete, it was driven south across the boundary line by Meeker's men. When the last stray-herd started south Buck rode over to the H2 punchers and told them to tell their foreman to let him know when he could assist in the southern roundup and thus return the favor.

As the Bar-20 outfit and the C80 and Double Arrow men rode north towards the ranch house they were met by Lucas, foreman of the C80, who joined them near Medicine Bend.

"Well, got it all over, hey?" he cried as he rode up.

"Yep; bigger job than I thought, too. It gets bigger every year an' that blizzard didn't make much difference in th' work, neither," Buck replied. "I'll help you out when you get ready to drive."

"No you won't; you can help me an' Bartlett more

by keeping all yore men watchin' that line," quickly responded Lucas. "We'll work together, me an' Bartlett, an' we'll have all th' men we want. You just show that man Meeker that range grabbin' ain't healthy down here—that's all we want. Did he send you any help in th' valley?"

"Yes, three men," Buck replied. "But we'll break even on that when he works along the boundary."

"Have any trouble with 'em?"

"Not a bit."

"I sent Wood Wright down to Eagle th' other day, an' he says the town is shore there'll be a big range war," remarked Lucas. "He said there's lots of excitement down there an' they act like they wish th' trouble would hurry up an' happen. We've got to watch that town, all right."

"If there's a war th' rustlers'll flock from all over," interposed Rich Finn.

"Huh!" snorted Hopalong. "They'll flock out again if we get a chance to look for 'em. An' that town'll shore get into trouble if it don't live plumb easy. You know what happened th' last time rustlin' got to be th' style, don't you?"

"Well," replied Lucas, "I've fixed it with Cowan to get news to me an' Bartlett if anything sudden comes up. If you need us just let him know an' we'll be with you in two shakes."

"That's good, but I don't reckon I'll need any help, leastwise not for a long time," Buck responded. "But I tell you what you might do, when you can; make up a vigilance committee from yore outfits an' ride range for rustlers. We can take care of all that comes on us, but we won't have no time to bother about th' rest of th' range. An' if you do that it'll shut 'em out of our north range."

"We'll do it," Lucas promised. "Bartlett is going to watch th' trails north to see if he can catch anybody runnin' cattle to th' railroad construction camps. Every suspicious looking stranger is going to be held up an' asked questions; an' if we find any runnin' irons, you know what that means."

"I reckon we can handle th' situation, all right, no matter how hard it gets," laughed the Bar-20 foreman.

"Well, I'll be leavin' you now," Lucas remarked as they reached the Bar-20 bunk house. "We begin to round up next week, an' there's lots to be done by then. Say, can I use yore chuck wagon? Mine is shore done for."

"Why, of course," replied Buck heartily. "Take it now, if you want, or any time you send for it."

"Much obliged; come on, fellers," Lucas cried to his men. "We're going home."